BIG!
THAT'S TEXAS!

BIG!
That's the fight between Joe Jarrett and Zach Thomas for the whole damn city of Galveston!

BIG!
That's Madame Elya, lady barber. Big heart, big scissors, big where it counts, big, BIG, **BIG!**

AND BIG!
Maxine Messimo—the big nekkid picture over the bar, the big gambling lady, the big quick-with-the-gun gal!

BIG NOVEL, BIG MOVIE, BIG STARS, BIG FUN!
THE BIGGEST, FUNNIEST, SEXIEST
NOVEL ABOUT THE GREAT, BIG
STATE OF TEXAS!

THE SAM COMPANY PRESENTS

FRANK SINATRA
DEAN MARTIN
ANITA EKBERG
URSULA ANDRESS

IN

4 FOR TEXAS

Co-starring:
CHARLES BRONSON and VICTOR BUONO

Guest Stars:
THE THREE STOOGES

Screenplay by:
TEDDI SHERMAN and ROBERT ALDRICH

Produced and Directed by:
ROBERT ALDRICH

A WARNER BROTHERS RELEASE

4 FOR TEXAS

BY DAN CUSHMAN

**BASED ON THE SCREENPLAY WRITTEN BY
TEDDI SHERMAN AND ROBERT ALDRICH**

YOUR ASSURANCE OF QUALITY · BANTAM BOOKS · NEW YORK ·

4 FOR TEXAS

A Bantam Book / published December 1963

Library of Congress Catalog Card Number: 63-21963

Bantam Books are published by Bantam Books, Inc. Its trade-mark,
consisting of the words "Bantam Books" and the portrayal of a
bantam, is registered in the United States Patent Office and in other
countries. Marca Registrada. Printed in the United States of America, Bantam Books, Inc., 271 Madison Ave., New York 16, N. Y.

4 FOR TEXAS

I

One hot July day, less than a decade after the War Between the States, a stagecoach was rolling westward from the Louisiana border across the continental heartland of Texas. It was a heavy vehicle and heavily loaded, pulled by a four-horse team on the level, but changing to six horses when the way became steep and crooked along the Neches and the arroyos above Furnass. The coach bore in peeling gold leaf the name and corporate insignia of the San Angelo & Arizona Express line.

It was already crowded and two men were riding on top with the driver when it reached Stone Junction and took on a passenger waiting with a canvas warsack, an alligator valise, and a Spanish-fork saddle.

He was a rangy man, with large shoulders, and that made things difficult. He took off his planter's-style sombrero, but there was nothing he could do about the pistol in the holster high at his side. He should have taken it off and put it in the valise, and he apparently realized that; but now it was too late and all he could do was move it around so it would not ram the elderly gentleman beside him, and suffer the added misery of a buttoned coat in deference to the women aboard. He was good-looking in a heavy-jawed way, although his eyes were a trifle narrow, as if they had become so by looking into the sun, and at off-guard moments there was a ruthless set to his mouth. He was thirty or a trifle more. When he spoke it was evident that he was a Southerner, but his clothes were of Northern tailoring—all except his hat. It bore in gold-stamp in its sweatband the name of Lalange & Cyr, New Orleans.

"Why doesn't the company put on an extra coach?" asked a woman, middle-aged and bilious, looking out at the station-master, who was repacking the baggage. "At least this freight can wait for the next one," she added.

1

Some express, wrapped in canvas, had been roped to one of the seats.

"I'm sorry, but that's premium express for the Maxon Brothers Hardware in San Saba."

"But why is it in a passenger's seat?"

"It *is* a passenger. It's paying a passenger's rate. Twenty cents a pound. Just pretend its name is George. Anyhow, it don't snore or chew tobacco."

"You think you're almighty funny, don't you? I may just report your name to the superintendent."

"You go ahead, and tell 'em I'm handling this job all alone when I ought to have one clerk and a wrangler helping me."

The woman, breathing her annoyance, turned away, but the feet of the new passenger hampered her.

"Sorry I'm so long-legged." He had a friendly voice, winning and attractive, and he smiled.

"Do *you* travel by the pound?" she asked.

"No, ma'am."

"George does," she said, pointing at the express. "I weigh one hundred four pounds. If they treat us like express, why does my ticket cost as much as yours?"

"Never mind, Louella," said her husband. "It's unpleasant for all of us. These trips are something that have to be endured. We talked about it before we left."

Then he said to the man, "We're from Hyvas Creek. That's up north. We've been to see our son in Shreveport. He had blood poison and a leg amputated, but he's better now."

"And that saddle you brought along," the woman said. "What happened, did you kill your horse?"

"No, ma'am. There's an old saying: you should never go out into Texas without a gun, a saddle, and a whisky chaser."

"If you have a saddle, why don't you have a horse?"

"There'll be a railroad through here soon," was the answer. "And we'll look back on these days as real adventuring. I'm a railroad man myself. My card, ma'am."

The card read: *Joseph T. Jarrett, Railroad Investments.* She wouldn't take it.

"My sister lost a small fortune in a railroad scheme," she said. "She was a widow, too."

"I'll assure you it wasn't *our* railroad, ma'am. We're bonded by Rothschilds in New York."

Her husband took the card.

They were so close that when the coach started, their knees knocked together. There was another seat, but it was even more tightly packed by extra express.

2

"They ought to be reported to the Governor," the woman said. "We wouldn't have to put up with this if we had anyone with gumption sitting in Austin."

"No, ma'am."

"This coach line will go broke one of these days."

The shares of the San Angelo & Arizona were selling at a solid $22 on the Galveston exchange, and the fact that it kept its coaches overloaded with pay cargo in no way depressed them. By paying no heed to comfort, but doggedly reaching its destinations winter and summer, in storm and the endless droughts, the company had destroyed all competition, even that of a St. Louis company whose coaches larruped along at eight miles an hour, and there was a belief that it had frightened off the railroads. For it was true that although the nation was well launched into the greatest railroad building era in history, scarcely a line had pierced into the real heartland of Texas.

They rolled out of Stone Junction and a breeze came down from the northwest without cooling the air. It was only 10:14 by Joseph T. Jarrett's flip-open solid gold watch. What the day would be like when afternoon came was dreadful to contemplate. There'd been no rain in a month and a half.

Jarrett looked at the watch longer than was necessary because he liked things of solid quality, and the watch, with its green-gold overlay floral design on fourteen carat yellow, was the best available. Instead of the figures 1 to 12, it had the letters of his name in a circle: J O E * T * J A R-R E T T. He had won the watch playing rouge et noir on a Missouri River steamboat, but he had had a Kansas City jeweler install the genuine ceramic dial. He liked watches better than anything in the world, outside of guns. His gun, over which he kept his coat buttoned on account of the ladies, was another flawless piece of equipment, made to order, with special ivory stocks and reverse-groove rifling, by Colt's Patent Fire Arms Co. of Hartford, Conn.

The bilious woman sat with her eyes closed. Nobody talked. The teams kept at a slow jog, and the dust of their hoofs came through the shrunken floor boards of the coach. Everything you touched left a coating of white powder on your fingers. Jarrett was so crowded he cold move only from one hip to the other. He was sweating, and his trousers stuck to him. He wondered about the women with their corsets. A woman could endure more than a man. They demanded more, but they could endure more.

The coach rolled down the straight road and road runners

3

crossed in front of it. There were a few dried-out farms, and the plains ran on to the gray-shimmering, flame-licking edge of the world. God, it was hot!

Another passenger, a stockman with a San Felipe ticket stuck in the band of his hat, finally spoke. "I thought the railroad was headed into Fort Worth."

"Not ours." Jarrett said. "Not the big line—the Dixie Gulf & Trans-Southern. Famed Cotton Route. We're straight across south-central."

"You're going to Floral City?"

"Yes, sir."

"I heard there were railroaders there thick as flies. Carpetbaggers and railroaders."

"I don't know as I like that remark," Jarrett said mildly.

"Well, nothing personal."

"Thank you."

"But I don't like railroads, and that's a free Texan's privilege."

"Yes, sir. It's a privilege we fought for—three times in less than forty years. We're allowed to dislike anything we care to."

"And I dislike the high and mighty railroads. Railroads take over the country, enslave the ranchers, steal the bread off farm tables. Look at poor Mrs. James up in Missouri. I been reading about her. And when her boys Jesse and Frank go out and stand up to the railroads, they hound them across the land. Of course, part of it was that they were with General C. W. Quantrell."

"I defer to no man in my admiration for Jesse Woodson James and his illustrious brother. I, too, am a Baptist, sir. And I fought for the South. But I also believe the time has come for good will, when we can all be prosperous together."

"I didn't mean you were a Yankee. I wouldn't say a thing like that, even if you are a railroad man. I regret saying anything out of line. And I'm all for being prosperous."

"Everybody gets short-tempered in this heat."

A cowboy spoke up. "How far you figure to get across Texas?"

"You mean today, or with the railroad?" Jarrett asked.

"With the railroad."

"Our destination is the Pacific Ocean."

"You'll never make it. There's not enough water out west for the engine."

"Not enough fuel, either," said the stockman.

"They won't need fuel. When they get past San Angelo, the water will boil in the sun."

4

"They'll never make it to New Mexico."

"I think they will," said a young Army wife, traveling with her captain husband.

"Thank you, ma'am," said Jarrett. "I was beginning to think this rocking, jolting wreck of a vehicle didn't have a single enemy."

The railroad was imaginary anyhow. He had sold stock in the corporation known as the Dixie Gulf & Trans-Southern, but it had never got beyond the promotional stage. A great idea, but the commissions, costs, and charges had eaten up every penny subscribed. All he had left were the stock and bond books, a hand-screw seal, and the charter under the laws of Ohio. Come to think of it, *he* was the Dixie Gulf & Trans-Southern now. He was the Cotton Line. Everyone else had been scared off by the creditors, and not a mile of track had ever been laid.

There was a dinner stop at one o'clock, and after that an eternity of heat. The evening meal was at Vik's Bridge. It was cool there, beside the shrunken remnants of a river. Two of the passengers, a dress-goods drummer and one of the men riding with the driver, got off to wait for the Fort Worth coach. The rancher, the cowboy, and Jarrett cut high card to see who would get to ride above, and Jarrett won. They were his cards.

"I always carry a deck with me to play solitaire with," he said to the women. "They give a man something to do besides going to saloons."

That night he rode in coolness under the stars, and woke up at the Little Brazos crossing. In the afternoon they reached Floral City.

II

Chickens were lying in the dust of Main Street, and the dust of the stagecoach drifted over them. A Mexican boy sat in a patch of shade beneath a brownish oak tree smoking a cigarette, and some men sat on the benches in front of a hotel. The buildings were mostly frame with false fronts that had twisted from shrinkage in the sun. People watched the stage from inside the saloons and stores and a barber shop, and came out after it had stopped. They did not move rapidly, even though its arrival was the big event of the day. To Jarrett's eye there was little railroad excitement, or excitement of any kind.

"Well, here's Floral City in full bloom," said the driver.

Jarrett sat for a while in the high seat looking across the vista of false fronts, shacks, and adobes with heat-shimmering roofs toward the prairie and a river. The river, where the bridge crossed it, was dry, but the teams had smelled water, so water was somewhere. A couple of patent windmills stood quiet in the distance.

"Floral City—what did they name it after, the cactus blossoms?"

"This is the biggest little town in middle Texas," the driver said. "Got the best water. No hardness in it. No alki. You're absolutely right about building your railroad in here. A railroad will make this into a town of three thousand people, just like Fort Worth."

Jarrett waited to get his baggage. Nobody came to carry it, so he picked up the warsack and valise in one hand and the saddle in the other. The hotel, just across the street, was a large, rambling two-story building with a verandah across the front, which looked as if it would fall down if anyone walked on it. A paint-peeling sign read: Planters House. Men sat and watched him from the green benches. He limped on both legs, his muscles responding slowly after the seat's confinement, and he realized that at thirty-odd he was feeling his age. His sweat-stuck pants came loose, and he appreciated the cooling flow of air around his hindquarters.

"Hey, caballero!" called an old man from one of the benches. "Why the saddle? It must be a pretty rough coach the Express is running these days."

He was a dehydrated old man with a face like an empty tobacco pouch. He wore a black hat with an insignia of the Mexican War and the Sam Houston medal on its band. Jarrett was glad to see the medal. When last he was in Texas, just leaving for the war, people were still taking it hard about Governor Sam opposing secession, refusing to swear allegiance to the Confederacy, and shooting his mouth off in general. They called him a Yankee, but that was ridiculous. What he really was was a rebel rebel. They sort of admired him for standing up and shouting down the whole state, or trying to, but they took it hard. Even when he was dead they were calling him a traitor. Some of the old fellows threw away their Houston medals, and some of them cut them in half, saying he was like Benedict Arnold, who had

had his leg buried with full military honors and the rest of him declared traitor. But the past few years had helped, and there was the medal again.

Jarrett made it the rest of the way before dropping his baggage and the saddle. "As I've often remarked," he said, "a man starting across Texas ought to take a pistol, a saddle, and a bottle of chaser."

"You don't need to bring chaser here. We got the best drinking water in the state."

The Mexican kid came over and opened the door. He was waiting for a coin, but he didn't get one.

"Bring my baggage," said Jarrett. "The saddle too."

"Si, caballero."

He stood for a time just inside the door, letting his eyes grow used to the dimness. The room had the smell of frontier hotels everywhere. It was big and dusty and had a barren look. There were some big leather chairs, and rubber plants stood in green tubs. As it was just as hot inside as out, nobody sat in the chairs. At the moment a German and his wife, fellow passengers, were registering. He waited until the clerk finished with them and had let them carry their own baggage upstairs.

"Yes, sir?" he said, turning to Jarrett. He wore little two-bit-size glasses.

"What are your accommodations?"

"We have one room left."

"One's all I need."

"You have to sign this. It's the new law."

"A hotel register! I've *heard* of these." He signed, using the ornate secretary hand.

"That'll be a dollar twenty-five," said the clerk.

Jarrett paid, the dollar being sharp and shining-new from the Denver mint. The clerk dropped it to test its ring.

"You also might bite it. On the other hand, there's them that drill little holes through just halfway."

"Sorry, but the country is full of railroad boomers. You know the type."

"Yes, sir. I'm with the Dixie Coast & Trans-Southern myself."

"Sorry. No offense."

"Then none taken. Do I get a key with the room?"

The clerk found a cigar box with a number of keys in it and offered Jarrett his choice.

"They all work?"

"Any key there will unlock any room in the house."

"I don't need to unlock any room but my own."

"Well, I wanted to let you know. We don't recommend the rooms for safe keeping. For people carrying large sums, we recommend the bank, the Lone Star State. Its vaults are explosion-proof, and are free to the guests of the hotel. Of course, I'm not saying there's danger of thieves. We're an honest town. Hardly a door ever locked, day or night. Of course, now with all the strangers, Yankees coming in—" He stopped, fearing he had given offense.

"I'm not a Yankee."

"No, sir. I didn't mean to suggest that you were. I only wanted to tell you about the bank, you being with the railroad."

"The other railroad fellows using the bank for pretty big sums?" Jarrett asked casually. "I just want to know what kind of competition I'm going to have, buying up land, water, et cetera."

"I believe so. They came in with a special guard on the coach."

"Ah-ha! It looks as if I'll have some competition."

"And they're making their disbursements spot cash. People are afraid of bank drafts here, after the war. I shouldn't be telling you this, but you being a Southerner, and those other gentlemen—one of them at least . . ."

"Is a Yankee!"

"Mr. Ansel, Jonas Ansel, from St. Louis."

"And he's the one that's paying the money out, the spot cash?"

"I believe so. He was the one who came on the guarded stagecoach."

"You speak as if there were some others."

"Oh, we've had quite a number from time to time. Right now there's Mr. Thomas, from Galveston."

"That wouldn't be Mr. Zachariah Thomas?"

"Yes." He leafed over one page in the register. "Zachariah W. Thomas, Galveston."

"He's staying right here?" Jarrett asked.

"Both of them. Mr. Thomas has the verandah suite. And Mr. Ansel is in eight, on the ground floor. He was afraid of high places."

"Have a cigar, Mr.—"

"Box. Walter Box."

"Have a cigar, Mr. Box."

"I'll save it till after supper, but thanks."

Jarrett himself shucked the foil from a cigar, bit the end off, and lit up. He had strong teeth, and a way of smiling with a cigar in his mouth that made people glad he was their friend.

"Tell me more. For instance, I'd like to hear more about this tycoon, Zachariah Thomas."

"Well, I figured everybody in these parts had heard of *him*. . . . But you're not of these parts." Jarrett had registered from Denver, Colorado. "Many enterprises. Ships, warehousing. That means cotton, mostly. And of course, being in shipping and warehousing, he's in the commission business. It all goes together."

"Also banking, brokerage, et cetera."

"Yes."

"And cordage, lightering, ship-chandlering, whisky, gambling, and the demimonde."

"Well, of course, that about gambling and the demimonde—people say those things. He might have some investments. You know how Galveston is."

Indeed Jarrett knew how Galveston was! His first memories were of Galveston—of the docks of Galveston, of climbing high staircases of cotton bales. How he got to Galveston he never knew. One story was that he had been brought ashore off a ship after his father and mother died from the yellow fever of 1839. Another story was that he had been picked up from a shipwreck, and he liked that one best. Anyhow, he knew Galveston, and from a time long antedating that of Mr. Zachariah Thomas, tycoon of shipping, cotton, brokerage, gambling, and the demimonde.

The clerk went on talking in his ingratiating voice. He was letting Jarrett know what a friend he wanted to be, willing to keep his eyes open and his ears, too, and to tip him off about what the other railroaders were about. He hadn't come to the point, but what he was seeking was a small retainer, and a little commission now and then for bits of information. He was willing to do this because Jarrett was in no manner associated with the Yankees and the carpetbaggers.

And while the clerk's precise, rather sibilant voice kept on, like a fly beating against glass in the hot, late afternoon, Jarrett thought about Galveston, and his old home, the vine-covered institution, the Lanternlight Orphanage, run by the Reverend Enoch Lantern, spare and tall, with Old Testament eyes and a disposition to match. Jarrett's flesh still rose in welts when he remembered the whippings old Lantern had given. And he had deserved every one of them. Yes, if ever he had strayed from the paths of rectitude it had not been

9

old Lantern's fault. Some kids could be won over by rewards, and some through the use of reason, while others responded to appeals to their pride, and some to kindness. But every so often you met one who had to have it beaten into him, and that one was himself, young Joseph T. Jarrett.

"Allow me to assure you, Mr. Box, that my firm, Dixie Gulf & Trans-Southern, always remembers its friends in a very substantial way," Jarrett said, when the clerk stopped talking. "By that I mean if our plans worked out, and you, for example, had some part in it, no matter of how secret and private a nature—well, sir, I wouldn't be at all surprised to walk in here and see you the *owner* of this hotel."

He smoked his cigar and allowed that to sink in. "Now this man, Ansel, is he making disbursements?"

"Yes. Very definitely."

"In large amounts? Or is it mainly a few dollars here, a few dollars there, and the rest Yankee big talk?"

"I wouldn't know about that. It is my understanding that, as far as Mr. Ansel is concerned, no large amounts have yet been paid over. But he has such amounts in hand."

"Big amounts are the sort of thing I, as a railroad man, naturally am interested in. Now, you say *in hand*. How do you know he has them in hand?"

"I put two and two together."

"Something you heard?"

"Something I saw, too. They went over to the bank. It was right in business hours, and pretty soon the door was closed and the front shades pulled. They do that when the big cattle-buying money comes in, but I never saw them do it for so long."

"So it must have been a very large amount."

"Definitely!"

"Just how much would you guess?"

"Well, this is only a rumor. But I have a cousin married to the teller. Well, I shouldn't be talking . . ."

"You go ahead, Mr. Box. Rest assured that you're talking to *a friend*."

"Well, I shouldn't be spreading such information, but . . ."

"Have another cigar."

Box took it, and saw that a folded banknote was with it. It was a ten. He put the banknote in one pocket and the cigar in another. Ten dollars was a week's salary.

"I was told it was a *hundred thousand dollars!*"

"Oh, come now, Box!"

"That's what I heard!" the clerk whispered vehemently.

10

"A hundred thousand dollars! There's not that much cash money in the whole South that the Yankees have overlooked."

"Of course not. The *Yankee* brought it in!"

"A hundred thousand dollars?"

"In cash. Gold!"

"It couldn't be in gold. Do you know what that would weigh? Four hundred and fifty pounds."

"Gold and gold certificates. It's the same thing."

"Well, if that's true, competition for my railroad is going to be very rough. Very rough indeed. But you know what? Just you sit tight and keep your eyes open, Box. You tell me every move they make. I'll get out a message on the Army telegraph, and by the gods, we'll bring in some money of our own!"

III

He told the Mexican boy to leave the saddle below, but to bring up the bag and valise. The clerk's eyes were on him as he climbed the stairs. He thinks I'm going to rob the bank, thought Jarrett. Right now he's weighing his advantages, one way and the other. Everybody is going to get rich from the railroad, and he'd like to get in on it, too, only how do you do it clerking in a hotel? However, the hundred thousand—if there was a hundred thousand—or the ten thousand, which was more likely—offered certain possibilities, one way and the other.

So what would Box do? First, he would go down to the sheriff's office and have a look at the Wanted posters. They would tell him nothing. There was only once that anyone had got out a Wanted poster on Jarrett, and that had been cleared up, absolutely. Next, Box would weigh the advantages of getting a percentage of the swag, in case there was a holdup, or of selling Jarrett out to Thomas and Ansel. This would take some time, and Box would have to keep everyone's confidence. In the meantime . . .

"You want me to go back after your saddle, Señor Caballero?" asked the Mexican boy, who came in dragging the bag and warsack as heavy as himself.

"No."

"How come you have a saddle, señor, and no horse?"

"You can always get a horse that fits, but a saddle's a different matter."

"You want me to watch your saddle?"

"No, this is an honest town." He gave the boy a dime.

"You can hire me all day for two bits."

"All right, I'll pay you two bits."

"To watch the saddle, Señor Caballero?"

"You watch for Señor Thomas and Señor Ansel. You *sabe*?"

"Sure. What do next?"

"Just watch for 'em."

He closed the door and looked at himself in the mirror. Do I look like a bank robber, he thought. The mirror was a good one of beveled French glass, and it reflected back his face with all its seams and blemishes. He needed a shave. The heat had left his skin oily, and the dust that came through the coach hour after hour had gathered at the corners of his eyes. He looked older, and heavier at the sides of his jaw, and more sag-eyed than he remembered.

What kind of a life have I lived, he thought. Too much Arizona, and too much Colorado and Wyoming. Too much living on beans and alum pancakes. And whisky under the oil lamps. There comes a time when a man has to settle down. He should never have hunted gold in Arizona. That was what had put the bird-track wrinkles at the corners of his eyes. He tried smoothing them out, but they went right back in again. And there was the hard-luck time when he had to take employment as faro dealer in Colorado. The poor light and the tobacco smoke had caused a good deal of eye strain. It had got so his eyes would burn in the daylight. Later he'd been up from dusk to dawn as night policeman in Cheyenne, and there had been the hard three weeks he had spent as detective for the Wells Fargo Company before, for some unexplained reason, he was dropped from the payroll. He had gone all out for Wells Fargo, and had covered, horseback, the distance from Fort Sanders to the Devil's Gate and back, a journey of 310 miles, in less than a week, going without proper sleep, tracking down the Pilot Rock gang, but they had discharged him without a word of explanation. All of those things had taken something out of him. It had left its stamp on his face. He liked to think it had taught him something, too.

He picked up the china pitcher and drank some of

the water. It was warm and flat. Beads of moisture were on the sides of the pitcher.

He took an interest in the water. Every man who had been long in the West took an interest in water. He tasted it again, tasted it for its real quality under the warmth and flatness. It was dead, but it had no taste—no alkali, soda taste. It was soft, like rainwater. The pitcher was as old as the hotel; it had all the chipped and crazed signs of age, but there was no stain from minerals. He poured water to wash with, and ran his hand inside the pitcher. For all the years water had stood evaporating in the pitcher, the glaze was as smooth as ever. If the railroad really was coming—and he'd had this reported both ways—such water would be worth a fortune.

A fortune! He took off his gun, stripped off his coat, his collar and tie and shirt. He dipped his head and let water run salty and dust-filled from his hair. How many years, how much traveling and using his brain and his gun, and being smarter than the other fellow—but no fortune. Nothing to show—two hundred dollars, or less than that. Good God, what had happened to his life? Here he was, past thirty, and his life on the tilted edge. No money, a saddle but no horse, nothing.

He took off his pants and let the water run down his body and legs. There was no towel in the room, and he stood by the open window and the breeze, lifting the cheesecloth curtains, cooled and dried him. It gave him an added contentment to scratch. Looking across one-story buildings and a wedge of street, he could see the bank, the only brick building in town. A heavy cube of a building, it stood with massive solidity, with a door recessed deeply between Grecian pillars.

A fortune . . . The water, which at that moment was cooling him, was very good water, and it was worth a fortune to anybody building a railroad. It was the water that had brought Zach Thomas and Jonas Ansel, and the hundred thousand dollars. Where the honey was, the flies would gather.

Naked, he lay down on the bed and looked at the ceiling. Presently he dozed, and a large horsefly kept beating his head. Its buzzing was endless. It confused the chalk-white gypsum plaster with the sky. The drone of the horsefly became mixed in Jarrett's mind with banks and honey. The fly was caught in honey, but it was not a fly, really. In his

13

dream it became a high-speed bellows, driven by steam power, forcing a blast of air through the purifying pots of the Denver mint. Ah, how brilliant and shining the coins spilled out, and men scooped them into boxes with shovels! The sounds of wagons and teamsters in the street outside his room became the clinking and the voices of shovelers in the Denver mint. He was wading in money, his feet stuck in money as if in quicksand.

Then a massive man, fat, in a silk hat, with a gold watch chain across his vest, came and stood over him. "I'm Zach Thomas," he said, "and that is my money."

"Stay away from that money," said Jarrett.

They struggled for the money, Jarrett at a disadvantage because he was wading so deep in it. But Zach Thomas was very fat—he had the terrible, wheezing corpulence of a whale. The fat slowly turned things in Jarret's favor.

"Never borrow and never lend," Jarrett said, quoting old Enoch Lantern back at the orphanage. "Save and have. He who hides farthings, shillings will find."

He awoke. He was lying on his side and the fly was crawling on him, looking for beads of sweat. He killed the fly and sat up. He found his wallet and counted his money. He had exactly $138 to his name. Over in Memphis, getting wind of big money and the railroad excitement, it seemed the most natural thing in the world to come over here with his old Dixie Gulf & Trans-Southern stocks, bonds, and charter and cut himself in on some of it. But things always looked different when you just woke up. Was he a damn fool, giving the clerk ten dollars? And promising the Mexican kid twenty-five cents?

"Maybe," he muttered, "I ought to rob that damn bank after all!"

IV

He dressed, except for his collar which he carried, and went down to the barber shop. A man was in the chair, lying back, and there was a hot towel over his face. He had on a good pair of boots, except they were too high in the heels.

The trousers were excellent, but were cut too extremely to the mode, close to his legs. He knew the type. Gambler type—gaudy, poor taste.

"Sit down, sir," said the barber, a powerful mulatto, with a good gold-tooth smile. "Paper, sir?"

It was the *New Orleans Picayune*. It had come in on the stage with Jarrett. He had read it through once, but he sat down with it again.

"Oh yes, times have been hard, very hard," the barber continued to the man under the hot towel. He stropped a razor and drew it across his spit-wetted thumbnail to see whether it pulled sharp and smooth. Then he put it on the shelf ready for use. It was obvious from his tone and the care of his preparations that this was no ordinary customer.

"Times were indeed *very* hard after the cattle market gave out. There's certainly no money to be made on hides and tallow delivered to tidewater. And as we don't raise cotton hereabouts it didn't look like us in this town was going to keep body and soul together, hardly."

"Why didn't they drive their cattle to Galveston?" the man asked, muffled by the towel.

"We *do* haul there, but it's a long effort. Six to eight days by wagon, camping along the way."

They were genuine Spanish boots. It was not that the heels were too high; they were slanted too far. It made them rather ostentatious. You could always tell the difference between a gaudy dresser and a true gentleman. Jarrett pretended to read while listening to the conversation.

"This *could* be a cotton country," the barber went on. "We commenced to hear talk of cotton as soon as we got wind of the railroad. And the ranchers—they said less about driving cattle away north for shipment on the U.P. To tell you the truth, sir, I thought it was *crazy*. Why, that's more extreme than driving to Galveston, even. Far more extreme." He seemed fond of the word extreme. "These cattlemen complain they have nothing to sell but hides in those tidewater slaughterhouses. Why, they wouldn't have even the hides left after driving to Missouri or Nebraska and the U.P. And besides that, they'd have to go up against the buffalo market."

He took off the towel and the man's face was visible. He was good-looking in what seemed to Jarrett a bold and cheap way. His face was large-boned, especially the nose and cheekbones, and he stared at Jarrett, and kept on staring. He gave no sign of recognition, or of friendliness; he simply stared. The barber got to lathering him and turned his head to the other side, and after that Jarrett knew he was watching in the mirror. He got his hand out from under the cloth to scratch a place where the lather tickled his nose, and Jarrett saw that he wore a very large diamond. His shirtsleeve was lace-inlaid in a most costly manner, but not in the best of taste. Gaudy, card-sharper type.

Jarrett ignored him for the paper. He kept looking at the same sentence while the man watched him in the mirror. Finally it made him nervous, so he walked to the window and looked out. It was a jolt to see another man watching from across the street. This one was tall, a shadowy form in a saloon door, and something about him was familiar. Familiar and alarming. Jarrett conquered the desire to escape. He drove out the thought that they were waiting here to surround him. Why would they? Nobody knew he was coming to this barber shop. And he'd done nothing.

Reflex had sent his hand to the butt of his gun. The man in the chair had lifted himself up, and the barber had stopped shaving and was looking at Jarrett. He went back and sat down. The man lay back then, and the barber went on with his work. The man continued to stare at him, and Jarrett stared at the paper.

Then suddenly it came to him. He knew who the fellow was —the one across the street. It was Matson—Blackie Matson of Wyoming. Matson, who had murdered three brothers of an emigrant family. Jarrett had helped arrest him when he was night policeman in Cheyenne. They had caught him with the brothers' teams, and he had been tried and sentenced to hang. But Matson was over there now, a lean, cadaverous, black shadow. He had escaped. He had followed Jarrett to kill him.

"Do you know him?" asked the man in the chair.

Jarrett flinched.

"Hey!" The man had raised up again, with the lather over his face.

"Were you talking to me?" Jarrett said.

"Yes, that fellow across the street, do you know him?"

"Which one?"

"The one that's been watching me ever since I left the hotel."

"That description means nothing to me, sir."

"You're not together?"

"No, we're not together."

He didn't like the man's questions any more than he had liked his way of staring. The anger which had so long been his failing was building up in him, but he clamped a lid on it

16

before it got out of control. If there was one good, sound adage in the West, it was never to start trouble in the other man's town.

"The fact of the matter was," Jarrett said mildly, "the way he was looking at me, and the way you were looking at me—well, it about convinced me *you* were together. And here you thought *we* were together! Ha-ha!"

"Ha-ha!" said the man in the chair, and it was like biting down on sand.

"Ha-ha—" The barber started to laugh, but the expression on Jarrett's face brought him up sharp.

"I thought you arrived in town together," said the man in the chair.

"What are you, the sheriff or something?"

"No, I'm not the sheriff."

"I came in on the stagecoach," Jarrett said, and his control was so good that he sounded casual, positively yawning-casual, as if the barber's bench were the most comfortable place in the world, and himself content. "He wasn't on that coach. Nor anybody resembling him. I can assure you, my good sir, that I became very well acquainted with all the other passengers; we were in most close proximity."

"Um!" said the man. He seemed to be admiring the excellence of Jarrett's syntax.

"As for meeting him elsewhere, it is distinctly possible that I have. I meet a great many people in my line; some of them"—and he met the eyes from the barber chair when he said it—"not of the best sort. My line happens to be securities, railroads. I might have seen him while I was appraising the various routes for the Kansas Pacific. Or again, I might have known him when in Dakota for the Rock Island, or in Wyoming for the Denver and Northern."

"You don't look like a railroad financier."

"Well, some people might not take you for a gambler, either."

That had slipped out, sort of around the clamped lid of his anger, and he noticed it struck home. The eyes were more probing than ever, but the lips peeled back in a smile. A smile was not always a good sign. In fact, with the real killers it was frequently a bad one. And here was a man, he thought, who could smile and smile, and shoot him dead. He didn't like it that the man's hands were covered by the cloth. He could be holding a gun at that very instant. He could be aiming it between Jarrett's eyes. The smile, which lingered, would be precedent to nailing him to the wall. However, Jarrett turned to page five of the *Picayune* and his hands were steady.

"We're all gamblers one way or another," said the man being shaved.

"Now, ain't that true!" The barber had sensed trouble and was doing his best to smooth things over. "Excuse me, but does that razor seem to pull a trifle?"

The razor was obviously passing through lather and beard like a spoon through lard.

"No, it's smooth, very smooth. You're a fine barber. In fact, you're the finest barber I've ever been shaved by, bar one."

"You mean bar none?"

"Bar *one*. And you'd have to see this barber to believe it."

"I'd be mighty flattered to."

The tension had eased. "So you're in railroading?" said the man.

"I am," said Jarrett.

"Forgive me, but I don't seem to recall your name in association with any line in this region."

Jarrett wondered how he could associate his name with anything, not having been told what it was.

"I'm with the Dixie Gulf & Trans-Southern. That's the Cotton Line."

"The what?"

Jarrett repeated the name.

"That's a new one on me. It must be one of those little spur lines off the Yazoo." He laughed and addressed the barber. "You can never tell the size of a line by its name."

Jarrett resolved not to lose his temper again. "The Dixie Gulf Trans-Southern," he said, "running from Savannah, Georgia, to west Texas, and eventually to the Pacific coast via Santa Fe, will be the true trunk line of the South. Unfortunately, because of present political conditions, we've been obliged to incorporate under the laws of Ohio; but make no mistake about it, we're a Southern line. More than seventy per cent of our capital has been subscribed in the Confederate States, England, and the Continent. We are convinced, sir, despite the recent conflict and its tragic conclusion, that the area from Savannah to middle Texas is the rich heartland of this nation. We propose to be its aorta and its jugular vein, sir. We feel that it is only a question of time before the South rises and gains through agriculture, business, and commerce what was lost on the battlefield."

He was quoting from the prospectus, as he had done so

many times in the past while selling Dixie Gulf stock, and he spoke with such conviction that he almost convinced himself. Yes, and he still believed it was a superb idea, and one that might be resurrected yet.

"Perhaps the line would be more familiar," he said, "if I explained that it is our purpose to lease the Mobile & Ohio trackage from Meridian north through Corinth, the segment laid waste by Grant and that brigand, Sherman, and bankrupt after the war. Recapitalization will thus allow us, and our shippers, the choice of markets, north or south, as seem most lucrative. Also, our palace sleeping cars will allow the traveler to be carried from Cincinnati to New Orleans, Mobile, Savannah, or any of the other great cities of the South, without the necessity of changing trains at Corinth or any of the other junction points.

"But of course our real goal is to tie the Atlantic and Pacific by means of an all-Southern route. This will terminate at the village of San Diego, which in my prediction will become a great city because of it. It goes without saying that we will have the warm, low Southern route, a superb advantage, while the trains of the Central Pacific, our Northern competitor, lie impacted in the Sierra snows. Sir, if such a line as ours had been functioning through the war, it might well have tilted the scales in our favor. But there's no use crying over spilt milk—or blood. What's done is done, and we look toward a bright tomorrow. The people who invest in Dixie Gulf & Trans-Southern will reap rewards beyond the dreams of avarice."

He had been carried away. He realized that the barber had stopped shaving, and the man had half risen in the chair.

"It sounds real good."

"It *is* good."

"But I still never heard of a Dixie Gulf & Trans-Southern."

"You will, sir, you will."

"I tell you what I *have* heard about."

"Yes?"

"I heard about a fellow just got in and made a lot of inquiries about the bank. He didn't deposit any money. He just inquired. What would you make of a thing like that?"

Jarrett stood up. He had the feeling that things had gone too far. "You're referring to me, sir."

"Barber, what do folks in Floral City do to bank robbers?"

"I don't know as we ever had any."

"Well, hereabouts. In Milford, maybe?"

"That's our sister city, thirty-eight miles away. Well, in Milford they hang 'em. They've hung two, one they shot, and one got away."

"The big one always gets away." The man looked at Jarrett very hard when he said it.

"I'm not a bank robber," said Jarrett. "The fact is, I expect to be bringing in one hundred and twenty-five thousand dollars in gold coin and certificates with which to purchase water rights in this region, and a person does not do that without making inquiries about the safety of those repositories which are available."

"And the gentleman across the street is your bodyguard?"

"No, sir!"

Then the conversation languished. Massaged and powdered, the man was brought upright in the chair. There he received other attentions—a neck shave, a rub, a few snips with the scissors, and his hair combed to a flowing feather-edge.

He was broader in the shoulders than Jarrett had thought, and when he stepped from the chair he landed on the balls of his feet as if he were ready to spring. He had a lithe power, a sure grace that reminded Jarrett of a mountain lion he had once seen bounding down a gulch side in Colorado, a creature all muscle and the nerve lightning that tensed the muscle—a bundle of smooth, cocked-and-ready deadliness. And he seemed so damned sure of himself! As if he had everything under control, and some to spare.

Jarrett noticed, too, that he had been right about the pistol. The man carried one, and it was on the left side with its handle turned right, and when he was in the chair it had to be pointed straight at him. All the man would have needed to do was make some trifling adjustment, cock, and pull the trigger. Jarrett couldn't help feeling like one who had just walked along the friable edge of a precipice.

"I'll be seeing you around, no doubt," he said in an effort to ease things at parting.

"Don't follow me too close, Jarrett."

"Let me brush your coat," the barber exclaimed. "There seems to be a mite of lint on the left shoulder." He whisked, stopping the conversation, and getting his tip. And he took a deep breath, filling himself like a bellows, after the man was out the door.

"Nice gentleman," said Jarrett, getting into the chair, which was still warm from the man's behind. He didn't like to sit in his warmth, and he squirmed forward. "Beautiful diamond.

A little on the yellowish side, but large. Hundred-dollar gun. Big tipper."

"Yes, sir."

"Who is he?"

"Why, I thought you was acquainted. I thought you railroad men was just having your little joke."

"Railroad men?"

"Surely you know that that was Mr. Zachariah Thomas!"

It jolted him, and it shouldn't have. He should have guessed. But he still had the vision of Zachariah Thomas as a massive, corpulent man like those cartoons the papers ran of Entrenched Wealth. Nobody had ever told him Zach Thomas looked like that—he had just assumed it. He'd lain there in his room and dreamed it.

"The Zach Thomas from Galveston? The man that owns Galveston?"

"Yes, sir! That's *the* Zach Thomas! He was sitting right in this chair!"

"I had him pegged for a gambler, and so he was," said Jarrett, being tilted back.

"Oh, I wouldn't call him a gambler. He's in shipping, banking, railroads—"

"A man who runs evil houses is the keeper of an evil house. It happens that I was raised in a God-fearing home. I was brought up amid surroundings where all gambling was frowned upon."

That was certainly true. By God, if Zachariah Thomas had shown up with a pair of dice at the Lanternlight Orphanage, old Enoch Lantern would have beaten him until he was lumpy as a knob-oak cane.

"I don't think it behooves me to comment on another man's livelihood," said the barber. "You *do* want a shave? I took it for granted—"

"And a massage, trim, shampoo, and tonic. Also some rose water and glycerine to get this damnable scale off my fingernails. This climate raises hob with them. I want everything, and twice as good as Zachariah Thomas. Because I'm just twice as good a tipper."

"Yes, *sir!*" said the barber.

V

He had a good supper. You always could find a good supper in Texas as long as you stuck to meat. Afterward he enjoyed a cigar on the hotel verandah, and he walked in the long cool of the evening down to the river. Everything was baked and dried through the day, but with coolness the odors were unlocked and you could smell the sage and the grass for a hundred miles.

He came back, giving only the briefest glance to the bank, where somebody was inside working late. Rigs and saddle horses were at the hitch racks. Music came from a cantina where the Mexicans hung out. He looked around for Zach Thomas, and saw that there was a light burning upstairs in what was probably his verandah suite. He was sure that Box, the clerk, had gone straight to Thomas with what he knew.

"Hello, Mr. Jarrett," the clerk greeted him.

"Hello, Mr. Box."

He walked to the stairs. One hundred thousand dollars, he thought—what a ridiculous story! When you met a man who never had had anything, and who couldn't conceive of real money, he always named figures that were too high. Ten thousand dollars now—ah, what wouldn't Jarrett do to get his hands on ten thousand dollars! A fortune.

"Señor Caballero!"

He had seen the shadow on the stairs; it had given his nerves quite a wrench, and his gun was out of its holster. He stood with it weighing solid in his hand—long octagonal silvered barrel, .44 calibre, special rifling, the most valuable thing he owned. But it was only the Mexican kid.

"Don't ever do that again, Pablo. You'll get killed doing that."

"Señor Caballero," the boy whispered, "there is a man in your room!"

"Who is it—Zach Thomas?"

"Eh?"

"Handsome, arrogant son of a— Well, never mind." He could see that Pablo didn't understand the gringo words. "Who is it?"

"I don't know."

"How did he get there?"

"A key!"

"What does he look like?"

"Tall. Black clothes. Black shirt, pants. Tall but hunch, like so. Long arms. Like—"

"I know." It was not Zach Thomas, then, but Matson.

"He's your friend?"

"No, he's not my friend."

"I save your life?"

"Maybe you did."

"Worth one dollar?"

"It's worth two bits." Jarrett gave it to him.

"Gracias!"

It was big money to Pablo. You never want to overpay a person, especially when your life is at stake. He'll only get big-money ideas. He'll commence putting things out for bids.

"You keep this up, Pablo, and you'll raise yourself to a dollar."

"Si, caballero!"

The hall was dark and quiet, and he could hear the sounds of voices through a distant open window. Men were on the street below. Boots and spurs sounded along the boardwalk. The Mexican kid was watching him from a safe distance.

Jarrett had his gun out, for he hadn't put it away. He tried the door, turning the knob gently, and keeping his body to one side. It was locked, just as he had left it. He wished now he hadn't locked the room. Now he had to use the key, and that complicated things. It gave Matson a better chance to kill him. However, he didn't think Matson would. Matson hadn't killed the emigrant brothers just for pleasure—he wanted their teams and wagons. Matson had never killed anyone for just the fun of it—there had to be a matter of profit involved. Small profit, perhaps, but profit. It made him feel more secure. It placed Matson in the business world.

Jarrett unlocked the door and let it swing open. From where he stood he could see the window, framing the last glow in the west. The door swung to a stop. Now he had to walk inside, or do something. But Matson solved the problem for him.

"Hello, Jarrett," he said.

Matson spoke moving. He shifted his position, in the event Jarrett would shoot, but nothing of the sort happened, of course. The fact that Matson was as wary as Jarrett himself was a relief, and Jarrett laughed. But the laugh had a hard sound. It came back to him, an echo, unexpectedly close.

"You son of a bitch," he said.

"Don't call me names."

"Eh?"

"You listen to me!" Matson said. "That's all over and done with."

"What's all over and done with?"

"Wyoming. This is a different country. I'm willing to let bygones be bygones. You do the same, too. It'll be better for both of us."

"All right, but light the lamp."

"It's your room. You light it."

"You were here first—I defer to you, Matson."

"What the hell, do you think I'm going to shoot you? If I wanted you, I could have had you a lot easier than this. I could have bagged you down by the river and pushed you into the quicksand. Instead, I came here, and paid that Mexican kid fifty cents to show me your room and swipe me a key."

Jarrett had to laugh. "He's quite a kid, isn't he? He's going to get on in the world. He'll be going around in two-hue leather boots and a silk shirt when we're under the sod, Matson. But just the same, *you* light the lamp. Getting here first wins you the privilege."

Matson pulled a shade, shutting out the sky, and struck a match. After the darkness it seemed very bright. Jarrett could see his black trousers and shirt, his long hand with the white fingernails that reminded him of the claws of a chicken. Matson lit the lamp and put the chimney on. He adjusted the wick. Then he stood looking at Jarrett.

He had a pair of dead-looking eyes. Up in Wyoming he had not displayed the slightest emotion when shown the exhumed bodies of the Weaver brothers. He hadn't even bothered to deny his guilt when he was faced with the proof. And when they sentenced him to hang he hadn't shown any reaction to that, either. He had the killer's greatest asset, a complete absence of emotion.

"What'd you do, break out?"

"No, they turned me loose."

The man was obviously telling the truth. "Who turned you loose?" Jarrett asked.

"The sheriff in Cheyenne. Those were stolen horses, just like I said they were. The Weavers were horse thieves. There's no law against killing a horse thief, on sight or any other way. I was supposed to get a reward, but they never paid it to me. They turned me loose and told me to leave town. I killed three horse thieves, and that was the thanks I got for it."

"Yeah, that's gratitude."

"So I said to hell with 'em. I always despised that town of Cheyenne. All those Army fellows, officers with their mighty ways, women that won't speak to you. I went to Denver, and down to the Sangre Basin. I got a job with a freight outfit—guard. I scouted down in the Nations, and then I came here. I'm pretty highly regarded amongst the freight outfits. I had a job offered me to ride shotgun on the Arizona coach line. I was down in the South, too. Along the coast. I was offered jobs there—guard and detective work. I just bring this out in case you still believe those lies up in Wyoming. I know you were a policeman there and were just doing your job. I hold no hard feelings . . . but I don't want you believing any lies."

He said it dead-eyed, with the eyes of a pike, or a barracuda, and Jarrett knew he was merely saying the conventional words, and that he didn't care what anybody believed, as long as it didn't interfere with the money he made. He stayed on the other side of the lamp now. He didn't act wary, but he was. And his cold-fish deadliness never changed.

"Where were you on the coast—in Galveston?"

"Partly."

"Who are you working for now?"

"That's none of your business."

"Don't push it, Matson. I hate your yellow guts. If I kill you in this room—"

"You're not going to kill me. You're going to listen to me."

"Why?"

"Because I represent some pretty big people, and I can make you some money."

"All right, I'm listening."

"Fine. I'm glad to see you get off your high horse. Haven't you got any liquor around?"

"I said I'd listen to you. I didn't say I'd drink with you."

"As you say. I thought it'd be easier if we were friends, but I can treat you either way. You know what's over in that bank?"

"One hundred thousand dollars?"

Matson stood perfectly still. It was his way of showing surprise. "So I was right!"

"What do you mean, you were right?"

"You did come here to get your hooks into the money."

In a way it was true, only Jarrett hadn't known about that particular money.

Matson went on, "You're no better'n anybody. I heard that was why you got run off from Wells Fargo. You were in with the Cap Rock gang and they found out."

"Pilot Rock gang."

"Cap Rock or Pilot Rock, it spells out the same thing—that you're exactly what you accused me of being." He got a bitter satisfaction from what he deemed to be Jarrett's admission. "And the way you tossed me into that louse-filled jail! Without tobacco or a damn thing."

"What do you want? Tell me, and get out."

"You came here to rob that bank."

"Alone? Let me look at myself in the mirror. I must be quite a man."

"You're a good man with a gun. And you can make friends. That's why I'm here talking to you. For instance, you've made friends with Zack Thomas already."

"We're as close as some brothers. Cain and Abel."

"You got acquainted. I could see you two chinning away like good fellows."

"We were talking about that hundred thousand dollars."

"What did he say about it?"

"Don't be a damn fool. There's no hundred thousand dollars. It'll end by being ten thousand dollars. Or five. Why would anybody have a hundred thousand? You could buy all of Texas for a hundred thousand, cash being scarce as it is."

"It's a *hundred thousand dollars!*"

He meant it; he meant it so fish-eyed earnest that Jarrett almost believed him. Now he was feeling a peculiar excitement, like one long hungry who has had a drink, a very small drink, of good French brandy. He could feel excitement running through him. He was no longer tired. It took all his will power to resist pacing the room. He forced himself to remain as dead calm as his visitor.

"All right, so it's a hundred thousand dollars. What about it?"

"We're taking it."

"We?"

"Us—and some others. Men I can trust. Men who served with me up in the Nations. Wagon guards—veterans, a lot of them—former Confederate soldiers."

"Outlaws."

"A man's a man, and a good man is a good man. I got some good men."

"Where are they?"

Matson didn't answer.

"I might tell you that Zach Thomas is already suspicious," Jarrett said.

"I know. That's why I'm here seeing you."

"He's suspicious of me. He saw you standing over there, and he's suspicious of you. He's suspicious as a rogue wolf, and unless I miss my guess he's got the fangs to match."

"All right, just forget I ever called on you." Matson started for the door.

It was a bluff, and Jarrett could have booted himself for saying, "Wait!"

Matson stopped, grinning. "Change your mind?"

"Say I *might* join you. What would you want me to do?"

"Get on the coach with him."

"What coach?"

"The one him and Ansel are taking the money on."

"They're taking it? Where?"

"Out along the line."

"The coach runs pretty crowded."

"His won't be."

"How do you know?"

"He's sent for a special one—for tomorrow."

"You know that?"

"I know it."

Matson was not really very smart, Jarrett was thinking. He was working for somebody, and it had to be someone of importance.

"How about the other fellow? The one on the ground floor who's afraid of high places?"

"Ansel?"

"Yes."

"They'll both be on it. Him and Ansel. They'll be out of here tomorrow before noon."

"And I'm supposed to be on the coach with them? How am I going to accomplish that miracle?"

"The money will be on it. You'll be on it."

"You mean I'll just naturally figure a way?"

"Yes."

"Thanks. After I get on it, then what?"

"If it goes out the stage road, nothing. We'll take care of things. But once it leaves the stage road, any place, you'll have to delay it. That'll be your job, just delay it. Give us

27

two hours and we'll be there. And of course we'll expect your help."

"How many men have you got?"

"Eleven—twelve counting myself."

"That ought to take care of things most handily!"

"There's one other thing," Matson said.

"Yes?"

"That Mexican boy. He knows I came here to see you. He knows too much. I want him got rid of."

"You're telling this to me?"

"All right then, I'll get rid of him."

"You mean you'll kill him?"

"Don't think I enjoy it. It just has to be done. One Mexican kid more or less—there's no shortage of Mexicans. I'll cut his throat and stick him down a badger hole."

"You son of a bitch! If that kid isn't around here tomorrow, I'll kill *you*."

"And wipe out your chance at a share in a hundred thousand? I think not."

"You try me, Matson!"

"All right, he's your problem."

"And about that hundred thousand—what's my share? You don't need to think I'll settle for a thirteenth."

"I'm not a coach robber."

Jarrett couldn't have been more surprised if he'd blandly denied being a killer.

"What in hell are you talking about—you're not a coach robber?"

"I'm not *robbing* that coach! I'm getting that money back to its proper owners."

"Oh, my God!" said Jarrett, needing a place to sit down.

"I told you I was a detective."

"You can call yourself by any name you like as long as I get my share. And if I'm to be the brains of this enterprise, my share will be exactly thirty thousand dollars."

"You'll get three."

"Three thousand? That's small change."

"Three thousand—and complete protection from prosecution."

"Your employers can promise that?"

"They can."

"Why, Zach is way up in political circles. He elects 'em. He tells 'em what to do. How can—"

"No prosecution. We're returning this money to its owners. If the job's done right, there may be a little extra. But it has to be done *right*."

"No warrant and no arrests?"

"Yes—but be on that coach tomorrow."

You son of a bitch, thought Jarrett, watching him go out of the door. You fish-eyed, killing, back-shooting son of a bitch. But a hundred thousand dollars! . . .

VI

Jarrett left at midnight in a livery rig, taking the Mexican kid along so Matson couldn't get his hands on him, and because he needed somebody to show him the way. Toward morning, with a ranch in sight, he turned the kid loose with five dollars and a warning.

"I ought to take your hide off for giving the key to Matson, but I'm telling you, stay away from him, because he'll kill you."

"Yes, Señor Caballero!"

He waited until smoke showed from the chimney, and then drove down to the ranch house. It was a small spread, running horses, and owned by a couple of bachelors named Fowler and McReedy. They asked him in for pancakes and sowbelly, and McReedy drove him down to the stage road.

"There's a bridge like you were looking for. And thanks for the ten dollars. I'll drive the rig back to Floral City tomorrow. But I don't fancy just leaving you. I better come back tonight, because if that coach is loaded to the racks like it generally is they'll pass you by."

"No, they won't pass me by. It's against the law for a public conveyance to pass a stranded man."

"Law means nothing to a coach company."

"Then I'll sue 'em and get rich."

He was at the crossing of a steep-sided little creek. The bridge was made of axe-squared cottonwood logs, and it was a simple matter to dismantle one side of it. All he needed to do was get below and shoulder-lever one of the beams out of place. He managed this, and then, sweating, he sat down and waited. The creek was dry-baked, with a little wetness farther along, and some green-scummed potholes. A few dwarf trees gave shade. He had a bottle of water and plenty of cigars.

29

He sat on his saddle. It was very hot. He hadn't seen a cloud since he came to Texas. Down in the creek, above a pothole, swarms of insects rose and fell in the sunlight. The road twisted away through the mesquite, and the heat distortion made it seem to stand on end like a sidewinder snake.

He was ready for a long wait, an all-day one, if necessary, and maybe on into the next, because Matson's information might be wrong. But in less than an hour a coach came in sight.

It was not the regular one, but was smaller, and lightly loaded. You could tell its lack of cargo by the way it rolled, pitching fore-and-aft on its leather springs. Two men sat in the seat, and one of them had a gun. On most runs the shotgun guard was dispensed with in favor of a cash passenger. A man inside was leaning out, looking. The driver slowed down. He was talking to the man who leaned out.

It was too far for Jarrett to see distinctly, and the heat rose making everything look as if it were being viewed through a cheap magnifying glass, but he knew that the man leaning out was Zach Thomas. He knew it by instinct, by a tingle at his nerve ends.

The guard stood up, holding the iron rack with one hand, and peering up and down the creek. The coach stopped altogether. Smiling, Jarrett walked down the road with his arms well away from his body. The guard leveled his gun. He beaded down so exactly that Jarrett could not even see the sun glimmer of the barrels, only their twin black holes. It looked like about ten gauge. Loaded with No. 2 buckshot, it would pattern out just about right to riddle him in a circle from chin to bellybutton.

"My horse got away," called Jarrett in his most pleasant tone.

"What?"

"My horse got away. I'm stranded."

Zack was saying something, and the driver was answering him. Another man was inside the coach, but he did not show himself, and Jarrett was aware of him only as a shadow. That would be the railroad representative, Ansel.

"Why, it's Mr. Thomas!" called Jarrett, as if he had just recognized Zach. "Am I relieved to see *you!* I seem to be stranded, sir, in this God-awful desert."

"Who are you?"

"Mr. Jarrett. Jarrett of the Dixie Gulf & Trans-Southern. Don't you remember? The barber shop." He started on as if now it was certainly all right, but a twitch of the shotgun stopped him.

"Mr. Thomas, the joke seems to be on me! Simple confession is good for the soul, and I'll own to startin' out tryin' to get ahead of you with these ranchers and their water rights, but damn if it didn't seem to backfire. Now, sir, you *do* have me at quite a disadvantage—"

"Where's the rest of 'em?" barked the guard.

"The rest of who?"

"The rest of your gang. This is the oldest dodge in the world, but I'm not being took in by it. Do you have 'em hiding along the crick?"

"No, sir! I'm alone, absolutely. You keep me covered, sir, and send somebody to inspect. And if I'm not telling the truth you have my permission to pull that trigger."

"Tell him to get out of the way, we're coming across," said Zach Thomas.

"Not across this bridge, you *can't*. It looks like something happened to it. It looks like the buffalo got under it and hoisted some of the beams away."

"There are no buffalo in this country."

"Well, something was at it."

After an exchange with Thomas, the guard got down, surly and mean, a slab-faced man with a drooping mustache, and came forward to have a look at things. He walked along the creek and saw nothing. Magpies were tilting and balancing on the limbs of the few trees, and any guard who developed an eye for such things could tell at a glance that nobody was hiding there, because magpies are the wariest birds in creation.

"It's all right," he said. "He's alone."

"Yes, sir, Mr. Thomas! You're as safe as a babe in his mother's arms."

The coach now came forward.

"I ought to kill you on general principles," said Zach Thomas. He had peeled down to his linen shirt in the heat, but his gun was strapped to him by its rather complicated harness.

"Fellow railroad men!" Jarrett said cheerily. "Courtesy of the road! We of Dixie Gulf & Trans-Southern always honor the other line's passes."

"How about it, Ansel—did you ever hear of a railroad financier by the name of Joseph T. Jarrett?"

Ansel was a small, middle-aged man with a face that reminded Jarrett of a lap dog's. He was obviously upset at the surroundings in which he had found himself. Despite the heat, he wore his jacket, a black one; and with his little hard hat on his head he looked as if he should be sitting in a hack in Louisville rather than in this beaten, heat-shriveled stagecoach.

"No!" he said, after blinking several times. "I have not. Nor have I heard of the rail line he purports to represent. This man is an impostor."

"Oh, I think you're dignifying him too much. He looks like a cheap swindler to me," Thomas said.

"Ha-ha! Oh, come, sir! I never objected to you because you were a gaming-house keeper."

"Don't push it too hard, Jarrett."

"What do you want to do?" asked the guard, not giving up hope, and fingering the hot metal of the shotgun.

"Well, first we've got to fix the bridge. You!" Thomas motioned at Jarrett. "Help him."

"I don't go in much for heavy labor. I was hoping you'd invite me into the shade of that coach while this man with the shotgun fixed the bridge."

"You can hope and be damned. You help fix that bridge that you dismembered, and maybe we won't kill you when we drive off."

"It's against the law in this state to drive by a stranded man with a public vehicle. It states specifically that any driver, and/or owner, of any public conveyance, outside a corporate limit, who knowingly—"

"Right there's where you hoodwinked yourself, Jarrett. Because this isn't a public conveyance. It's a private one leased by me, and we're passing you by."

"You do, and you're a dead man by twelve o'clock."

It brought more of a reaction than he had anticipated, and he backed up with his hands very wide, showing there was no possible threat from his own gun at the moment.

"Wait," said Zach. "This is interesting. I want to hear this. What are you threatening me with?"

"I ain't threatening. That's just exactly the point. I'm trying to save your hide."

"You mean that black-shirted killer from in town?"

"Yes sir, that black-shirted killer. He made me an offer, and a mighty princely offer too, to help him kill you."

"You were supposed to be inside the coach and him outside."

"You hit it on the head, sir."

"Well, I'll be damned."

"You want to know how much your life was worth?"

"Yes."

"You ain't going to like this."

"How much?"

32

"I was to get three thousand dollars. I said I thought your life was worth thirty thousand dollars. But he said *three* thousand."

"So you settled for three."

"I pretended to."

"How can I be sure of that?"

"Why, you can have my gun. I'll be riding right inside where you can watch me. And I'll be able to tell you some other interesting things, but not out here in the sun. No, sir, I'd like very much to be inside that coach while I'm telling you."

"Such as what?"

"Such as who it was wants you killed."

"You told me. That black-shirted—"

"Now, why would he want to kill you? He's nothing but a gunman. He was a scout and a guard for some freight outfits. And all of a sudden he shows up here to kill you. Why? I should think you'd be curious to get to the bottom of a thing like that, Mr. Thomas."

"Get his gun," he said to the guard. "Hand it here. This is a nice piece. Colt, special bore. Your name engraved. Why, it really is Joseph T. Jarrett! That's a mighty fine gun. Mighty fine."

"Shall I get in the coach?"

"Get in, get in."

"Thank you, sir. I'll never forget this favor."

He got in the coach, and Ansel recoiled from him as if he were a gila monster.

Zach Thomas said, "There's one thing I don't understand. Why did you put yourself out there like a pigeon at a gun-club shoot? Why'd you take a gamble like that? Most men would have killed you already."

"I'm a good judge of human nature, Zach. And as soon as I saw you sitting in that barber chair I thought, there's a man whose life is worth a heap more'n three thousand dollars, and he's bright enough to know it. I said to myself, 'Joe Jarrett, at three thousand dollars you're being underpaid.' I said, 'Joe, Mr. Thomas is going to reward you a heap more than that for saving his life!' "

VII

Zach Thomas seemed to be in no hurry to find out who had designs against his life. He was enjoying testing the balance of Jarrett's gun. He weighed it, right hand and left hand, drew out his own gun and tested the twin balances of both, and tried each of them in his holster.

"I'll keep this to remember you by," he said to Jarrett.

"I know you're just joking, sir. The Zachariah Thomas I heard tell about wouldn't do a thing like that."

Outside, the guard and the driver labored and cursed the bridge, and finally got it back together to allow the coach a perilous, tilted passage across. It rolled on up the road, which wound through resin brush toward the slot passages of some distant mesas. It was so hot the rabbits wouldn't get out of the road, but sat crouched in the shade with dust kicking over them.

"Who wants to kill me?" Zach Thomas asked.

"I can't give you their exact names, but I—"

"You know, I knew you were going to say that."

"I can give you the town where they live."

"Just name any town in Texas and you'll find somebody who wants to kill me. I've won too much of their money."

"Yes, sir. But this town is Galveston."

It had less effect on him than Jarrett had hoped. He went on, "I figured we could strike up a little plan. The two of us could maybe be partners, a sort of Let's Keep Zach Thomas Healthy and Wealthy Society."

"That's a jolly idea! We could be partners. Me and all my property, and you with your hand-made gun and good, beaming smile."

"You're taking the wrong attitude—"

"That may be so." Thomas looked at his watch. "It is now exactly an hour and twenty minutes before noon. Noon was when I was to die. Noon was when this attack was to come. Noon or before, right?"

"That's only approximate. Good God, man—"

"You said I'd be a dead man by twelve o'clock. I'll wait till twelve o'clock. And if those so-called attackers don't show

34

up, I'm going to kill you. I'll kill you because it's what you got coming."

"Man, use your head—"

"No, I'll use my gun." He took aim. "Yes, I'm going to kill you because it's justice. Because you got on this coach, making use of my good nature and my confidence, obviously for the one purpose of robbing me."

"No, Thomas. I urge you as a—"

Thomas cut him short. "Time will tell. I'm going to take a little nap. The secret of traveling in these vehicles is to rest. Don't use one bit more energy than you have to. Breathe deep and slow. Relax. Think pleasant thoughts. Think about cool waters."

Ansel said, "Perhaps there really are some bandits. If so, I think some precautions are called for."

"Like what?" asked Zach, eyes closed.

"We could turn back."

"Maybe when I've had my sleep we'll talk about it further."

He really means it, thought Jarrett. He doesn't believe a word I said, and at the stroke of twelve this man really intends to kill me.

The coach rolled on monotonously. Zach Thomas breathed slowly and deeply. His eyes were closed, or almost. Only the tiniest slits of eyeball could be seen—the whites of his eyes, and a man could not see out of the whites. I have only to lurch with the coach, Jarrett thought, and I'd have him. But the gun was there, almost pointed, and a twitch, a slight angling, the hammer, the trigger, and *crash!* That would be it. The finish. It gave him a strange giddiness, and a sickness in the pit of his stomach, the pit of his guts, the pit of everything. Down, down, down, spinning into blackness, unending and eternal. He shivered. Ansel beside him cleared his throat. And one eyelid of Zach Thomas seemed to tremble.

"Nice day," said Jarrett. "What was that name again—Ansel?"

"Ansel. Jonas Ansel."

Ansel did not take his eyes off the gun. Seated as he was, shoulder to shoulder with Jarrett, he was probably frightened, the poor fellow, that Thomas might miss. It could happen very easily on the rocking, swaying stagecoach. Ansel had the eyes of a cornered packrat.

"Mr. Ansel," Jarrett said, "I wonder if you'd mind changing places? The sun gets you most abusively where—"

"Stay where you are," said Zach Thomas.

"You're not what would be called a sound sleeper."

"I sleep one side at a time."

"Is that dorsal and ventral, or port and starboard?"

"Port and starboard. I swap hands now and then with the gun."

"Town ahead," called the guard.

"There can't be," said the driver.

"I can see the window reflections."

"It's not a town."

"It's a house then."

"It's no house either. I pass here every week."

"It's somebody signaling with a mirror," said Jarrett casually.

Thomas lowered the gun—not all the way, but a breath-giving trifle. "How about it?" he asked, leaning out.

"It could be a mirror. It's coming from beside that little mesa," the driver said.

"Ask him if it's Blackie Matson," said Jarrett.

"It's somebody on a horse. It has to be, the way the light's moving. I saw Injuns, Comanches, out in New Mexico, and—"

"God damn it, get off this road!" shouted Zach.

The driver obeyed, and started whipping the horses.

"How many are there?" Zach asked, holding fast.

"I can't tell!"

With practiced hands, the driver kept the coach weaving around the worst of the prairie roughness as he steered a course aimed at passing the mesa on the side least suited to ambush. It hit a slight depression full tilt, with its wheels momentarily off the ground. Zach Thomas had to use both hands to save himself, quickly holstering his pistol as he did so. Both Jarrett and Ansel were half knocked from their seats. All three men were sprawling and tangled, but when Jarrett got free he had recovered his pistol.

"Maybe I ought to collect my three thousand, Zach!"

"A man's got a right to be wrong, hasn't he?"

"Here they come!" called the driver. "There's four or five of 'em."

A bullet from far off struck dirt and made a dull bumble-bee sound glancing away through the heat. A second bullet winged through the coach, scattering slivers, one of which hung like a porcupine quill to Zach Thomas' cheek. He cursed and pulled it out, and blood followed in a bright streak, mixing with sweat and the filming dust.

For half a minute all anyone could do was hang tight while the coach careened over the bumpy ground. There was a depression which in other seasons had been a shallow lake, and the driver took the outfit into it. The bottom was clay, dried and curled into squares the size of a man's hand. It crunched with a sound like hail on a canvas roof as the wheels rolled over it. The guard was shooting.

Three of the riders were far back, but a fourth, following a different route, came in close, and Zach, taking a long unsteady aim, pulled the trigger. The man pulled around as if stung, and went head and shoulder foremost off the far side of his horse. The horse went down with a roll of dust, and got up almost immediately, side-trotting off to keep from stepping on the bridle, leaving the rider a blue-shirted, still form on the ground.

"That was a lucky shot," said Jarrett. "That had to be a dog-lucky shot."

There was no doubt of that. The man had been a good two hundred yards away.

The lake bed ended and the driver commenced pulling his team in a wide circle, as if to regain the road.

"What's going on?" Zach yelled.

"We'll never outrun 'em with these teams. Our only chance is make it to Mesa Wells."

"Keep rolling! I *want* 'em to catch up."

The guard kept shooting, his buckshot falling short and pounding patterns of dust.

"When are *you* going to cut loose?" Zach asked Jarrett.

"Whenever I won't waste bullets."

Two men had ridden a long cut-across from the mesa and dismounted, their horses visible in a clump of resin brush. There they waited for a dead shot when the coach passed, but the driver had spotted them. He managed to bring the coach around in a full-speed turn by means of reins and the brake, but the sudden action sent everyone grabbing and sprawling. Ansel had gone to hands and knees on the floor, and both Jarrett and Thomas fell over him. Above, the guard, who was reloading, dropped both cartridges and had to hunt for more.

At that instant two guns exploded almost in unison. The guard was hit and knocked to the back of the seat. He sat with his boots sticking out and the gun thrust in front of him. He stood up as the coach lunged on, and pitched head foremost over the side. Somehow one boot became twisted in a seat brace. He hung head down, a dead and heavy weight, his arms dangling, hands almost to the ground. The front wheel on that side kept banging and scraping his head. His face, turned toward Jarrett, seemed to be looking in at him. It was a bloody face, bullet-smashed, with a gaping hole where his nose had been.

"Get him loose up there!" called Jarrett.

"I ain't a-holdin' him!" answered the driver.

Then a heavier wham of the coach wheels jerked the man so that his boot sole came loose and he fell free into the resin brush.

Zach Thomas, taking a box of cartridges from his coat pocket, got up to take the guard's place. He tried to get out of the door, but the door, when opened, swung back and forth, threatening to spill him to the earth. He came back inside and crawled through the window. His long legs with their expensive trousers were all Jarrett could see of him as he wrapped himself around the top edge of the coach; then he hoisted himself up, with only his good Spanish boots in view. After they were gone from sight he must have given a command to the driver, for he turned the coach toward the other side of the mesquite brush.

The ambushers now made the mistake of looking for a new position. Zach hit one of them and he reeled out, clutching his chest with both hands. The other man went crawling, and Jarrett's bullets went on both sides of him. He was having no luck at all, and Zach shouted down, "What the hell's the trouble? Maybe you don't *want* to hit 'em."

"You just got in another lucky one, Zach."

"I'm always lucky."

"And modesty isn't one of your traits!"

"You don't have to be modest in this world, you have to be *good*."

Two riders were in pursuit. Jarrett would freeze down, but each time he pulled the trigger a sudden movement would lift the gun and he would fire off at the gray-blue sky, or else the floor would drop from under his feet and the bullet would lift dirt in a streak fifty or sixty yards too short. But he kept shooting, and his gun grew hot in his hand. It felt as if it had been all day in the sun, and then it felt as if it had come from a blacksmith's forge, and the powder commenced gumming and making the cylinder stick.

He reloaded, spit on the cylinder at the worst sticking place, and fired again—just a snap shot to see if the gun would work—and a rider was hit. He went off his horse as though he had been low-bridged by a clothesline. His horse simply ran from under him and he was left rolling in the dirt.

"How's that for shootin', Zach?" Jarrett yelled. "That's the way we shot in the circus."

"Every bullet has to go some place!"

The other rider decided not to continue. Like the dog chasing the train, thought Jarrett, that didn't know what he'd do with it if he caught it. The man dismounted with a sliding of boots, went to his belly with a rifle, and commenced levering bullets into the back of the coach. Every one of them went through some place, tearing slivers of oak, leaving a burnt smell, a smell of sulphur and saltpetre.

"There's a very peculiar thing, Mr. Ansel," said Jarrett, reloading again. "How in the world could any of the sulphur and saltpetre stick to 'em after all that distance? Mr. Ansel! Mr. Ansel, do you hear me?"

Ansel was on hands and knees so close against the floor that his back was bowed. Jarrett tried to help him back to the seat, but he wouldn't cooperate.

"Ansel! Mr. Ansel! We're out of rifle range. You might as well be comfortable."

His hand came away warm and slippery. There is a certain slick-sticky quality possessed by nothing except blood. Jarrett looked at the smear of red over his hand and wrist. Ansel had been hit, and hit bad. It had gone through him under the armpits. There was blood on the floor, and a dug-out place where the spent bullet had mushroomed, leaving a shine of new-turned lead.

"Ansel!" he called again. The little man looked at him, but his eyes lacked focus. And with each bound and twist of the coach his body rolled as if in swivels of jelly.

"You poor devil! You poor little railroad man. And you played it safer than anybody else."

"Everything all right down there?" called Thomas.

"I'm just lending a hand to Mr. Ansel."

"Is he all right?"

"He ain't complaining."

He went through Ansel's pockets. He had a wallet with a thick sheaf of money—he was carrying five hundred, at the very least. Jarrett put the money in his own pocket and tossed the wallet aside. The wild progress of the coach seemed to increase, but he braced himself against it and went on with his investigation. He found some cigars, a bottle of patent medicine, a picture of a leathery-faced woman. Across Ansel's vest was a massive watch chain with a lodge insignia that looked rather like a gold flatiron with stars and scimitars and mystic insignia in white ceramic and sapphire chips.

And the watch! Jarrett was a fancier of watches, and this watch was something to behold. It was of heaviest gold, and was almost a clock. What a weight of watch and chain for a little fellow like Ansel to carry around! Time really meant something to him. Jarrett held it swinging on its chain, a solid half-pound of watch at the very least, with engravings of trains, trees, buffaloes, and steamboats.

"There they are!" Zach Thomas shouted.

"Get 'em, Zach!"

There was an inscription:

> To Jonas Ansel . . . for
> 25 years of unwavering loyalty.
> Thaddeus Markam, Pres.,
> Texas-Interstate Ry.

The front of the watch flipped open. The figures were of filigree gold, elevated. He closed the watch, and heard music. No doubt of it, above the banging of the coach and the explosion of gunfire he heard the sound of bells. It took him a second to realize it was coming from the watch. It was twelve o'clock, and the watch chimed the hour.

He realized that the horses were running away, and knew the driver must have been hit. He could see the reins streaking along beside the wheels. He put the watch in his pocket just as the driver went headlong to the ground. There he lay among cactus, face down.

"Hey, who's driving the coach?" Jarrett called.

"I am!" Zach answered.

"Why don't you use the reins?"

"I can't reach 'em." Zach was on his stomach, with his boots braced on the luggage rail.

"Put on the brake."

"To hell with the brake! I like to be a moving target."

"Target for who?"

"They're up ahead. I thought you said there'd be an even dozen. I killed an even dozen already."

Ahead he saw some gullies and the face of a mesa. A smooth-looking swale rounding the mesa seemed the only route possible, and the horses were headed for it. Horsemen were there, dismounting or arriving at a gallop. He saw Matson, knew him by his stiff gestures as he thrust his rifle, giving commands.

They'll riddle us like cheese, Jarrett thought.

The coach thundered on. There was still plenty of run in the horses. The way was slightly downhill, and the coach, overtaking the wheelers, frightened them to an even wilder gallop, and the leaders had to outrun them. Mesquite bushes whipped the sides and cast off brownish twigs. The bushes roared beneath the coach floor, and Jarrett could smell the hot gum, and the dust of the flying screwbean pods. Presently the coach mounted a steep, curving pitch and skidded, with only two wheels touching the ground. Ahead was the mesa face, which looked much lower than from a distance, and here were men and horses.

The coach door, swinging open, caught a bullet that glanced over Jarrett's head. He saw a man standing not ten yards away, levering a rifle. The picture of him was a half-second frozen in time and space. Jarrett shot him, and the man sat down on folded legs. There was a shocked, slack look on his face. It was the picture Jarrett carried with him as the coach rolled on and bullets tore it from both sides, and from the rear.

He kept firing. Men had scattered and were crawling for cover; a couple of them were riding off. One of them was shot in the back—Matson had done that, he knew.

When his gun stuck, he had no spit left to soften the burnt powder, so he poured Ansel's patent medicine over it. It had a smell like brandy. It cut the powder cake and dripped black syrup. He wiped the gun on Ansel's coatsleeve and reloaded.

He decided to try some of the medicine on himself. It contained about forty per cent alcohol, and gave him a quick bolt of energy. It tasted like the very devil, but once it was down he could feel new life running through his veins. He tilted the bottle and drank the rest of it.

"Ee-ya-hoo!" he shouted. "Roll, you wagons!"

"Ee-ya-hoo!" Zach answered. "Run, you bang-tailed buffaloes." He had no control over the teams, so he swung the whip, driving them to an even wilder gallop. The coach kept rolling.

There was a steep rise and a steeper descent. "Hold it, we're going over the jumps!" Zach called. The coach climbed, and left the ground. Jarrett had a sensation of flying, with no seat under him, no floor, nothing. Then he was on his side, and he could see sky through one of the doors.

Ansel was there, close to him, and Jarrett had the ridiculous feeling that Ansel was dancing with him. He was entwined in the man's arms and legs, and both of them were turning. Then there was a crash, and dirt filled all the air. He couldn't see or hear for dirt.

And then everything stopped. He lay content and tired. He

41

didn't want to move—he didn't want to do a thing. Nothing seemed important. He could hear the horses kicking and smashing; he could feel the tug of them on the coach. Someone looked in on him, but he was content just to lie there. He wanted nobody to disturb him. Not then, not ever.

VIII

Some time must have passed, for the sun, shining through the broken roof, had made his shoulder hot. The horses were still demolishing the coach. Then he knew it could not be the horses. It was not like the smashing of hoofs. Rather, a creak and jiggle, creak and jiggle.

Dirt was in his throat and nostrils. The harder he tried to breathe, the less air he got. He managed to extricate himself from under a seat, from under Mr. Ansel, and move up through one of the windows.

That noise was Zach trying to rip a board off the coach, and he was too preoccupied to see him. Jarrett felt for his gun. He had dropped it when the coach overturned. He lowered himself again, and looked for it. It was under Ansel— a strip of the ivory handle was visible. The front sight was tangled in the dead man's clothing and he had a hard time pulling it free. Then he stood up again, through the window.

Zach was still working on the plank. It was a tough strip of oak, and it was held by screws. He had no screwdriver, and they held tenaciously. He was using the barrel of his gun as a pry, working a wedge along to keep the crack widening, and the fingers of one hand were bleeding. Then, as he gave a final heave, a screw gave way and the board was loose. It flew back with a snap like a released bow, and as Zach exhaled, money spilled from a sack. They were gold coins of large size, almost as large as dollars, and they ran with a heavy music into the dirt. Zach waited until the gold stopped, and then pulled out some currency. There was more currency, and more, flat-wrapped in bank wrappings.

Jarrett slowly lifted himself up through the window. He used his elbows, and never for an instant failed to cover Zach Thomas with the gun. He did not make a sound. He stood clear, and Zach still had not seen him—he was like a man mesmerized, staring at the money. Now and then he would reach and touch the sack from which the gold had burst, and more coins would fall with a clinking music.

"Nice, nice," said Jarrett.

Zach spun and started with his gun, but he checked himself. He froze as a man might on waking up and finding a rattlesnake coiled beside his bed, a rattlesnake that the slightest twitch of a muscle would startle into striking. For Jarrett's gun was cocked—and it had a honed hair trigger. And Jarrett was squinting down the knife edge and V sights exactly between his eyes.

"Drop it, Zach. Drop the gun."

Zach dropped his gun. The act seemed to give him great pain. The gun fell at his feet.

"Give it a kick so it won't tempt you. Now, what is that stuff you took out? Is that money?"

"Don't get any ideas, Jarrett, please. Don't get yourself into trouble. This kind of money will never do you any good."

"I ain't looking for trouble. Trouble I've had in plenty. But chiefly for *want* of money. And I *do* enjoy the sight of it. Some people like to look at pictures, and some at sunsets, but I like to look at money. I even like hearing it. I like listening to the jingle of gold coins. There's no music like it. Those old yella boys! Look at all that money! And to think that Enoch Lantern told me that the meek would inherit the earth!"

"Who?"

"Enoch Lantern. My old spiritual advisor."

"You had one?"

"I did. He used to tell me, 'The meek shall inherit the earth.' But later on I found out you had to have rich relatives. Then he used to say, 'Turn the other cheek,' but the only place it worked for me was in a barber shop. So I saw that these ideas were real good, but they had to be tuned up to the special conditions."

"He didn't say anything about pointing guns at people who just saved your life?"

"No, he didn't, but if the situation ever comes up I'll check into it."

"It's come up, Jarrett. I'm talking about us. About me—Zach Thomas, your friend, the man who picked you up when you were stranded and on foot, and gave you a free ride, and got on top, taking all the risks, driving that mudwagon through hell and gunmen while you rode safe and sound inside with heavy oak to turn the bullets away."

"It would be an untruth to say I hadn't been giving that

43

some thought. I've been here looking at you and that money and thinking about a lot of things. However, the saving of lives I see the other way around. I've been thinking how I came out here in a livery rig at my own expense and tore down a bridge just to get aboard and save your life. And you were hard to convince. You were going to shoot me at the crest of noon, remember? I had to argue and argue, and all the while I was double-crossing those boys back there, Blackie Matson and the rest, who wanted to pay me cash money, three thousand dollars."

"I never intended to kill you."

"No?"

"Of course not." He started forward, but a tenseness in Jarrett's trigger finger checked him.

"Don't make me!" Jarrett said. "After saving your life, I sort of feel a proprietary interest in it. And I *have* saved it. Come to think of it, I'm saving it over and over just by not pulling this trigger. It's got to be a habit, almost. Don't make it a bad habit, Zach. Don't make it one I got to break."

"Oh, I wouldn't want you breaking any habits. The fact is, I'd like very much to be your friend. Not just now, but forever."

"Why, that's right neighborly."

"I was figuring we might join in and pick up this money *together.*"

"It *is* salvage in a way, isn't it? Like a shipwreck. You get fifty per cent for towing 'em into port."

"Ten per cent for stagecoaches."

"I thought it was fifty."

"We might stretch a point and make it fifteen."

"If we get to stretching points, I'll make it a hundred."

He went around and had a look at the money. There were several more sacks of it—flat-packed currency that had to be pulled out. The burst sack kept spilling gold coins every time he jiggled it with his boot.

"Well, I'm tired of standing in this sun," Jarrett said. "I got to get moving. Pick it up, Zach! Gather it all up and put it in one of those carpetbags from the boot. No, let me empty the bag. And I'll take that gun of yours while I'm about it."

"You'll hang for this. That's railroad money. Nobody gets away with that much railroad money. They'll follow you to the end of the world."

"That they may do, but I'll have some fun on the way. Gather it up!"

"Take a fourth of it. You know how much a fourth is? Twenty-five thousand!"

"No, Zach. Gather it all up."

"You were talking about somebody named Enoch Lantern. I've heard of him. Galveston. Lanternlight Orphanage. A great man. Oh, he'll be proud of you! Think of him, if not of yourself. And I'll split fifty-fifty, Jarrett. Share alike. How about it?"

"All right, I'll divide with you half and half. We'll take turns caring for all of it. You had your turn, and now I'll have my turn. I'll write you when your turn comes next. Keep gathering it up. Tromp those bills down hard. Use your foot."

"You're a coward!" Zach said through his teeth, loading money.

"Now, Zach—"

"Yes, you are. You stand there behind that gun, a coward. You haven't got the nerve to face me. A yellow coward."

"I don't like being called a yellow coward."

"You're like all cheap thieves, you don't like the truth. I'll go back to Galveston and be a bigger man broke than you'd be with a million. Because you're not the man I am, Jarrett, and you know it."

"Now, Zach! You're headed for trouble."

"You're yellow. You're afraid of me."

"Now, Zach!"

"I saw you in the barber shop and thought, 'Now, there's a cheap Yankee.' I knew you were with that Blackie. Cheap gunmen. No guts. When the payoff comes you're the little men who had to have the drop. You haven't got the guts to face me. I'm a better man than you are, Jarrett. And you know it."

"Zach, I'm good-natured, but don't push me."

"You're queasy-gutted."

"No—"

"Prove it, then. I'll shoot it out with you toe to toe." He laughed. He had the smile and the eyes that made Jarrett feel like a worm. Jarrett's every instinct was to wipe the smile off Zach Thomas' face. He wanted to throw the gun aside and show the arrogant son-of-a— Whup! thought Jarrett. The fellow almost had you. It's what he's trying to do, Jarrett. Don't let your pride get mixed up in this. Pride is pride, but money is money. A hundred thousand—that's too much to mix up with pride.

He eased slowly and laughed. "No, Zach, I ain't going to fight you. And I'll tell you why. I'll tell you with a story about this fellow named Dade Walkup back in Colorado. He had a gambling house, and one day a mine owner named

45

Charlie Rhue came in and was betting real heavy at faro. He was betting the same cards to win and the same cards to lose all through the deck, and having such an almighty run of luck that Dade got scared he'd lose the joint, so he rang in a cold deck on him. Well, Charlie lost everything he had. He lost twenty thousand dollars, and his mine, his solid gold watch, his diamond ring, and he walked out broke. Then pretty soon it came to him that he'd been cold-decked, so he got his gun and came back. He sent word inside:

" 'Tell Dade to get his gun and come out a-shootin', because I'm here to kill him.'

"So they went in and told Dade, who was in his office, but he wouldn't go out. So Charlie says, 'Tell Dade he's a thief, and he runs a crooked game. Not only that, tell him I said he doesn't know who his father was, and his mother don't either.'

"But Dade still wouldn't come out. Then Charlie insulted him as he'd never been insulted before.

" 'Tell Dade that he's the lowest thing I can lay my tongue to. Tell him he's nothing but a Yankee and a Roman Catholic.'

"Well, when the boys came in with that he really had Dade sweating, but he still wouldn't go out and fight him.

" 'No,' he says, 'I'd like to favor Charlie, but just look at it from my viewpoint. If he gets killed what's he got to lose? Why, he's nothing but a pauper. But look at me. I'm one of the wealthiest men in this camp. I got a gambling house, a mine, twenty thousand dollars, a solid gold watch, and a diamond ring. I'm not afraid of Charlie, but I'm a gambling man and I don't like the odds.'

"And that's how it is with me, Zach. I'd like to accommodate you, but you're looking at a man with a hundred thousand dollars, and as far as I can see, you're broke. You go and find another stake for yourself, Zach, and I'll fight you on even terms."

Slowly, very slowly, Zach Thomas filled the bag with money. At last he had it all. The gold was very heavy.

"It's lucky I brought my saddle," said Jarrett.

"Yeah, it's almost as if you had this in mind all the time."

"Do you mind saddling me a horse? I'd like that big-rumped bay. And I'll take the blaze-face mare for a pack horse."

"I'm not a hostler. I don't mind gathering money—"

"Zach, you ought to know I couldn't do that job of saddling while you're here waiting the chance to find a gun

46

some place and shoot me in the back. I'll just have to kill you. It's the only other choice. In one way, letting you hostle is like—"

"I know, you're just saving my life."

"Some day you can pay me back."

"Mr. Jarrett," he said fervently, "I will. Some day I'll pay you back with one hundred per cent interest!"

IX

It was fine to have a saddle. He certainly knew what he was about when he brought that saddle. Being prepared made all the difference in the world. It meant the difference between comfort and discomfort, success and failure. He was a rich man now, and he felt like one, much more than if he'd had to ride bareback. He led the mare with his baggage on her, except for the money, and that he kept in front of him, between his waist and the pommel. The other team he drove with him, hazing them along a mile or so, not to inconvenience Zach, but merely to keep him from getting over to the road, where he might hail a passer-by, and call the sheriff.

He could well imagine the story Zach would have for the sheriff, trying to make out that Jarrett had stolen the money, instead of just taking charge of it, which was a different thing entirely; and that he had been in with the bandits, Matson's right-hand man, seen together in Floral City, et cetera.

"Now, you wait for me, Zach," he had called back from long pistol range, after keeping him out in the open as a precaution. "You wait for me right there, Zach. I'm going in to deposit this money in a safe place, but I'll be back with an undertaker for poor Mr. Ansel."

"You son of a bitch!" he could hear Zach shouting. "You'll find out you made the mistake of your life leaving me out here on the desert."

"Now, that's no way to talk about Texas."

"I'll catch up with you, Jarrett. You better kill me right now, because I promise you—"

"If I killed you there'd be nobody to sit with Mr. Ansel. Besides, who would explain about the money? The railroad company is going to be mighty worried about their money. They're going to take some convincing, and from what I hear you're a great convincer."

"For God's sake, Jarrett, at least leave me a horse."

"Walkin' ain't bad if you wait till the cool of the evening. You'll find Fort Worth is in that direction, whilst Galveston is thataway. And on the other hand, if you prefer the joys of Baton Rouge, you'll find it yonder."

And so they had parted.

He dropped over one of the low, prairie rims and nothing was visible then except the mesas and the illimitable circle of the sky. It was very hot, and the sun reflected from the ground as it would from water, underlighting his hat brim and making him narrow his eyes. There was a dense quality to the Texas sun you found nowhere else, not even in Arizona. The heat and brilliance made it hard to see over a couple hundred yards in any direction. He pulled his hat to his eyebrows and tied a black kerchief across his cheekbones, cutting down the glare, and it helped, just as snow glasses helped in December in the Rockies.

He watched for the glint of riders—for field glasses, a silvered spur, or a concha. Or for gunshine. Often the first sign of riders, even though they might be quite close, as close as half a mile, would be a shine of metal in the brilliance.

But there was nothing. He was the only moving thing in all that great country. He rode southeastward across land that was as flat as a griddle. There was a shallow dry wash where the brush grew in shrunken, brownish clumps, and he dismounted to rest in the shade. He used the money for a pillow; and it was pleasant, from time to time, to move and feel the metallic grating of gold pieces. The watch chimes roused him at each quarter hour and he would get up for a long scrutiny of the back trail, but there was no pursuit. Finally he decided to count the money, and was shocked to find only ninety-six thousand and a few extra dollars. Had some of it been overlooked? It annoyed him to think of being taken for almost four thousand dollars. He was, in a way, responsible for the full amount. What he should have done was count it right there on the spot and force Zach Thomas to an accounting. If it was four thousand short, Zach should have signed a slip, an I.O.U., something to balance the ledgers. He tried smoking one of Ansel's cigars, but they were cheap, crooked-burning, with an ash that looked like coal cinders. They certainly didn't taste like cigars belonging to a man who would be entrusted with a hundred thousand dollars.

48

He wondered who the money belonged to, anyway. Well, obviously it belonged to him, Joseph T. Jarrett. He had saved it from Matson and his gang, and that made half of it his by rights of salvage. The other half, which could be considered the short half, $46,000, he intended to return to its rightful and proper owner and/or owners when and if they presented themselves with *proof*—and within a reasonable length of time. But that didn't mean Jarrett was going to put any ads about it in the paper.

A breeze sprang up, rustling the leaves, and he rode on again. He got to thinking that it was simply preposterous that all that money would be on the coach. He examined the currency and held it to the sun. It wasn't counterfeit—when the sun shone through it you could always tell. It baffled him. There just wasn't that much money in the South, but it was in the sack, and he had it. And, oh God! would there be a manhunt! A man and money hunt.

He decided it was time to stop and think about where to go. It was cooler now; some of the shimmer and flame was gone, and the horizon had shape. Here and there, widely separated, were plumes of dust that could be wagons or riders or dust devils.

It was only a question of time until they picked up his trail. What's the main thing that a fugitive does to set him apart from other people, he thought. Why, he runs. The thing was to do the least expected. He hit on it, and laughed in wonder that it had not occurred to him before. He would go to Galveston. He would beat Matson and Zach Thomas both to Galveston. There he'd be, walking around in his new clothes, looking like a financier, and *being* a financier, and who would ever believe he was a fugitive? No matter what story Zach told. How could he ever prove that Jarrett was even on the coach? He couldn't. Nobody would believe him. They'd all think he went down the deep coulee with the money himself.

Then there was the other thing—those fellows who had hired Matson. Who were they? Well, they were men with ten thousand dollars to hire gunmen, for one thing. It opened a whole new world of opportunity to him, the world of big, easy money.

"Jarrett," he said, "it ain't the money you got, it's what you *do* with what you got that determines the successful man. Why, the secret of this ninety-six thousand might be more important than the money itself. There must be a lot of opportunity some place, or this kind of money wouldn't be floating around."

Part Two

I

A breeze, blowing through the open window, carried a heavy fragrance of flowers. It was the most characteristic smell of Galveston, the one for which that Gulf port was principally celebrated; but Harvey Burden, president of the Merchants & Shippers State Bank, and leading citizen, turned his back on it. He walked around to the side of his carved mahogany desk and blew his nose, one nostril at a time, into a spittoon. Afterward he patted his nose and face with a folded cambric handkerchief. He was a large man, large in face and neck and hands, large in every way, and the handkerchief did not go far. By the time he put it away there were already beads of sweat on his forehead and coursing down the folds of his neck.

"Bah! This heat, and dampness! And those damned, stinking roses!"

He had said it now for the thousandth time, one could tell by his deep and violent fervor. Of all the odors in the world, Harvey Burden most disliked the odor of flowers. He disliked all flowers, but roses the most, and he referred to them all by that name.

He was a Northerner originally, and there had been a time when he enjoyed smelling flowers. But it had been in another climate. It had been in a place where there was winter and summer, fall and spring, where things had a brightness, where they were light and brisk, and not cloyed with the inevitable, insufferable muggy heat of the tropics. And where there was a clean breeze, not one that passed over the God damned rotting tide flats down the island. These fermenting essences! These odors of death! Yes, that was it. That was the key to it, he thought, mopping his face of its perspiration: the smell of death. The smell of Galveston, the Oleander City, always reminded him of the morning after in an undertaking parlor.

He was very fat, but very powerful. As a boy of fourteen he had walked down to Cincinnati and learned the trade of ironmonger. It was there, he said in his lighter moments, that he had learned how to sweat. By the time he was twenty, Burden was known as the most powerful man on the Cincinnati docks. He had fancied himself as a wrestler and made a tour on a showboat meeting all comers, but an Irishman in Owenstown came in with a lump of scrap metal in his fist and broke his jaw. It led to a riot when the Irishman's backers failed to collect. A deck hand set the boat adrift, cutting off town reinforcements, and it took half an hour with clubs and fists to control the situation, and by that time Burden had a mangled jaw that never set right, giving him a cross-bite that he recompensed for by a peculiar, pointing purse of the lips. ("He always looks as if he was ready to spit," people said of Harvey Burden.)

After his wrestling accident he gave up muscular activities and became clerk in a warehouse. The hard times of the 'fifties broke his employer, and he took over the place on lease. He leased steamboats during the off season and used his warehouses—he acquired more and more of them—to store cargo and wait for market opportunities. He took to visiting the best tailors and restaurants, and he put on weight. He engaged in the cotton commission business, moving to New Orleans, and when the war broke out he was one of the most influential men in the Confederacy.

"We all have to fight, but each in his own way," Burden said at a banquet in the winter of 1861. "The soldier fights with a gun. The ladies make lint for bandages. The little children save their pennies for Confederate bonds. And it's up to us of the warehousing and shipping world to do our part, in our own way. Dollars are our cannon and cotton our sabers. With these weapons we got to go forth into the lists of trade and make the Confed'racy felt and respected in the markets and the financial marts of the world. We got to *withhold* cotton, and then we got to *supply*. Timing is the thing. And these fellows at Montgomery will have to learn that when it comes to finance, nothing takes the place of a banker; or in business, that nothing takes the place of a businessman. I say, give us freedom to act and we'll go a long way, internationally, toward winning this *wah!*"

One would never have guessed, hearing him, that he was the product of an Ohio farm.

In New Orleans he was on the warehousing committee, and early saw the danger of Union gunboats in the Gulf. He was able, however, by the multiple numbering of bales, to make each one do the work of two, beating the Southern embargo by which it was hoped to bring cotton-hungry Europe to terms, and transferring his stocks to some warehouses that he had farsightedly leased in Havana and Tampico. He had intended replacing the bales with the new ginning from up the river, but that proved unnecessary when the Union fleet under Farragut fought its way up the river and took the port in the spring of '62. He was thus left with a gigantic profit, or a potential profit as soon as the Havana and Tampico bales were shipped, but the occupation had come too suddenly for him to liquidate his New Orleans accounts and transform them into gold. Gold was in very short supply, and he was forced to accept one-to-five in order to get out with specie instead of depreciated Jeff Davis paper. Still he made quite a killing.

"Understand I'm not meaning to censure them that stayed behind in New Orleans," he said later, addressing the Shipping Club of Galveston, "but I was not of a kidney nor of a mood to grovel under General Butler and the rest. No, my course was clear. I came here to Galveston, the Queen Cotton Shipper of the Texas Gulf, to continue my fight to keep our cherished Confed'racy on a strong financial footing by the only means possible. And I say, let's not continue our tragic mistake of withholding cotton from the world markets. Trade is the secret of winning this wah, as you warehousers and merchants of Galveston right well know. What we need is a business administration up in Montgomery. I say, turn things over to the businessmen and things won't get in the shape they're in. I say, help the businessman and the shipper and in that way we'll get the dollar, and pound, and French franc credits we need; and here at home we'll be on a sound footing so we can pay our taxes, and in that way truly support our brave boys in the field."

Burden had been a leader right from the start, even winning some battle fame and the temporary name "Admiral," when he loaded his own cotton on a barge to stop cannon balls and ordered it forth, a so-called "cotton-clad," to battle a Yankee gunboat. This sacrifice of his property went a long way toward stilling the jealous tongues that carried stories of his New Orleans coup and named him a Yankee money leech, bleeding the South, and depositing all his cotton exchange as Spanish gold funds in Havana.

As things turned out, Harvey Burden needed every cent of his gold deposits. He invested in Galveston expecting an after-war boom, but the Union occupation raised havoc with that. There were ten people to bribe then for every one during Confederate control, and you couldn't lend a dollar on any collateral but what the debtor went into bankruptcy, and then the Northern houses discounted you out of existence.

He had invested heavily in the bank. It was full of mortgage paper he didn't dare foreclose, but instead he had to lend more and more in the hope of keeping folks in business, or otherwise he'd be saddled with dozens of losing propositions, and debts and taxes, and the bank would be broke. Then the greenback inflation hurt, and hurt bad, because he had lent coin, and the damn Northerners and carpetbaggers turned up with their legal-tender rule, and he had to accept greenbacks at face. That was the thing that really hurt Galveston. Every business house in town felt it. Oh, Burden had had some tight months back in those times of '66 and '67 when he juggled this and that, and kept the town and his old creditors alive!

And things weren't too good yet. The main reason they weren't too good involved the really big thing he had done to save the town. He had brought in a man, a gambling-house owner, an expert on pleasure domes, the man who had done so much in a single six-month period to raise New Orleans from its doldrums and make it the mecca of a hundred steamboat excursions from up the river. He had formed an association with the other business leaders of Galveston and had brought in Zachariah Thomas. And it had been fine. The city had sparked to the arrival of new money. But lately it had been not so good. They had the business, but they also had Zach Thomas; and of late he, Burden, was being blamed for him.

Zach had grown too big, he was controlling the town; but Burden said, "Very well, I got him, I can get rid of him." He had a plan. He had a scheme to wipe out Zach Thomas' business control, send him to the penitentiary, or kill him. . . .

It happened that Zach was a heavy stockholder in the bank. The bank had a great deal of uncollectable mortgage paper on ranches midstate—whole counties of them. However, with the railroads finally reaching Texas, it was easy to hope that a lot of the land, with its water and coal seams, might be worth a great deal. To make it very easy for Zach Thomas to believe, to provide a bait the right size for the fish, Burden had gone to the grandiose lengths of raising one hundred thousand dollars in cash money from five of the leading business men in town, and from himself. It was all in cash—gold and gold certificates.

"Would you like to see a pleasant thing?" Burden asked Zach Thomas one day, and showed him the hundred thousand dollars.

"Good Lord!" said Zach, and it was a pleasure to see him left almost speechless for a change. "Where did this come from?"

"Railroad money. I haven't said anything about it. Competition, you know. Oh, how the Houston bank would like to move in on this! I do believe that this new account, the Louisiana, Texas and Southwestern is likely to turn into something."

"But why so much cash?"

"They have to have it. This mustn't be noised around, for obvious reasons. It would send land and water values skyrocketing. But they're going through by the Floral City route. And here's the bad thing—well, not bad, but the thing that prevents us from really cashing in—we own a lot of that land up there, or *could* own it—it's a mere matter of putting our paper through the court, but we can't do a thing. We can't serve L.T. & S.W. as a repository, and at the same time use our information to squeeze prices on our land and water. But I guess there's nothing I can do."

"No, not ethically," and there was a long, thoughtful look in Zach Thomas' eyes. He seemed to look right out through the bank wall, and across the Gulf, and not even stop there. His eyes seemed to look off forever.

"Harvey, I can't quite agree with you about the ethics. They're going to buy from somebody. And after they get moving through the country, word will go around. The prices will go right up, only we won't be getting anything. Some speculator will buy up the deeds and liquidate the loans. We'll get what we put in—at inflated dollars, instead of the good pre-war gold that was lent in a lot of cases."

"True, true."

"What if *I* took that paper, saying nothing?"

"But I couldn't give it to you, Zach. Of course, I'm leaving right now for dinner, and the door is open. It's in there in the fireproof files. The ones by the far wall. It's classified according to counties. I never look at it from one month to the next. So if some of it were to disappear, who would know the difference?"

"Thanks, Harvey. You go ahead and have a good dinner. I'll keep watch of things."

"By the way, a Mr. Ansel is going to pick up that money in a couple or three days. He's already armed with the surveyor's preliminary. He'll be at the Palmetto House. I dare say ten dollars in the right hand would give you access to his room, and you could see exactly where they plan to run the road."

"He's really doing it? Ansel is taking this money, and paying out cash, not checks?"

"Absolutely. You know how ranchers are. They want to see the money. With gold and gold certificates in hand, he can buy for fifty or sixty per cent of the check price."

"But a hundred thousand dollars in a suitcase!"

"That's railroads for you. They have all the money in the country."

"It can't be. He wouldn't carry that much all in cash."

"Well, Zach, you just saw it."

"Yes, I did, didn't I?"

After Zach left with Ansel—Ansel was a real railroad man, hired from the L.T. & S.W. for this special task, no questions asked—all Burden had to do, it seemed, was wait a decent period for the deals to be closed, money transferred, etc., and then get the money back. There were men about who did such jobs. He had one particular man in mind, a fellow named Matson who had done some guard work for him. He had faith in Matson because he was wanted for murder in Kansas, and Burden had the political influence to protect him from extradition. Played strongly, it was a perfect scheme—but Matson, unaccountably, had failed. Ansel was dead, Thomas alive, and some person unknown had got away with the money.

The frightening thing right now was, how much had Zach Thomas guessed? What facts did he have? He was very sharp, very suspicious. If he ever started putting it together, Burden was as good as a dead man. He had to find out and strike first. It was kill or be killed. But he was really tackling somebody when he came up against Thomas. He mopped his face. Ah, God, it was hot!

There was a deferential knock at the door, and he opened the drawer of his desk, checking to see that his revolver was there—a Colt, cap and ball, five-shooter, Secret Service model.

"Yes?"

It was only Dwight Franklyn, his pussy-footing assistant cashier. He looked to make sure there was nobody following him. But Zach wouldn't have knocked or sent Dwight. He'd have rammed straight in. He was the kind of man who would come in jovially with a big "Ha-ha! How are you, Harvey?" and shoot him.

"Mr. Burden . . ."

"Yes, Dwight. Yes, damn it, what is it?"

"There's a man to see you."

"No. I said nobody."

"I'm afraid he won't go away. He has a gun."

"You mean he pointed a gun at you in this bank? Call the police!"

"Well, he's been here before. I came late one night, and I just happened to see him leave your office. He's a guard, or a detective."

"Oh!" Burden lost some color. His skin looked spotty. Then he commenced to sweat harder than ever. "The fool. The—"

"Sir?"

"Nothing—send him in. Hurry, damn it, send him in!"

"Yes, sir."

What if Zach saw him and knew who he was? Why can't I have people with some discretion? Why am I always saddled with fools? . . . There was another possibility. Maybe Matson was not a fool, but came openly in order to blackmail him.

"Matson! Come in, come in. Close the door."

He came in, and looked at Burden with a dead-eyed scowl. He had obviously come in no mood of apology.

This man is too dangerous, Burden thought. I'll have to get rid of him. And that meant kill him. How much has he told his confederates? I could kill him now, not with the pistol, but with my hands. . . . All he needed do was to get close and grab him. Burden was extremely strong, but the important point was, he knew how to use his strength. He knew how to get a man helplessly off balance, and use the principles of leverage. He could snap Matson's back over the edge of the desk. Or he could use his hands and a knee —he had done that once to a man who jumped him on the docks at Natchez. *Crack!*—if he lived to be a hundred he would never forget how that man had turned limp as a slice of liver in his hands. . . .

"You're a fool, Matson, to come here in broad daylight. This is a dangerous thing for both of us."

"I need some money."

Burden laughed and wiped sweat from under his collar. "You saw the sign that said 'Bank' and knew it was the place to come for money! If you have some money here on deposit you'll be paid. Otherwise, not a penny. What have you done, that you expect money?"

"You know the agreement we made," Matson said.

"Indeed I do. We made an agreement that envisaged some

kind of efficiency and success. You were to receive quite a substantial sum of money—when you *succeeded*. But you *failed!*"

"It wasn't my fault we failed. There was somebody else had wind of that money."

"Who?"

Matson ignored the question, and set his lips in a tight, vicious line.

"Listen to me, if you know the identity of the man who took that money—"

"I do, and I'm keeping it to myself. I'm not taking the chance that you'll double-cross me and get it back on your own. I'll get it back, and I want the reward."

"You'll get a reward, yes."

"Twenty thousand dollars."

"That's extortionate! If you think—"

"I lost some men out there. They were friends of mine. Some of the boys took it pretty hard. Some of them had the idea you slipped up. They figured there were too many knew what was going on. They even thought maybe there wasn't any money at all, and that you—"

"Do you mean they know *I* hired them?"

"No, they don't—if they did you might not even be alive."

"Don't ever be so bold or so foolish as to violate my instructions in that matter; because if my identity should ever—"

"When the boys get paid they won't care who you are. Shell out that money, Burden."

"What money?"

"Their pay, and mine. We were to get ten thousand, split up."

"Exactly! You were to get it when the bank's money was returned! There was no provision for the event of failure."

"All right. I'll go out and tell 'em you said that."

"Hold on. I'll pay you two thousand."

"It's not enough."

The trouble was, this would have to come out of his own pocket, whereas the previous expense, steep as it was, had been split six ways.

"I'll pay you three," Burden said. "I understand several men were killed. You were sorry to lose your friends, yes— but look on the bright side. That leaves each of you a larger split. Three thousand dollars—as a retainer. And if you can get the money back, well, the old agreement holds. Plus this three thousand. Take it or leave it."

Matson stood thinking about it. He was not a smart man,

but he was clever in a purely animal way. He was clever the way a lobo is clever.

"It might occur to you, Matson, to sell me out to Zach Thomas. If you do, I'll see to it you're turned over for that Kansas noose."

Matson winced at the mention of Kansas. "Why, you fat son of a —"

It was as far as he got, because Burden, who rather expected some such response, had walked around the desk, and with a quickness unexpected in a man of his bulk, hit him in the neck with a hand chop. It wasn't his best blow, but it stunned. Matson started for his gun, a reflex movement; he lifted it halfway from its holster, but staggered and hit the wall. Timing himself with precision, Burden waited and kicked him savagely in the groin.

Matson sank to his knees, and his gun fell. He could not breathe; his face turned dark. He fell to the carpet on his side and writhed for a few seconds. Then he lay there getting his breath. He had made scarcely a sound. At last he pulled himself to a chair and sat in it, arms wrapped around his lower abdomen. And breathing deeply, he filled his lungs.

"Don't ever call me fat again," said Burden.

Matson looked at him. There was no hatred or anger in his eyes—no emotion of any kind. He just sat looking

"Now, I'm going to give you three thousand, and five hundred more for yourself. You will present this slip to Mr. Franklyn, the man who let you in. Mind you, this isn't a reward. It's no acknowledgment of obligation, nothing. It's just thirty-five hundred dollars to prove that I still have the confidence to give you a second chance. This is a great deal of money for a man like you in times like these. Mind you save some of it. I recommend our depository. Our regular savers receive one and a half per cent interest, annually. They are making their dollars work for them. I advise you to do likewise."

Matson got to his feet and took the slip. He wadded it ungraciously and stuck it in his pocket. His gun lay on the carpet. Glancing at Burden and reaching gingerly, he picked it up and put it in its holster.

"You will see Mr. Franklyn, and you will wait while he gets you the money. After that you will go out the side door. Don't be so foolhardy as to come here again. You are to divulge my name to nobody. Believe me, if you do, I'll have a way of knowing."

Matson started to leave.

"No, wait! I'm not finished. With all expedition seek out the hundred thousand if you can. Don't ever get so foolish as to think you can keep it for yourself. We bankers always have a way of learning these things. But there's another matter, even more immediately important. Zach Thomas is alive. He will probably be able to identify you. As long as he lives, none of us will be safe. Unfortunately—and I mean that from the bottom of my heart, because I am quite fond of the man—unfortunately, I say, he will have to be disposed of."

"What do you mean? Killed?"

"Yes," Burden said, sweating and patting the sweat away. "Yes, killed."

"How do you want it done?"

"When I hire a man to come in here to clean my spittoon, I only expect to arrive and find it polished in the morning. His means of accomplishing it are no concern of mine. I assume he knows how to polish brass, or I would not employ him."

"Killing a man is a lot higher-grade thing than polishing a spittoon."

"Perhaps, but you get my point. I'm not telling you how to do it. You do that job, Matson, and I'll pay you the added sum of two thousand dollars. Now, I don't want to hear any more about it, because two thousand is far over the usual price paid for the simple act of killing a man. Down on the docks the price of a man's life runs as low as fifty dollars."

"You just want to pay more because he's a friend of yours, and maybe you want a neater job?"

It sounded almost as if he had a sense of humor, but that was something Matson definitely did not possess.

"I am paying the top price because I know I am hiring the top man in the field."

"When do you want it done?"

"Five minutes from now if you have the chance, which you won't. Tonight if he returns. . . . Tomorrow. . . . But soon. Every moment that passes is an added danger to all of us." He turned away. "Well, what are you waiting for?"

"The two thousand."

"I will pay on delivery. I will pay when you deliver the meat." He laughed. It was the kind of laugh one might get from a machine by turning a crank.

"Go, now. Get out of here. . . . God, it's hot!"

"I hadn't noticed," Matson said.

"You wouldn't. You're not human. You have acid in your veins—acid and gall and copperas."

After Matson had gone, Burden needed something to buck him up. He poured whisky, and added water from the cooler. The water was warm, warm as blood. There was no ice in all the town—the ice ship wasn't in from New England. Not even Zach Thomas' Gold Coast or Madame Elya's had a fragment of ice. He sat at his desk and drank, shuddering and scowling.

There was Dwight Franklyn's rap again.

"Yes? Did you pay him?" Burden asked.

"I wanted to verify this."

"In heaven's name, do I need co-signers in my own bank? It's verified—pay him, pay him."

"Oh, and Mr. Williams and Mr. Aikens have arrived. That leaves only Mr. Saigon. He's—"

"Already? A'' right, tell them I'll be there directly."

As Franklyn turned away, Burden spoke again.

"Damn it, Dwight, why haven't we any ice here?"

"But there's no ice in the city. We can't—"

"Dwight, that's why you'll never rise to the top in the banking business. *Can't* never did anything. Your vocabulary shouldn't include the word 'can't.' See that that cooler is supplied with ice!"

Good God! Now he was going to have to face them and tell them their money was gone. The hundred thousand put up by Aikens, Williams, Burns, Mitchell, Saigon, and himself, the élite of the city's business aristocracy, $16,700 apiece as bait to lure the big fish, the tiger shark, thinking all but about two thousand apiece would come back. Thinking they might even show a profit, when charges were brought in regard to the stolen mortgages and Zach Thomas was cut up among them. Now he had to ask for more: their share of the $5,500. He would ask each to chip in $750. It would give him a small profit—$350 for himself. And why not? He took all the risk. He was the one who had to face Matson. He was the one Zach Thomas would come looking for.

He went to the door of the mahogany-lined directors' room and stood outside for a moment, straightening his tie and his linen jacket.

"You filthy sons of bitches!" he muttered; then he put on his best bland, unruffled smile and walked into the room.

"As you may have guessed, gentlemen, from my message, there's been, ah, a little hitch. The money has disappeared —but wait! Now, let's be calm. I have every anticipation of recovering it. And of seeing the ultimate, permanent departure of Zach Thomas. However, Rome was not built in a

60

day. It will just take a bit more effort than we first anticipated . . ."

When Burden emerged from the meeting he received the disturbing news that Zach Thomas had just returned to the city. He changed to a fresh shirt and tie, cursed the day, which had grown even hotter, and had a hack called.

"Madame Elya's," he said to the driver. "And snap to it, man! Hurry!"

Not that he was anxious to go. No, he wasn't, most definitely. But he wanted to get it over. He who hesitates is lost. Procrastination is the thief of time. A brave front wins more than a cowardly behind.

He went unarmed. Even Zach Thomas at his predictable worst would not shoot an unarmed man.

II

"Madame!" said the French maid, coming into the room. "Madame Elya."

"Not now, Marie! Please!"

"But, madame, it is an important visitor."

"I *have* an important visitor. Mr. Thomas is having a bath. Surely you realize I can take no customers."

"But this gentleman is here to see Mr. Thomas. It is the big banker!"

Elya Carlson made a movement of impatience. She was usually a very serene woman—tall, blonde, and beautiful—but the day was highly special: it had marked the return of Zach Thomas.

"Oh, very well. Tell him—"

"To come in?"

"No, of course not. Surely we have something here he can do to make his time pleasant. Pour him a champagne."

"It is warm, madame."

"A brandy, then. Take him the French periodicals. Take him down to the shop and have him choose a lingerie for his wife. The fans are working. Surely you can make him comfortable."

61

"Yes, madame."

She moved around the parlor, putting small things in order, removing a man's dusty hat from a gilt-finished Louis XIV chair, his dusty and wrinkled trousers from the floor, and his dusty Spanish boots, one from here and one from there. It was quite obvious that the wearer had felt right at home, and had shed his clothes on his way through.

"Marie!"

"Yes, madame?"

"Take these."

"Shall I burn them, madame?"

"Heaven forbid!" Madame Elya said, laughing. "Mr. Thomas would never forgive us if anything happened to these clothes. As you see, he became attached to them."

There was a slight music in the way she talked, a Swedish twist to the words, and in the way the final syllable of a sentence was left hanging. "You can see that they are favorites of his, or he would not have kept them next to him so long."

"He must have had a very hard journey, madame."

Madame Elya picked up the last item, a sock that sweat and grime had turned to crooked stripes. "Here. Take these out and have them aired and washed—in that order."

"Yes, madame."

There had been splashing in the adjoining room. Now it stopped. "Who's that girl out there?" called Zach Thomas.

"Nobody you'd be interested in, Zachariah."

"Let me look and see."

"Shall I go in, madame?" asked Marie.

"No. I'll take care of Mr. Thomas."

"Send her in with some soap," called Zach.

"*I* will bring the soap!"

"Did I hear somebody say 'Burden'? Did I hear that sweaty name?"

"He is waiting outside."

"What does old satchel-gut want?"

"I don't know, darling. Shall we ask?"

"No."

It was impossible to tell from Zach's tone what his present feelings were about Burden. You never knew when Zach spoke to you whether you were his best friend or his worst enemy.

He kept on splashing while Elya finished straightening the things in the apartment. In the center of the room, like a throne, stood a barber chair. She adjusted this and turned it with the hand of a professional. She was the famed Galveston lady barber.

"Elya, what are you doing?"

"Straightening up for you, Zachariah."

"Send in that girl to wash my back."

"*I* will wash your back! All Swedes are expert bath attendants. In Sweden everyone goes in bathing together, naked. It is considered the very best thing to do. And the wonderful steam baths that sweat all the poisons from the pores! It is what you need after this terrible journey of yours —a steam bath."

She went through an archway carrying several very thick towels, and in an inner room, scarcely smaller than the one featuring her barber chair, Zach Thomas was sitting in a large gold-plated tub. Several buckets of steaming water stood beside the tub, and Zach was in lather to his chin. He was leaning forward, and in his mouth was a large dark cigar. He did not seem to be in a very good humor.

"What does Burden want?"

"I don't know."

"Is anybody with him?"

"No, Zachariah."

"Have any suspicious-looking strangers been around here the last day or so?"

"Only the usual."

"No cold-eyed fellow about six feet, likes to dress in black, name might be Matson?"

She stood thinking. "Why?"

"I think he's going to try to kill me."

"Oh?"

With a long brush and with easy strokes, she began to wash his back. She kept dipping the brush and washing the soap out of it.

"You are joking, yes?"

"I never joke about my own life."

"Why is someone always looking to kill you, Zachariah? You are such a nice man."

"I try to be, but what a bad time I had this trip! Very bad. And so many peculiar, unexplained happenings. Money tossed around like cottonseed. A fortune of one hundred thousand dollars sent out to little cattle towns by hard-fisted railroads. Men stranded and carrying saddles on their backs. And a country swarming with bandits. Men showing up, clickety-click, right on time. Do you believe in fate, Elya?"

"Fate?"

"Do you believe in some blind power guiding all those things to a certain place at a certain time, and do you believe that that particular scene was written long ago, long before any of us were born, written since the beginning of time? Do you? Well, I don't. I think when anything becomes too damned providential, the hand of a man is there. Yes, I do, Elya. I believe somebody has been stacking the cards. In this case, I have a very strong feeling that I was handed a cold deck."

"More hot water?" asked a girl in the doorway.

"That will be enough, Susie."

"Bring it in!" ordered Zachariah.

"I hope it don' get too hot for you, sir."

She was a beautiful girl, dark and very Southern.

"I doubt whether you will ever be able to make anything hot enough for Mr. Thomas, my dear."

"Now, that wasn't nice," said Zach. "You're hurtin' Susie's feelings."

"I'm not a bit nice. You have been away a long time, and *I* am furnishing the warm things for you."

"Elya, darling!"

"Zachariah!"

"Come in with me, Swedish style."

"No, Zach."

"Elya, did you ever know a man named Jarrett?"

"No, Zach. Why so many questions? Did he also try to kill you?"

"Worse, he took a hundred thousand dollars from me."

"You are always talking about those great big foolish sums of money."

"There's nothing foolish about a hundred thousand dollars. A hundred thousand dollars is about the smartest thing there is."

"Poor Zachariah!"

"It was there. I saw it, I felt it. And I'll feel it again."

"Why do you talk about money when I am here? Isn't your Elya better than one hundred thousand dollars?"

"I love you both, darling. Each in a different way."

Zach spent a long time in the tub. Afterward he lay down and a large Negro man came and gave him a massage. Marie brought him some fresh clothes and he got in the barber chair. It seemed as if he had forgotten about Harvey Burden, but after Elya commenced preparing him for the razor he said to send him in.

"You're looking well, Harvey," he said when Burden entered. In fact, Burden looked rumpled and wrinkled. And the long wait had done his temper no good. However, he smiled, and went over to shake the hand that Zach offered from under the cloth.

"You're looking well, too, Zach. I hope everything went well."

"Why, haven't you heard?"

Burden did not know what to say. "I heard some reports. I hope they were false."

"You act nervous, Harvey. By the gods, you act like it was harder on you than it was on me."

"It's that Richter riverboat." It flashed in his mind as an excuse. Zach had asked to have him foreclose on the old Richter boat because he had some crazy idea about turning it into a floating gambling house. "I haven't been able to do it. The note is due, but the interest showed up at the last minute, and—"

"I want the boat, Harvey. But it's nothing to get so upset about."

"This heat! How do you stand it? And the perfume on top of it! I'm sorry, Elya. Not your perfume, or the tonics or lotions. No, not at all. It's the flowers. The damned, cloying flowers. Those damned, stinking roses! They hang and ferment. Do you remember the time there was a tornado and the whale washed up on the beach? Everyone complained of the smell. But I tell you I found it a relief. Yes, I did. It was a relief from those stinking roses. Funereal—that's what they are."

"Oh, come, Harvey! Let's not get morbid."

"What else can a man be but morbid?"

"He can be spiritual, Harvey. It's a question of mind over matter."

"No, damn it, sir, not in this heat."

"I've been experiencing a little heat myself," Zach said. "I walked for a day and a night across the desert."

"Dreadful! But how . . . ? Damn it, Zach, I knew I shouldn't allow you to start out without an escort."

It was a foolish remark, and Burden knew it instantly. Who in heaven's name ever worried about Zach? Of all people able to take care of themselves, Zach was the one.

"Why, thanks for your concern, Harvey. You sound right fatherly."

"Well, yes, I do feel that way toward you. As if you were my son. I really do, Zach."

"I knew you had sentiment for me, but I never knew it was that kind. Did you, Elya? Did you hear what Harvey just said? As if I was his son?"

"Yes, Zach," she said, spreading lather with her long fingers.

Burden said, "How about—what was that man's name—the railroad man? Ansel? I heard—"

"He got took dead."

"No! Murdered? Horrible. Tragic."

"And his money was stole."

"Shocking. I knew it should have been left on deposit. I strongly advised against taking it out of the bank. Gone, all of it?"

"Every beautiful piece of it."

"They'll get the thieves. Believe me, that much money doesn't disappear without a trace. But tell me this—were the mortgages transferred? That would make all the difference."

"The difference between it being my money and their money? I'm glad to tell you we can rest easy on that score. We never transferred a thing. And that highwayman never touched a piece of our mortgage paper. He knew when he was well off."

"Ha-ha!" Burden didn't know whether to laugh, or show concern, or what. It was a very ticklish thing when you set out to fool Zach Thomas. Just one tiny slip and he would *know*. It was a relief when Elya covered Zach's face with a towel. At least he couldn't lie there and look at Burden.

"All these sad doings seem to be fresh news to you, Harvey," Zach said, muffled and steaming.

The remark was too simple and innocent. He knows something, thought Burden, he suspects. The towel was removed, and Zach's eyes were on him. He had a very penetrating gaze. Burden always had the feeling that Zach could see an inch beneath the surface. Another thing that made him nervous was the fact that Zach was covered with the barber's cloth. He must be carrying a gun—he carried one everywhere; he probably had it with him in the bathtub.

It would be Zach's idea of a great joke to lie there with the gun drawn, aimed, and at some unexpected moment, as a punctuation for one of his remarks . . . bang! He remembered one time when Zach was having trouble with a gambler named Sutliff; they had quarreled over debts and women; and one day, perfectly innocent, Zach had said, "Why, there's a fly right on your vest, Sutty" . . . and bang! He had killed him.

"Gosh, Sutty was standing right behind that fly!" Zach had said. He thought it was *funny!* It showed the sense of humor he had.

Burden said, sweating, "I heard rumors. Yes, rumors. I was just praying they weren't true."

"Harvey, did you know there was a great big bead of perspiration hanging on the end of your nose?"

This is it, thought Burden. He is going to kill me. He'll shoot me through the upper jaw and it will blow the back of my head off. He had seen a man shot that way, and the vision of it made him sick. No, he won't do it here, thought Burden. Not here in Elya Carlson's salon, the most beautifully appointed place in the city.

He sat down in a slim-legged chair upholstered in silk tapestry. He noticed the rug at his feet. It was white silk, Persian. If he should shoot me here I'd bleed all over this chair and rug, he thought. Zach wouldn't want that to happen. He felt safe as long as he stayed on the white rug.

"You *are* sweating, Harvey. Why don't you go over and stand by the window? Open the window for Harvey, Elya."

"No. I'm fine here. This is all right."

"Why don't you sit in this wicker chair?" asked Elya. "It's much cooler."

"No, this is perfectly all right. Now, these thieves—"

"Thief. Mr. Joseph T. Jarrett."

"Jarrett?" That was the man, then, whose name Matson would not mention. "Jarrett, Jarrett," Burden whispered, as if memorizing it.

"You know him?"

"Jarrett? Oh, no. No. I thought there were twelve of them."

"Did *I* say twelve?"

"No—or did you? How did I get it in my head there were twelve?"

It had been a bad slip, the kind that might cost him his life.

Zach said, "There might have been twelve, or more than twelve—I don't know. The country was crawling with 'em. I was shooting 'em like tin ducks in a gallery. And just when everything seemed fine, there was this fellow . . . You know, Harvey, here's a funny thing—the first time I saw him was just like this. I was lying there getting shaved, and he was sitting over there, like you. I could have shot him so easy, so very easy. . . ."

"Let's not talk about such things!"

"Why, Harvey!"

"It's this heat. This damnable heat."

"And the roses."

"Yes, those damned, stinking roses."

"Listen, here's something else peculiar. That money. I know it came from the railroad . . ."

"Yes, yes, it did!"

"But do you know they didn't even mention it on the telegraph? All they were worried about was Mr. Ansel. It seemed so—well, so *unrailroad*. The L.T. & S.W. is, in fact, the first and only railroad I ever heard tell of that was more interested in a man's life than in their money. All they wired was how about them sending a hearse for Mr. Ansel's body. I could see they didn't know much about a body's keepin' qualities in Texas. The only way would be to pack him in hot sand like the Apaches used to do. It shrinks 'em down to the size of monkeys. Little Mr. Ansel, he'd have shrunk down to the size of a tomcat. So that wouldn't do. You can see how his family would have felt unpacking him out of maybe a shoe box? So I wired back not to bother, I had sort of conducted services on my own."

"Zachariah," said Elya, with the razor in her hand, "your Adam's apple is bobbling."

He lay still with his chin up, and Burden was able to breathe easier. "Dreadful, dreadful," he said. "Poor Mr. Ansel. I'm simply sick at all this. Every time I think of that good man . . ."

"I didn't realize you were so close. In fact, I thought you'd met just the one time."

"But a human life, Zach. Just general principles!"

"I always said they were the best kind to have."

"Yes, yes." There it was again, one of those hidden-edge remarks.

"I'm sure glad you're a man of general principles, Harvey. That's what occurred to me out there on the desert. There I was in that stagecoach, and they were shooting, and the bullets were whizzing around, and a big oak splinter came and got me—you can see the mark yet, right in my cheek—and I got the awfulest *feeling*. A suspicion like, a little bitty hunch, that there was something had gone on in the back room. People kept showing up that *knew* too much. There was a blank prairie, and all of a sudden riders from everywhere! Fellows walking carrying saddles. Everybody knowing about the money! And I thought to myself: Zach, wasn't it lucky you didn't sign over those bank mortgages and accept the money, because if you had you not only would lose it, they could take you for fraud and embezzlement. But then I thought about you, Harvey. I thought: Zach, isn't it lucky you have your good old pal Harvey

Burden in that bank ready to cover up for you! A man with general principles."

"And I would, too. I would."

"That's what I was saying, you would."

"Did it seem to you," Zach said when Burden was gone, "that Harvey was sweating just a bit more than usual?"

"It was very hot. And he is very fat."

"True. But it ain't that hot. And he ain't that fat. And he jumped as if a hot poker touched him when I said that name Joseph T. Jarrett."

"Darling, who cares for Joseph T. Jarrett?"

"Say you were a common bandit, instead of a very uncommon barber, and say you had a hundred thousand in stolen money, what would you do? You would head for the Indian Nations. But say you weren't a common bandit. Say you were an uncommon bandit. An uncommon smart one—or you thought you were—what would you do? Why, you'd say to yourself, 'I'll go just exactly where they least expect me.' You'd say, 'There's something very peculiar about this money, and the peculiarity lies deep in the heart of Galveston.' That's what you'd say. And you know what? You'd come *here*. Yes, darling, when you want to catch a fox you got to think like a fox. And just as sure as anything, while that posse was combing the mesquite, Joseph T. Jarrett was headed *here*."

III

After many years, Jarrett looked at Galveston again.

"Never go back," people said. "It will never seem the same." "You'll be disappointed, it'll look smaller, it won't be like you remember it." "You can never go home again."

But it didn't look smaller, and he wasn't disappointed. He'd forgotten many things, and their reacquaintance pleased him. Things of memory kept turning up on every side. He had forgotten the town was so green, and crowded, and busy. He was jostled by cattlemen, Mexicans in big-rowled spurs, sailors, gaudy West Indian Negroes with rings in their ears, yellow girls with beautiful bosoms and smiles that challenged his manhood. Had it been that way before? Who had changed, he wondered—the town or him?

"I've been away a long time," he said to himself. "Too long a time."

"Carry your bags, sir?" asked a colored boy.

"Hack, sir?"

"Hack, yes." Am I crazy, he thought—the whole country teeming with deputy sheriffs, and I ride down the street in an open hack? It was bad enough coming down on the little stern-wheel boat from Houston, but at least he did not have an entire city to think about, and people looking out from the very courthouse. But he got in the hack and sat there in his desert-dirty clothes, with his sweat-and-dust-caked planter's hat on his head.

"Store your bags here, sir?"

"The alligator valise, yes. The warsack, yes. This one I'll keep."

He laid the carpetbag at his feet and kept his coat open, with the gun butt hidden, pointing toward his hand.

"Where to, sir?"

"The Lanternlight."

"Where?"

"The Lanternlight."

The driver got in the hack, but he didn't start. "Sir, you know you're the first man that ever got in my hack and said, 'The Lanternlight?' "

"I am?"

"The very first. I was thinking that maybe, just maybe, you was makin' a mistake. We got a place here called the Ship's Lantern. I thought that maybe was the place."

"No, the Lanternlight. It's an orphanage."

"Just a moment, sir. I believe I know a man that's better able to get you away out there than I am."

He did not mind sitting. Great trees shaded the street, and on the Gulf breeze there was a fragrance. The air was heavy with smells and perfumes and memories. He could breathe the odor of the flowers, the green leaves, the wood rotting along the mudflats, the damp cotton bales, and all the vinegar fragrance of the waterfront. He could take the fragrances apart and put them together, and when they were put together they smelled like Galveston. The city of his thousand dreams.

In a while the man came back, and there was a coach following him. This was driven by a gaudy and powerful West

Indian Negro. He was far and away the most flamboyantly dressed coachman Jarrett had ever seen. Good God, he thought, are they trying to call the attention of the entire Bay area to me? Why don't they blow a horn and bring them over from Bolivar?

"This is Prince George. He drives folks out to the plantations and right up to the Lanternlight."

"Yes, sir! I am at your service, sir." Prince George had an accent more English than the English, as was common among colonials.

"How much do you weigh?" asked Jarrett.

"Fourteen stone, sir, give or take."

"I bet you can give and take plenty!"

"I haul to the Lanternlight free of charge, sir," he said, misinterpreting.

"Just only for the tip?"

"Yes, sir!" he said, showing a powerful set of teeth, among which two gleamed like nuggets of gold. The two gold teeth were engraved, or rather, had relief designs, Corinthian in nature. He wore large flat earrings that looked like scimitars. The gold bracelet on his right arm was of the size that would fit an ordinary man's leg. His skin had the hue of dark, oiled bronze.

"Put that carpetbag right at my feet," Jarrett said, changing to the other hack.

"This bag?" Prince George said, deft and bland, and Jarrett knew that he knew by the weight that it was gold. Nothing weighed as much as gold. You always knew when there was gold in a bundle by its lump-weight like a cannon ball.

"These bags stowed here. And *this* one by your feet!" said Prince George importantly. Then, mounting to his high seat, his silk hat and cockade on his head, his long whip held vertically, he drove off grandly.

They took the steam ferry to the mainland, Jarrett remaining enthroned in the carriage, smoking a cigar. The ferry made several stops, and finally he and Prince George were the only passengers aboard.

They went ashore at Mobile town, so called because a Mobile, Alabama, concern had once attempted to dredge out a ship canal and promote a city there. It was designed to put Galveston out of business, making its island position a liability, but a storm blew in with sediment that not only filled the canal but impacted the docks with muck; and now the warehouses were falling into disrepair, and the only boats

71

at its docks were a couple of barges that had been towed over by a little peanut-whistle tug. Negro children by the hundreds waded the littoral looking for shellfish.

"They can't improve on Galveston," said Jarrett. "It's been destroyed by flood, and sediment, and hurricane. It's been outflanked upcoast, downcoast, and on the inside, but she's still the queen city of the Texas Gulf. You can destroy her, but she rises again like the phoenix."

"It is famed, sir, far and wide. It's the oldest city in the United States of America!"

"St. Augustine to the contrary, that's something they can't take away from us. The first and the best. Just look at Mobile Town, yonder. I can still remember the spiel which the promotors were giving, about you should buy city lots because they would be worth more than those in Galveston, but the storm turned it into a crawdab fishery."

Railroads, dredge canals, and all developments be damned, Jarrett thought with a swell of loyal pride. Galveston was and always would be the chief, and he meant the largest, finest, gaudiest, and fastest-money town in Texas. When it really hit its stride, nothing could stop it. It would end up bigger than New Orleans.

With a hundred thousand dollars a man could do himself proud in a growing town like Galveston. There were so many opportunities. There was cotton, of course. Then there was the beef, which would surely come. He'd read in the paper about some scheme for loading beef from the Galveston abattoirs (still to be built) into the ice ships from New England, it being pointed out that the hulls were already cooled down to forty degrees Fahrenheit and would remain so through the fast steaming time it took to return, setting up a shuttle service that would cut the transportation cost for both ice and beef by approximately one third, and beat the railroads all hollow. Then, too, sulphur had been discovered. It was oozing right out of the ground at a place up on the Brazos River, and from sulphur came the acid tanning solutions which would make Galveston the leather capital of the country. It would mean cow leather would be cheaper to produce than buffalo leather, which had to come down by Missouri River steamboats, fighting its way through the Sioux and the killin' Blackfeet.

And besides, there were the yams, the fruits, the fish, and the location on the Gulf which made Galveston, and not New Orleans, not Baton Rouge, and certainly not St. Louis, the ideal and ultimate point from which the strips of railroad steel would radiate to all the West to Denver, Kansas,

Santa Fe, and even to the Comstock Lode of the high Sierras. Any man who cared to look at a map could see it plain as day.

It gave him a real good feeling to know he was arriving just at the start of all this, and that he had the capital to invest. He hadn't the slightest doubt he'd double or treble his money the first year. The thing you had to do was to incorporate and sell stock, and then pull your money out and use it over again, and over and over. It was the way financial and industrial empires were built. The only thing that worried him was what to do with the money until that time came. How was he to explain it if folks commenced asking questions? It wasn't what happened next year that worried him, it was what would happen today, tomorrow, or next week.

"Here we are," said Prince George, jarring his reverie. "The Lanternlight Orphanage!"

He had turned in through the arch and pillar entrance to an old plantation and was headed up a long crushed-shell drive. The place had once belonged to a family named Charbannon who had come there in the very old days, the Spanish days, even antedating Lafitte and the pirates, and raised rice and legumes and made brandy to supply the sailing ships. They had become very wealthy, but the Charbannon line had run out, as families will, and by the 1850's nobody was left except old Justinn Charbannon, who had got religion and left his house and holdings to the Reverend Enoch Lantern. What folks said Enoch had done was go out and scare the very devil out of the old man with his stories of fire and brimstone, and souls screaming into the night wilderness of eternity; and Charbannon, who had led a very gay youth, extending into late manhood, and was responsible, it was said, for the remarkable similarity of all mulattoes from age five to fifty-five throughout the Bay area, was chastened at last, and made peace with his Creator by willing the plantation to Lantern on his deathbed. Lantern had promptly started an orphanage; because Galveston, through the activities of others like Charbannon, as well as the sailors, the swashbucklers, and assorted ranchers, caballeros, and cotton buyers, had accumulated more waifs than any city in creation.

"Yes, those poor waifs, those poor, fatherless children!" Lantern would say, fixing some merchant, broker, planter, or judge with his falcon's eye and with his hand out for donation. "I know a man of your position and esteem in the community will be most generous," he would say, not too

73

subtly hinting that esteem was a thing that might be lost, and he himself was capable of lambasting him right from some pulpit, where he was forever showing up as guest speaker. And it was always *fatherless* waifs, not motherless. Lantern's money-raising prowess was phenomenal, and it was one of the things Jarrett most admired him for. "A blackmail unto God," he had called it in his more relaxed moments.

One time, Jerrett remembered, there was a fellow named Boggley, who was a big planter and had his own dock, who wouldn't contribute a cent. Lantern called on him and pleaded, and threatened, and finally he attacked him from the pulpit of his own church, the Bethany Baptist, ripping into him for the sin of cupidity, but it only made the man the more stubborn, and he went around saying hard things about Lantern, trying to tie his name up with Miss Ermaline Dubbins, who came from England, or New Jersey, or some place foreign. It was a filthy piece of scandal-mongering if there ever was one, and one day Boggley was walking down the street and Lantern was waiting for him in his omnibus carriage which he used to haul freight, and kids, and everything else, and he jumped out with a long cow whip and started letting him have it. Boggley ran with his arms around his head, because one of those Mexican lashes could shave your ear off right tight to your skull. Old Lantern was keeping up with him, and bringing that whip down about every fourth step, cutting Boggley's shirt to pieces and making hunks of his hair fly. He chased him inside the Mace & Geltwood Exchange, where the stairs were too narrow to swing the whip. Later on, Boggley got a shotgun and carried it around with him, saying he was going to kill Lantern, and he never did contribute a cent—but it was noticed that some of the other tight purses loosened up. And that was how Lantern kept things going.

"I hear the old Reverend Lantern passed to his reward," said Jarrett.

"Yes, he has crossed over the River Jordan."

"They better have had that boat in good shape, or they'd hear from him. I'll bet he don't cotton to no sloth in the afterworld any more than he did here."

"No, sir! That is what I have heard, sir."

"Who's directing the orphanage?"

"Miss Ermaline Dubbins."

"All alone?"

"She has very little help, sir. You are acquainted?"

"I'm a graduate."

They drew up before the wide porch of the house. Beyond

were some great double doors with fanlights and brass fixtures. The house had double verandahs, and was two-storied, with what looked like a bell tower on top. When Lantern took the place over, whole wings of the house were crumbling, but he had built new brick pillars and put in supporting timbers to prop it up, and as it became more and more crowded he added wings, most of them consisting of houses he had obtained free in one way and another and had bullied people into moving over on rollers by mule power. These he had fitted together and more or less tied in with the general architecture by means of lath, stucco, and gingerbread façades. The big surrounding areas that were fields under Lantern were still fields, and many a hot and blistery hour had Jarrett spent in them with hoe and shovel.

"You want me to wait?" Prince George asked.

"I'm afraid it might be a long wait. Or maybe it won't."

"I'll wait. Let me take that bag, sir. I can see it's heavy."

"No, no, I don't mind."

He went to the porch and stood for a time. At a distance, through the early heat, he could hear singing. The song had not changed. It was Miss Ermaline's own composition, a hymnlike song of very simple tone structure, entitled "May the Lanternlight Always Shine."

There were children on benches under the trees, and the unmistakable figure of Miss Ermaline leading them in the singing. What a beautiful woman, he had always thought, and it occurred to him that almost ten years had passed since he had seen her. She would be middle-aged now, but some people were beautiful always.

He walked through the old door, the visitors' door, feeling a twinge as he did so, for during his time it was barred to the children; and he went into the big bare room that had been the main hall under Charbannon, and on to Lantern's office library. An oil portrait of the old gentleman himself, almost lifesize, hung on the wall, and the artist, backing him with a rendition of clouds, mountains, trees, and a waterfall, had made it look as if thunders were rolling from his brow. A rough-hewn man, old Lantern, he had always looked to Jarrett as if he had been put together with a hammer and nails, without any sandpapering around the edges.

Even now, with Lantern in his grave, the portrait was disconcerting, and Jarrett got to worrying about the money, and whether he had made a mistake in getting hold of it as he had, in a rather questionable way; maybe it would call down on him the lightnings of retribution. It was almost a relief that old Lantern was dead, because otherwise he would, Jarrett felt, be able not only to see through the carpetbag to its contents, but also inside Jarrett's mind and conscience, and would ferret out guilt everywhere. Lantern had a very penetrating gaze where money was concerned.

The singing went on for a time, and after that he could hear voices chanting lessons. Then, quite close, he heard Miss Ermaline lecturing a boy.

"I'm glad to know," she was saying, "there is still honor among us. Honor, in the final analysis—"

Jarrett spoke, completing the sentence, "—is all that a man has."

She stopped suddenly, and then he heard her coming to the door.

"Why, Joseph! Joseph Jarrett! I knew that voice."

She came in, and he grabbed her and lifted her off her feet, and ran around the room with her while she struggled to get free.

"They'll see you, the children! I have to think of the children."

"Oh, damn the children!"

"Don't say a thing like that. He'll rise from the grave," she said, glancing at the portrait.

"He might, at that. If anybody could do it, he would. Ermaline, I came back to marry you."

"No, you didn't. You probably came back to hide from the sheriff."

He shot her a quick glance. "No, I didn't!" he said, in too quick denial.

"I was only joking, Joseph. My goodness, but you're filthy. How long since you've bathed?"

"You mean washed all over with soap?"

"Yes!"

"'Better hands grimed with toil than a heart black with sin.' He said it."

"He never said it. He said cleanliness was next to godliness."

"I do admit to being a bit worn and dusty. But I've been engaged in honest toil. And while we're on the subject of shabbiness—no offense, now—the place looks a little beaten around the edges. Am I right in guessing that you have missed old Enoch since he passed away—him and his famed money-raising powers?"

"You always were hard to fool when it came to money."

"They ain't contributing, are they? Those plutocrats of

"Right! I'd much appreciate it if you'd lend me that money back at fair interest—say, five per cent. Five per cent on a hundred thousand dollars amounts to five thousand per annum."

"One hundred thousand dollars?" she cried.

"Yes, ma'am. That's what's in that carpetbag. Or almost. I met some unscrupulous people who got away with almost four thousand, but—"

"Joseph, there was a hundred thousand dollars stolen from the railroad up near Floral City."

"There was? Now, ain't that a coincidence. When did this heinous robbery take place?"

"I read about it in yesterday's paper."

"Oh, I ain't seen that yet. I'll have to read about it. I don't read the crime news. I find it degrading. Generally I buy a paper and turn right to the stock market and financial news. But to the business at hand. I want to sign a note. Yes, I do, I insist. I want to sign a promissory note indicating I received this money of yours on loan. I know you may think it's not necessary, but it'd make me feel a lot better to have it legal."

"Joseph," she cried, "you'll never get away with it! Nobody would believe you borrowed it from us, or that we had it to lend."

"But I *am* borrowing it, and you *are* lending it. We got truth on our side, and Reverend Lantern said, 'Him who on his side has truth, then—'"

"Truth cuts no figure with a sheriff. That gang over there at the courthouse—"

"They don't worry me. Sheriffs and courthouses have great respect for capital in the hundred-thousand-dollar class. And we'll have the note as evidence. If there's one thing I learned about the law, it's that you can't argue against documentary evidence. If it's stolen money, they'd have to prove it was *you* rode out and took it. They'd have to say you robbed that Floral City coach, or whatever it was, and you can just see for yourself how silly that would sound. There isn't a jury in the land would entertain such a thought for one minute."

He commenced taking off his coat. "I'm going to leave the gold coin here. It's a mite heavy, and I want to pay my first year's interest right now, just in case something interferes. As for the rest, I have a mighty commodious lining in this coat, and I'd take it kindly if you did some padding and sewing. I rather fancy putting as much as possible up in the shoulders so it will improve my manly appearance. The rest

I can sort of blanket around. Miss Ermaline, this coat may be a bit threadbare at the cuffs, and it may be a bit grayed out by the Texas sun, but with that padding I'll have the finest-feeling coat in the states and in the territories. 'Clothes maketh the man,' said the poet, and I aim to walk out of here one of the manliest men in all Christendom."

"This filthy coat? I'll sew the money in a coat, but it will be one that looks respectable. You're leaving here in the Sunday preaching clothes of Enoch Lantern!"

"Now, Miss Ermaline—"

"Do you think anyone would arrest you in the clothes of Enoch Lantern? They wouldn't dare!"

"You really think that, Miss Ermaline?"

"I know it!" she said, with her head up. "For five years I've been waiting for someone to fill the clothes of Enoch Lantern. And you are that man! Anyone who can take a hundred thousand dollars away from a godless railroad and bring it to the Lanternlight Orphanage, Joseph, *is that man!* Reverend Lantern would be *proud!*"

"Well, I hope so."

"Just keep that interest coming in!"

"Amen," said Jarrett, "and hallelujah!"

IV

"I'm most sorry, sir," said Prince George to Jarrett when he came out wearing Lantern's preaching coat, white vest, turn-down collar, and gray stovepipe hat, "most sorry, but this hack has been spoken for by another gentleman."

"That gentleman happens to be me."

"Why, my goodness, so it is! You looked totally like a new man."

"How do you like him, George?" asked Miss Ermaline.

"He's magnificent. Do you know who he looks like? He could double for Lord Archibald Dunstin, who I used to drive for in Jamaica."

"You forgot this," said Miss Ermaline, handing him a gold-headed walking stick. "Sorry there's no sword in it."

"Of course not. Enoch never carried swords, only buggy whips."

"And derringers."

"And derringers."

The gray velour stovepipe hat was topheavy, and the reason lay in the derringer that was mounted in a special spring-snap holder. When Jarrett was handed the hat and saw the derringer mounted inside he could scarcely believe his eyes. But now that he thought about it, a lot of the things old Enoch Lantern had done were not the acts of an unarmed man. As far as he knew, he'd never been called on to draw the derringer. However, it had been there, right enough.

"You certainly do sit up with good erectness in that hat, sir," said Prince George. "I can tell at first glance you've worn plenty of top hats before."

He had to sit with his spine as straight as the barrel of a Sharps rifle, or the hat would fall off.

"This carpetbag feels a certain amount lighter than when you went in," said George.

"A little gift for the children."

"You're a fine man, Mr. Jarrett. You must have made a *very* important contribution."

"A small memorial," Jarrett said, sitting with his hands crossed over the gold-headed cane. What he should have was a pair of faun-colored gloves. The white vest wasn't right, either. When he got to one of the better haberdasheries he would buy a vest of embroidered silk, in either peach-down or apple green. He rather fancied himself in apple green. A girl in Kansas City once told him green went well with his eyes.

"It couldn't been a *small* memorial, judging by the weight."

"You can never judge by weight. One time I had a hundred dollars all in nickels and dimes."

"Ha-ha! Oh, I say that's ripping, Colonel Jarrett."

"My rank is major, brevet grade."

"Major. Major Jarrett. I'm relieved you left that money. I really am, because there's a lot of shady characters frequenting this city of late. In fact—I didn't mention it on the way out because I didn't realize you was such a close friend of Miss Ermaline—but as we took the ferry over here there were certain fellows watching you. Plug-uglies, Mr. Jarrett, of the worst order."

"In Galveston, in broad daylight—"

"Broad daylight means very little to some of the people in this town. They're high and mighty, and swing a lot of weight. They do their jobs broad out, making sure they have their own witnesses. Also they have their own lawyers. You see, they make everything legal. They do that to increase the dignity of their own courts."

"These plug-uglies, you say—they represent other people, then?"

"They do. They belong to a Mr. Zachariah Thomas."

Jarrett touched his side to make sure his holster was set right. "I've *heard* of him."

"Yes, sir. He's been gone of late. There was the most far-fetched story. To wit, that he was robbed of a hundred thousand dollars. Ha-ha! Of course, nobody in his right mind would believe that. It places him on the wrong side of the robbin' transaction. On the other hand, there was a rumor which said it was him robbed a railroad man of a hundred thousand dollars. That seemed more reasonable, only the figure was too big. A hundred thousand dollars! But, say it was even only *ten* thousand dollars, and he was robbed of it, and say he saw the robber here in Galveston, well, Major, broad daylight wouldn't stop him. If it was only ten cents it wouldn't stop him. Zach's not the type that takes robbin' easy."

"You know, you're a pretty smart fellow, Prince."

"*Me?*"

"Yes, you."

"I just try to keep my eyes and ears open."

Had he been listening at the window, Jarrett wondered? Had Miss Ermaline said something to him while he was changing his clothes? Or was he merely an alert coachman?

"All right, you're so sharp, tell me how much money I have in this carpetbag."

"Right now?"

"Yes, right now."

"Why, that's easy. You ain't got any money at all in that carpetbag. I could tell by the way you handled it. Not reverent like when you went in. And it was lighter. On the other hand, I see your shoulders are a lot more muscled than they were before. You know what I think, Major? I think you got a small fortune sewed up in that coat. And there'll be a lot of paper currency with bullet holes through it if you're not alacrit and extremely cautious."

"Alacrit?"

"Yes, sir. That's what the word alacrity comes from."

They had a long wait for the ferry, and crossed in the cool of evening. It was night when they reached Galveston. The ferry docks were quiet. George drove to a quay where there had been warehouses at one time, but a fire had passed through, probably during the war—one could still see the char signs high on the sides of old buildings—and the area had been paved with tile brick. It had rained, and water stood in the low places in the tiling.

"All quiet, as quiet as death," said Prince George. "As quiet as the tomb."

"Stay clear of the shadows."

"Yes, sir. One thing about Mr. Zach Thomas, he pays the funeral bills."

"Oh?"

"Yes, sir. One time this fellow, Chad—he's the chief of Mr. Thomas' plug-uglies—well, there was a fellow making trouble at the Four Winds, one of Mr. Thomas' establishments, and Chad just grabbed him and threw him through a wall. There was sort of a weak spot there and he crashed through. It killed him, Major. In passing through, something severed his head about half off his shoulders. Doc Wedloe sort of wired his head back down, but he died of the black putrids. I heard that Zach Thomas paid his doctor bill, funeral, everything."

"Just out of the goodness of his heart?"

"Yes, sir. Another time a gentleman committed suicide after losing all his money. He shot his brains out with a derringer. And Mr. Thomas paid for a fine funeral. Fourteen carriages and plumes. I drove in it."

"You think Zach would pay for my funeral?"

"Yes, Major, I do. Only Miss Ermaline would never stand for it. She'd claim your body. One thing you can rest easy about, Major, is that if anything happens you'll have a decent funeral."

They drove around the quay, off the tile facing, and under some trees that dripped warm rain. The drip had a faint fragrance. Bats were flying like swift shadows, and here and there, in an infrequent post lamp, their eyes would shine. There was something about a bat that always made it seem to be looking at *you;* one almost felt there was a human intelligence shining out. Jarrett closed his coat over the white vest, not only because of the target it made, but because the bats would see it and swoop in, and one of the most unpleasant experiences imaginable was getting one of those fiery-clawed creatures tangled in your clothes.

"Bats!" he exclaimed in disgust.

"Yes, sir. Bats will give you hydrophobia. Also the bubonic. They lay it to the ship rats that come in on the three-masters from Africa, and the burlapers from India, but it's my opinion the bubonic is carried by none other than bats.

83

I'd rather be bit by a swamp rattler than a bat. Then, there's vampires here, too. The Commercial Club gentlemen, Mr. Burden, and Aikens and all the rest, claim there ain't. They say it's a superstition. But I know of a three-year-old child that was killed dead, sucked out by a vampire bat. It was as big as a hawk. His mammy saw it. There it was, fluttering away in the night, like a piece of gauze. Black gauze, Major, like the veil a widow wears. In fact, I've heard that the vampire bats are ghosts of the ravenous dead."

West Indian Negroes were the most superstitious people in the world, Jarrett knew. They were so superstitious it made things really happen. They cast spells and killed each other even at great distances, on other islands, because their belief was so strong. It had gone so far that there had been a law passed against it in Louisiana. A lot of it was said to go on in the Bay region of Galveston, and when he was a boy a whole witch and sorcerer community was broken up down the island. The area even then had been full of free Negroes, Spanish-Indian Negroes from the islands, and they were the worst kind. Their women had the most beautiful bosoms in the world, and they really knew how to minister to a man. But their superstition gave him the skin crawls.

"Where in the devil are we going?" he asked, rousing from reverie.

"I just want to show you something, Major."

They had come out onto a wide expanse of dock that gave a hollow clopping sound under the horses' hoofs. He recalled the section as a boy. It had been one of the best then, the old Western Steam Transportation wharf and warehouse. Now it was almost abandoned. A heavy steam dredge was tied up at one end. Farther on was a gigantic old river steamboat. The tide was in movement, but the steamboat lay like a great, impacted ark. It looked like a palace boat of the old Mississippi days, but what was it doing there, in Galveston?

Prince George stopped the carriage. "Look at that lordly ship, Major. That there is the old *Weymount Castle!* One of the palaces of the Mississippi in her day. A floatin' palace, that's what they called her! Her floors were of teak and her woodwork was carved Honduras mahogany. Still is. The grand salon had sixty-six pillars done in ivory coat over the wood, and there were Persian carpets on the floors. But you never saw anything until you saw the grand staircase. Ebony! It led to the rooms of state, and the captain's quarters, and the observation."

Its paint had fallen off, revealing the whitish planking and superstructure, so that even in the dark it looked like old cheese. It gave off a smell of water rot.

"What's keeping it up?" Jarrett asked. "A shallow bottom?"

"No, sir, Major! You definitely are wrong there. That boat floats. It has outlived 'em by the score. And do you know why? Because of the African redwood planking? It was imported from the Gold Coast by sailing vessel. You can just imagine the cost, but it won't ever rot, not even in salt water, never. There's only one thing that boat needs, and that's paint, and polish, and elbow grease."

"How about a new steam equipment? It seems to me I can see rust holes through the chimneys."

"I ain't suggesting you sail it. It's only good for the coastwise trade, and you know how the Yankees have taken that over."

"What are you suggesting?"

"Mr. Jarrett, Major, you're a capitalist. You got your clothes stuffed with money that isn't earning you a dime. What's more, it's only a question of time before those fellows over at the exchange or the Four Winds skin you naked as a cat."

In sudden irritation he said, "Why don't you let me worry about that?"

"I *want* you to worry about it. I want you to do some real hard worrying about it. And I know the harder you worry the more you'll see that this boat here, the *Weymount Castle*, is a floating palace. It's sitting there, waiting to be reborn. Reborn as a floating palace gambling house! The one and only location that Zach Thomas hasn't taken over for his own."

"I want no fight with Zach Thomas."

"Then you better get a long way out of Galveston, because when I saw the looks in that Chad fellow's eyes, I could see you were in for trouble from his employer!"

V

Jarrett got out of the hack and walked down the dock. He was annoyed with that king-size, beaming, gold-toothed Prince George who had somehow inserted himself into his life, and in the short space of eight or ten hours had made himself indispensable. He was no ordinary coachman, that was certain. His livery alone had cost more than most coachmen had tied up in a horse and rig; his gold teeth and earrings were worth a hundred dollars, and there was his bracelet besides. He had a set of carved cameo buttons that would have been the envy of Queen Victoria, and his carriage and team were absolutely the finest in port. He probably had money tied up in the boat himself, or was steering suckers for a commission. Still, it wouldn't hurt to look.

As Jarrett walked down the dock he had a front view. If the boat were in any condition, if it were seaworthy enough to sail along the coast as an excursion yacht, then he might be interested. But as it was, no, thank you. No, Prince George, you beaming, golden-tooth promotor, no, *no*, and NO!

As he walked, the hack followed him at a distance. It was so quiet he could hear the hoofs as they struck, resounding from water under the dock with a peculiar, liquid echo.

A light was burning somewhere deep inside the boat. He could not see the light, actually, but a reflected glow of the light, giving some of the old salons a golden, peach-hued luminescence. He fell to imagining the boat as she had been, a glory of light and of sound, sailing the mighty Mississippi. Racing the *Magnolia* or the *Natchez Queen.* The string orchestra playing waltz music, and couples executing the swift circles of the dance. That grand old boat had seen it all, and now, bathed and mellowed by starlight, it was almost possible to imagine it that way yet. But no!—no investment.

He had walked farther than he realized, and he started back. The hack was no longer in sight. Then he saw that it had somehow got in between two of the warehouses. "Now, how the devil?" he muttered.

Then he realized it wasn't Prince George's hack. He stopped and stood quiet. There was a driver, a man standing alongside, and a man in the carriage with what looked like a set of mother-of-pearl opera glasses. The man was peering at the boat. He lowered the glasses and spoke, and his voice, coming clearly across the thirty or forty yards of distance, gave Jarrett a start of recognition.

"She's living there, all right," said Zach Thomas.

"She's not only living there, she's barricaded in there," a man answered.

"Barricaded? How do you know?"

"Anybody waiting inside with a Winchester repeating

rifle is barricaded, in my estimate. She'd have killed me if I hadn't gone belly down crawlin'."

"She was only warning you off, Chad."

"No, she'd have killed me," Chad answered.

"How does she eat? And what ever happened to her husband?"

"You shot her husband. Have you forgotten?"

"I did no such thing."

"You talked about it, and he ain't around."

"I told him I'd shoot him if I caught him in one of my places again. He was a cheating gambler. He had tallow under his fingernail and marked the cards with it. Then he'd wear those smoked glasses and the grease showed up plain as crayon."

"Anyhow, he's gone. And she's here."

"I want *her* gone by next week."

"So do I!" the man muttered truculently. "But this is the deputy sheriff's job! Or a constable's. What do we elect constables and pay our taxes for, if not to serve papers and perform evictions?"

"Do you pay taxes, Chad?"

"You do, and you pay plenty."

"We sent a constable down here with a notice and she shot it to pieces while he was trying to nail it up."

"Well, there you are. What good will I be to you dead?"

"I don't know, Chad. But don't think I haven't been giving it some thought."

"I'd be *no* good at all to you dead. Why don't *you* come down here and talk to her?"

"Why me?"

"Because women go crazy about you, especially when you're all dressed up."

"Yeah, they do, don't they?"

"You bet they do! Believe me, Mr. Thomas, if I was you I wouldn't worry about any woman, any place, any time. But don't try going in there tonight. That bald-headed wrestler keeps watch. He's always where—"

"The Billy Goat?"

"Yes, the Billy Goat."

"He sounds like *your* type."

"I'll get him just right sometime, and break him in half. Don't worry about the Billy Goat. I'll take care of him, if you take care of her."

"Maxine."

"Yes, that's her name."

"A very beautiful woman."

A match flared and Thomas' face was revealed, lean, tough, with its strong nose and glinting eyes. He was smiling, and he had a panatela cigar between his teeth. He waited for the sulphur to stop flaring, and puffed the cigar in clouds.

"All right, Chad. So be it. You dehorn that so-called Billy Goat, and I'll seek ways and means with little Maxine."

"She ain't so little, boss, and she's all woman."

"The very kind who find me unresistible."

The thing that set Jarrett's anger to rising was that Thomas was so obviously serious. He did consider himself irresistible to women. And it was at the same time so obviously foolish. He was a cheap, brassy swaggerer, and any woman, aside from those of the lowest order, would be repelled by him. A rack of bones, some muscle—granted a cat-quickness and an intelligence—but beyond that, what? At the bottom, he was a cheap tinhorn gambler. Jarrett had had him pegged from the start.

"I never thought you'd go into the steamboat business, Mr. Thomas," said Chad. "None of these old boats are making much money. I been told the insurance is awful high on old bottoms. Gosh, you take that old hull out on the Gulf and the first good sea would break it into driftwood."

"What are you talking about, Chad? That boat there is historic. There's no wood even for sale any more like went into that boat. They'd make little jewel chests out of her 'jumbe wood, chairs out of her casings, and violins out of the stuff they used to plank her with. Her chandeliers you could string and use for necklaces, and her rugs could decorate the tent of a caliph. Why, two governors were on hand for her christening, the President of the United States sent a message of felicitations, whilst on board never did such an assemblage of ladies and gentlemen, both domestic and foreign, dance to such music. They danced the lancers, and the sabers, and my own maternal uncle, Colonel Merriweather Zacchary, led the grand quadrille!

"It has what we call a *sentimental* value. That's why I want to get hold of it, one reason, and turn it into a gambling ship. The other reason is, I know it's what that woman has in mind, and it's only a question of time before she finds some damn fool who will put up the money. I wouldn't like that, Chad. I wouldn't like having to run 'im out of business. Funerals are getting higher and higher priced all the time."

"Gosh, I just thought you were going to haul cotton."

"No, I'm going to haul the people that haul the cotton and grow the cotton. And the cattle. And the sugar cane. I'm going to farm the farmer, and ranch the rancher. I'm going to cultivate 'em with champagne and rare viands, with music. I'll harrow 'em a little with faro, roulette, and chuck-a-luck. I'll sail down the coast and collect the rich and the wealthy from Sabine and New Orleans and Mobile. And when I bring 'em back they may not be so rich and so wealthy, but they'll have had an experience. Experience, Chad, the great teacher. They'll know what it's like to have been robbed and still had their money's worth. They may not have their money, but by the gods they'll have memories!"

Then his tone changed. "That woman has to get out of there! Drive me to the bank. No, it's too late. Drive me to Burden's house. It's the bank's job to foreclose on this. Interest be damned! It's up to Burden to do this. When you have a mortgage, you can foreclose it."

Jarrett stood quietly not thirty feet away, not revealing himself by the slightest movement, as the carriage rolled past. The rich aroma of Zach Thomas' cigar lingered for a minute afterward.

VI

"Mist' Major?" said Prince George in a hushed tone. He was walking.

"Here I am."

"That was Zach Thomas?"

"It was."

Prince George came up with a loaded whipstock in his hand. The lash had been cut off, and a wrist loop substituted so the stock could be used like a long sap, or a sling shot.

"I was worried about maybe he had some of his bully boys and was planning on raiding that ship, so I hid off. If they did it at night that poor little gal wouldn't be able to aim."

"She ought to have a shotgun."

"She does. She's got a four-gauge swivel gun loaded with

carpet tacks, lead slugs, pieces of chain, and what not, but even so— You like to go down there, Major? You want to talk to her about going into partnerships, maybe?"

"I'd prefer going there when she's able to aim."

They rode far down the waterfront and along a log corduroy road to the town's one place of amusement described by Prince George as not being Zach Thomas'. It proved to be a lot surrounded by shacks, cribs, a bagnio, a saloon serving a weak, sweetish rum in large mugs for five cents a mug, a barbecue with whole pigs roasting, and a cockfight arena where sports of all races stood tight-packed in a swelter, watching the pit, and betting through commissioners who sat on high stools with the signs of changing odds posted in their hats.

Jarrett won $50, which he passed on to Prince George for his day's service, and engaged him again for the following morning. Then he went to his room in the Congress Hotel.

Next morning he awoke in the hot sunlight, with birds singing in the trees outside his window. He packed his carpetbag with soiled clothing, intending to have Prince George turn it over to some laundress, his experience with hotels being far from good on this score, and then went downstairs to breakfast. He was on the terrace finishing his coffee, made syrupy Spanish-style with extract, sorghum, and hot milk, with enough cascarilla to make his eyes bulge, when Prince George appeared in a new white and blue uniform at the carriage entrance.

"You look well this morning, Major."

"And I feel well." Indeed he did; the cascarilla and coffee extract made him feel like swinging from the treetops.

"Take the bag, sir?"

"Laundry."

"Yes, sir. Where to, sir?"

"The stock exchange."

"Yes, sir!"

He drove through the entrance gate and among the crowds. Pedestrians were everywhere, and wagons cluttered the curbs, unloading cargo on the walks and the store ramps. It was a town of strong smells, and sweat and excitement. One heard French, Spanish, and a dozen varieties of English. There were a number of sidewalk cafés, most of them with their chairs leaning inward against the tables while black men with buckets dipped full from the morning water wagons sloshed down the floors and spread wet palm mats in preparation for the day's business. But at some the usual customers were at table, men in planters'

90

hats, Island rattans and Panamas, men carrying pistols and derringers, and wearing sash belts around their waists; men sitting all day, drinking centavo coffees and talking money in millions; talking of the market, and politics and revolutions.

There had been a clamp-down on swashbuckling expeditions from New Orleans, with an arms inspection of about one ship in six going down the Mississippi, but Galveston had not fallen under official scrutiny, and as a result it had become the staging point for a dozen expeditions a year, and the planning place for hundreds. South American generals and presidents in disfavor escaped to Galveston and waited their chance to return, often bringing with them their treasuries, on which they lived in incredible splendor, while would-be generals and heads of state mapped strategy, sought shipping and arms, and offered I.O.U. bribes and political preference.

"Stock exchange, Major?"

"That's what I said."

"You was very, very lucky with those chickens last night, Major. With your luck at chickens, I don't guess I'd ever play the market."

"You don't understand these things, Prince. The market is not a gambling house. It's a place where one buys and sells portions of the business world. Railroads, shipping lines, mines, and smelters."

"I understand, Major."

A wagon had backed into the street, blocking it, and they had to stop.

"Move the wagon!" George called out. "I got an important passenger for the stock exchange."

The wagon driver, a powerful Negro, apparently had no intention of moving. Instead, he notched the brake and wrapped the reins around it.

"What you say?" he asked, getting down.

"You heard very well what I said."

"I don't believe I heered you right. Who you think yo' is in yo' fine clothes and hifalutin' talky-talk? Yo' is addressin' a free American citizen!"

"I'm talkin' to a teamster that's blocking the street of this city. I'm talking to a man that's looking to get his head knocked in."

"Who by?"

"Me by!" said Prince George, hefting the loaded crop.

There was something too accidental about it, just too damned accidental. Jarrett stood up in the carriage and had a look around. Besides the usual crowd that gathered for an argument with the chance of a fight, there were a number of men he didn't like the looks of. They were spaced along the sidewalk, one by a barrel, one by a saloon door, another coming up behind, and all too casual, too intent—and too obviously the kind of toughs a man could hire for a few dollars for special jobs. The kind of men Chad would get hold of. And he saw a man he took to be Chad himself.

"George!" he cried.

"I ain't troubling this fellow. He's troubling me. He's blocking the street, and—"

"Let's get out of here."

"Begging your pardon, Major—"

"I said get out of here!"

"Yes, sir!" He suddenly understood, and seemed more alarmed than his employer. He tried to get the horses to back, but the colored teamster grabbed them by the bridles.

"Let go!" cried Prince George, cutting at him with his whip.

The teamster reeled back, freeing the team and casting his hands up for protection. A lash mark spread claret against his ebony cheek.

"Hey, there!" yelled one of the toughs. "What are you trying to do, you damn foreigner?"

The horses freed, Prince George managed to back the carriage, but there were people behind him and all around him. It went off-angle and crashed into a wheeled stand filled with oranges. Oranges rolled across the brick pavement. People from all around were snatching them up.

"I'll pay for them," Jarrett said to the mulatto owner. "How much are they? A dollar will do, won't it?"

The man grabbed the dollar, and asked fifty cents more for the stand.

"To hell with you!"

"Boss, boss!" George was saying. "Here's the Angel."

"Who?"

"The Angel. You know, I was telling you."

A short, powerful man stood looking at Jarrett. He had taken him to be one of Chad's toughs, and a bad-appearing one at that.

"It's about time you showed up," said the Angel.

"What do you mean, time I showed up? I made no appointment with you. I made no appointment with them, either."

"I'm the Angel—didn't he tell you about me?"

92

"You know, about the boat," said George.

"All I remember was about a beautiful woman with a swivel gun loaded—"

"Him, too! He's here to protect your investment. You can *trust* him, boss!"

"If you have that money—" The Angel looked at the carpetbag.

"That's just soiled laundry," said George. "The Major has it sewed in his coat."

Jarrett didn't know what to do. He might as well be robbed by Chad's men as by George and this "Angel," but he had to make a gamble one way or the other. By now they were closely surrounded. One of the roughs came staggering in, pretending to be pushed, but his object was plain. He wanted a chance at the carpetbag. Prince George, turning, came up with a right fist that knocked the man down. Others came in, and the Angel charged, goat-fashion, with his head down. Clubs and saps appeared, but they seemed to have no effect on him. He drove one of the men against a hitching rack, where they grappled.

For an instant the Angel seemed to be at a disadvantage, but Prince George, leaning tall and limber from his vantage point on the side of the coach, swung the whipstock and the man went to his knees, the Angel coming up with a knee and mashing his nose in.

Jarrett meanwhile attempted to get off on the far side. He had no fancy for free-for-alls, and he dreaded getting Lantern's clothes torn. On the other hand, he did not dare draw the gun, because a gun once drawn is useless unless fired, and there were too many people about.

He stood tall in the carriage, his top hat making him seem much taller, and shouted, "I'll fight any man in the crowd for fifty dollars!"

It brought a stop to everything except a tussle which a couple of sailors had got into just for the fun of it.

Jarrett saw Chad, and thrust a long finger at him. "You greasy pig! You're the head of this gang. Come and fight me."

Chad did not mind being called a greasy pig, or anything else, and he wasn't afraid to fight. But what he wanted, obviously, was to get his hands on the carpetbag. Jarrett knew that, and abandoned it in the carriage as he swung down.

"How about it, pig?"

"Yah, I'll fight you."

"Hold my coat!" Jarrett cried, stripping it off.

"I'll take it!" said the Angel.

Good Lord, thought Jarrett when the Angel disappeared, dodging through the crowd, now I do have to fight this fellow!

"He's carrying a gun!" said a tall, loose-jawed man.

"I'll take it off."

"Keep your hand away from it!" said Chad.

"I could have shot you right between the eyes any time I wanted to."

A man wearing a badge came pushing through the crowd. "You're shooting nobody between the eyes, mister. What's going on here?"

"You tell me," said Jarrett. "What kind of a town do you have here that a gentleman can't ride down the street in his carriage?"

"Who are you?"

"My card, sir."

"Oh, railroads."

"I'll have that card back, sir, if you don't mind."

Like all policemen, this one wanted to be sure of a man's influence before he started shoving him around, hence, although he knew who Chad worked for, and wanted to do nothing offensive to Zachariah Thomas, he wanted to be careful with Jarrett also.

"This here blackfella," said Prince George, waving at the wagoner, "blocked the thoroughfare whilst I was trying to drive my fare from the best hotel in town to the stock exchange. Major Jarrett has got a big put-and-take order on the telegraph between here and Philadelphia. A thing like this could look mighty bad for Galveston."

"All right," said the policeman to the crowd. "Clear out."

"My carpetbag!" cried Jarrett. "Somebody stole my carpetbag!"

He couldn't imagine how it had disappeared. He had turned, watching Chad and the others, and it was gone from behind him.

"There he goes, he's running with it!" cried someone near him.

One of Chad's men was briefly visible, dodging in and out of the crowd, and he had the carpetbag. Jarrett drew his gun and beaded down exactly on the middle of his back, but there were people beyond and at both sides, making the shot too risky. Anyway, a dead man would prove quite a complication.

"I've changed my mind, driver," said Jarrett, resuming his

seat and sitting with hands folded across the gold-headed walking stick. "I've decided to go to the bank and make a small withdrawal from my account."

"Which bank, sir?"

"Any bank. Just any bank at all."

VII

"What in the devil is this?" said Zach Thomas, hurling the carpetbag at Chad, who let it hit him without a change of expression. "This is filled with reeking socks and sweaty shirts."

"It's what you told me to get, boss."

"I told you to get the money. I said it might be in a carpetbag. I said there was six, eight thousand in gold. You could feel that much money like a tailor's flatiron."

"I didn't snitch it. It was Lefty got it. He—"

"You were head of that expedition, weren't you? Did you search his room?"

"McKnight is doing that. He's at the hotel right now."

"He might as well save his time. He wouldn't hide it in a hotel room. He wouldn't leave it out of his reach. Did he have any other bags? Did he have an alligator-skin valise?"

"This is positively all he had, boss."

Zach Thomas, pacing his office above the Sunny South, his most luxurious casino, restaurant, and temple of pleasure, was in a savage mood. He had a way of smiling when he was angry, and looking at things through narrowed eyes, and working the muscles of his jaws. Chad was not an observant man, but he had a certain animal alertness, and he knew when he saw the jaw muscles working that he would have to go easy, because Zach Thomas might strike as quick and deadly as a diamondback. He might, for instance, put a bullet right through him.

"Now, what could have happened to it?" Zach mused in his velvet voice. "He had it when he got off the boat. I talked to the captain. It was Jarrett, no mistake, and he wouldn't let the carpetbag out of sight. He sat with it between his feet the whole way. Then you went out yesterday, and you followed him—"

"I sure did, boss. I didn't lose sight of him for one second. I followed him all the way to the ferry."

"All the way to the ferry! He went somewhere and hid it. You should have got on with him instead of running back to me. But never mind, Chad. I don't expect you to have muscle and brains both."

"Thanks!" Chad said gratefully. "I sure am strong, all right."

"But now, Chad, I'm going to ask you to try something. I'm going to ask you to *think*. Did he have something in that coach, anything at all, a paper bag, maybe? Did he have something he might have hid? Could he have passed it to some confederate?"

"Most everybody's on the Confederate side—"

"Oh, for God's sake! Try and think, was there anything—"

"I'm thinkin', boss! I'm thinkin'!"

"Try sitting down. Close your eyes. Now think."

"I know!" Chad cried in a moment.

"Yes?"

"Well, he was in his shirtsleeves when he drove off. He rode off in his vest and shirtsleeves. In his vest and a stove-pipe hat!"

"In other words, he took off his coat."

"He did something with it."

"He couldn't carry much in a *coat*."

"It was padded so he looked like the heavyweight champion of the world. But when he took it off and handed it to the Billy Goat—"

Zach Thomas cursed.

"He ran off with it and never came back!" said Chad. "I guess he was scared of me, too."

"You damn fool! You damned, fat-headed fool." A fine Turkish carpet was on the floor, and Zach expended his anger by hurling his cigar down and grinding it deep into the fabric. "I'd rather *Jarrett* would have that money than the Angel. Jarrett would hang around one or another of my places until he lost it. It would be just a question of time and percentage, because a fool and his money are soon parted."

"Yah, boss," Chad said, eager to please. "I heard you say that before, boss."

"Well," Zach said bitterly, "I guess I sent a fool on a fool's errand. Whatever happens to it, the Billy Goat will see to it that Richter gets enough to pay the interest on the *Weymount Castle*."

"Why don't we—"

"Go out and find Harvey Burden," he told Chad. Then he picked up his hat and said, "Never mind, I'll go over there myself."

He needed some air. There were times, in periods of stress, when the walls of a house pressed in on him. It always happened when he was oppressed by stupid bouncers, and muddling help in general. Good God! When a man paid what he did to bouncers, gun guards, informers, to the police and the sheriff's office, and to prosecutors and judges, you would think some of the load could be taken off his shoulders. The fact was he couldn't even send a gang out to crack a skull, toss some troublemaker in the bay, or horsewhip a faro dealer found stealing, without he had to smooth it out afterward. A while back he had killed a man after great provocation, an armed man with notches in his gun, and he had been forced to submit to arrest, bail, and a hearing because the sheriff and prosecutor were worried about an investigation by the Union brigadier over in Bolivar, and the carpetbaggers holding forth in Austin.

What he actually did was furnish his own law enforcement, and at the same time pay the city and county. He paid the officials twice, in fact, once as a taxpayer, and again as graft. You'd think they'd appreciate it, and if he needed somebody taken care of, they'd be willing to oblige. But, no—he had to pay them extra, and suffer the indignities of a search and seizure besides.

"Son of a bitch, dirty son of a bitch," said Zach.

Sometimes when he got to thinking about inefficiency, and petty crookedness and lack of gratitude in the world, he wanted to walk and walk under the blue sky and never go inside the limits of Galveston again. After all, he had had a good Christian home. Nobody had had a better upbringing than Zach—right up until he was eleven years old, when he ran away with the medicine show, intending to become a doctor. Then he'd run a museum in Chicago, operated the shell-game circuit, and become an exhibition shot in the Bell's Wonder Shows, a circus. He had been in California and started around the Horn, and been shipwrecked off Manzanillo. He was in Panama when the war broke out, and he leased boats to run the blockade into the Gulf ports, coming to Galveston for the first time and meeting Harvey Burden.

How Burden had impressed him at that time! Burden was the first grade-A fat and overbearing man of wealth he had ever met. He was what Zach Thomas had aspired to be. He could still remember how he sat spellbound and listened all one afternoon while Burden talked millions in an aura of French brandy and Cuban Corona cigars. But that had been a long time ago. The big fellow had overextended himself and bought cotton options like a damned fool, so today one good kick at his credit structure and the whole thing would come tumbling down like a chimney without mortar. One of these days, Zach was thinking, it would be up to him to deliver that kick. But not for a while. He needed Burden for a front, and he had too much of his own tied up in the bank.

"Is the boss in?" he asked, walking around behind the cages where the large vault door stood open, and to the private stairs.

"I'll tell him you're here," said Dwight Franklyn.

"Never mind, I know the way."

VIII

"No, I tell you, no, no, no!" Harvey Burden was saying. He was panting, short of breath from excited annoyance, and striking his desk with a fat fist, a fist as big and white as a leg of boiled pork. "No, damn it, no, you exceeded your authority!"

Facing him was a short, bald-headed man, Samuel Leach, his head cashier. "Mr. Burden, you're the boss, but—"

"No, I tell you, no such authority was ever given you. In small amounts, yes. But ninety thousand dollars! If there turns out to be some trouble concerning this transaction—"

He stopped suddenly, seeing Zach Thomas. His face was flushed, and the vehemence of his speech had left his lips thick and moist. He turned pale and mottled, and Zach realized that he must be the last person Burden wished to see at that moment. But he recovered with a resonant voice.

"Oh, Zach! That's all, Leach. Zach, my boy! Very glad to see you. I was—"

"What was that about?" Zach asked as Leach departed.

"Oh, that! That fool! Do you realize—" Then Burden commenced to curse. He had a vile tongue, and his way of cursing, with deep feeling, in a tone such as others might use for prayer, made the words seem worse.

Zach said, "Don't tell me he accepted a deposit from that coach robber, Jarrett?"

"You knew!"

"Well, that's fine. What could be better? We have the money back."

"Damn it, sir, he accepted the money and *no questions asked*. He made no examination, nothing. He certified it, every banknote, and signed the deposit. Had it countersigned. I tell you the money is now part of the bank's responsibility. Jarrett can write a check for that, all ninety thousand dollars of it, and if this bank doesn't honor it he can *close our doors*. Yes, he could. He could start a run on this bank. I tell you he could ruin us!"

"What do you suppose he did with the other ten thousand?"

"I don't know." Blowing and exhausted, he fell into his chair. "Oh, God, it's hot!"

"Let me see the money."

"Zach, I can't let you see the money. Do you know what I think? I think this whole thing is a trap. I think he's a government man. No, he's not a government man—he's working for the Tadloe interests in New Orleans. They're out to smash us. They know we've overextended ourselves on cotton futures—"

"Close the door."

"You close the door!"

Burden really had to be upset to assume such a tone to Zach. He was perspiring so much that his handkerchief was soaked, and he threw it in a desk drawer.

"Oh, God, it's hot!" he said again. "This is the hottest day we've had. And the dampness— Oh, to get out of this son-of-a-bitching town to where I could breathe!"

"It's not hot at all. It's nice and cool to us who have clear consciences."

"You have no more of a clear conscience than I have."

"I just borrowed from the bank, Harvey. I haven't been lending to myself. Do you know what we call it when bankers lend to themselves? We refer to that as dipping into the till."

"Sir, I resent that allegation!"

"What's the matter with you? There's nothing in this for you to get worked up about. I'm the one who ought to get worked up. After all, that money was stolen from me, in a manner of speaking."

"Yes, yes. It's this heat. I can't think clearly, I can't sleep at night. If we only had some ice."

His hair stuck to his scalp, and his shirt to his chest. Every time he got up from sitting, his pants stuck tight to the inside of his legs. It wasn't so bad except when Zach came around. The day could be almost bearable, he wouldn't even be thinking of the heat, then Zach would come and perspiration would flow from every pore.

He walked to the water cooler and looked out of the window, half expecting to see Aikens, Saigon, or one of the other partners rushing over, having heard about the money. Word of it was bound to get out. It was the biggest cash deposit ever to come through the wicket. He was going to have a rough time with Saigon. Aikens, Williams, Burns, and Mitchell he could handle—but Saigon! Good Lord, the man had fought duels for less.

"I'll fight him!" Burden muttered. "But I'll take my choice of weapons." He did not notice what he was doing; in his agitation he had taken hold of the back of a chair, and it broke in his heavy fist.

Zach said, "My thought is, if we could bring in the sheriff and sort of attach the money, as far as Jarrett is concerned, and then look up his record and get him out of the country, or hang him, or get him killed trying to escape, why then—"

"No, no. It would never work. We'd be in over our ears." There was a rap at the door. "Yes, what is it, Dwight?"

"That man is here!"

"What man?"

"Mr. Jarrett. He wants to make a withdrawal."

"No, not the same day of the deposit."

"He's out there?" asked Zach.

"Yes."

"Send him in. I'd like to look at this depositor."

"I'm here already," said Jarrett, stepping in. "Well, Zach! You're looking well. Tanned, lean, and healthy."

He came in carrying his gray stovepipe hat by means of a hand thrust deeply into it.

"What do you have in that hat, a pistol?"

"Zach, on my honor, I haven't got anything in this hat a preacher wouldn't carry."

"Well, sit down. We're not going to kill you *here*. It would give the bank a bad name. A man deposits ninety thousand dollars and gets killed by one of the directors when he tries to make his first withdrawal—why, it'd be all over town. People would talk. How about it, Joe? Did you know I was a director of this bank when you sent that

100

fellow here? Are you hatching up some kind of a plot? Did you think depositing it in my vault would be a perfect way of keeping me away from my money?"

"I think you got this money confused with some other money. Yes. You see, this money is some I borrowed. I signed a note for it. That other money, the salvage, I sort of got rid of."

"You sure go through money in a hurry."

"I got expensive tastes."

"I'll see to it you get an expensive funeral."

"That's all provided for. This money would immediately fall under attachment to a charitable institution if anything happened to me. In fact, no judge of probate, or jury either, could possibly decide against this institution, it's so estimable."

The muscles were working at the sides of Thomas' jaw; it was a danger sign, and Burden saw it, whether Jarrett did or not. He got around behind his heavy mahogany desk and sat down on the edge of his great chair, ready to go to the floor, protected from bullets. In that position he watched, and mopped his face with a fresh handkerchief. His lips moved, although no sound came, and he prayed: "Oh God, Thou Almighty one on high, let these two wolves kill each other with their first shots. Oh God, put bullets through the hearts of both these sons of bitches. Oh God, I'm the best contributor to the church in this town. I've done that for You, You do this for me."

"That's my money, Jarrett," Zach said. "And no legal technicality will keep me from it. It's mine, and I want it."

"Some day there'll be something you want and can't get."

"Not in this town. I own it, and I run it. Don't I, Harvey? Harvey, here, is the biggest businessman in town. Tell him, Harvey, how I am in this town."

"Well, of course, Mr. Thomas is one of our most important citizens."

"Jarrett, you've heard that old poem about playing aces in another man's town."

"It's my town, too, Zach. I first saw the light of day here. One way of looking at it, I'm a home boy and you two are interlopers."

"I could walk to that window and wave a handkerchief," said Zach, "and marksmen would kill you as you stepped into the street. I could blow you up with giant powder as you rode in your carriage, and they'd never find the fragments. Or I could make you disappear—just vanish. Eaten up by the gar and 'gators out in the lagoon. But I don't want to. I

101

think you could be valuable to me. I can see a way we could both stay alive, and each have an easier life on account of the other.

"First, I take over that money, which is mine anyway. Then I stake you into one of the biggest, newest, fanciest, and most glittering establishments ever seen on these coasts. I'll give you a decent wage and a percentage. Who knows, you might even get to be a hundred-thousandaire on your own, honestly. I think that's fair. More'n fair. What do you think about it, Harvey? Don't you think that's fair?"

"Yes, yes. More than fair."

There would be no shooting. Burden had to get up and free his sweat-slick pants from his crotch. He went to the cooler and drank a tall glass of the tepid water. From the window he saw Saigon walking up the street, a colored boy going before with a sun parasol. "Oh God," he whispered, "don't let him come here and give the play away." But Saigon, he saw with relief, had gone up the stairs to Harrison Williams' brokerage house. That could be good or bad . . .

"I'm not offering you this proposition just on account of the money, Jarrett," Zach was saying. "Here, have a cigar. Harvey, pour some of the Napoleon brandy. I must apologize for the bank having no ice. This is warm as sweat. . . . Well, as I was saying, I like a man working with me who can take charge. Not a *yes sir,* and *no sir* sort of fellow. In fact, I've been thinking I might want a man who could take complete charge while I took a sail to Europe to visit the spas and make a tour. In fact, Harvey, here, would welcome a change, too. We all need a vacation—"

"Oh, do I! If I ever get out of this son-of-a-bitching town, by this putrid bay, away from the heat, and dampness, and the God damned stinking—"

"Yes, he needs a vacation, too—an even longer one. So you see the opportunity in being my second in command? Naturally, I'm not offering it to you right off. You'd have to prove yourself. And we'd have to start off with a clean slate. You'd have to release that money, et cetera. No hard feelings. No recriminations. Just release it. Oh, I'll bet we'll have lots of laughs about that whole business out there by the coach! I can just hear us laughing about it right now. Ha-ha!"

"Ha-ha," Jarrett echoed. "You make it sound very attractive. And don't think I'm not flattered. I am. And under other conditions I might say yes like a shot. However, I have an idea I've been working on. A very big glittering idea of my own."

102

"What is it?"

"There's an old riverboat down by the docks. It was a palace ship off the old Mississippi trade. The *Weymount Castle*. It occurred to me—now don't laugh about this just because it's different—but I thought I might turn it into a gambling palace. A floating palace of chance. Of music and ballroom floors and curved staircases where young gentlemen could drink wine out of ladies' slippers."

"You son of a bitch!" Zach snarled.

"No!" said Jarrett, with the hat in his lap. From deep inside it came the unmistakable click of a derringer pistol. "Now, Zach! You didn't want to shoot a big depositor; well, I wouldn't want to shoot a big director."

"You won't get away with it, Jarrett."

"I'm gettin', I'm gettin'."

"Stay away from that boat! That boat is going to be mine."

"I believe you're holding a coat of mine hereabouts."

"Yes, yes," said Burden. "See Mr. Franklyn about it."

"Walk out of here and it's war, Jarrett," Zach said.

"I been thinking I might change the name of that boat to the *Ophir*. The *Golden Ophir*. What a name for a floating palace of chance! Because Ophir is where the Queen of Sheba came from. And she brought golden ingots, and the rarest jewels, and frankincense and myrrh. Although I sort of thought we'd specialize in the best charcoaled bourbon and the French wines. Also I been considering *La Maison Rouge*. And dressing everybody up in red. Red swallowtail coats!—wouldn't that be gaudy? At any rate, whatever I name it, and whatever I do, you boys are invited to the grand opening."

Part Three

I

It was an awfully old boat. He knew last night it was old, but the shadows had smoothed it over, had given it an added dimension, a glow of romance, of memories, of the old days on the Mississippi. Last night ghosts had lived there, and its empty staterooms, windows were like the eyes of the past, a memory of lost voices, and music, and forgotten laughter. But by merciless sunlight it was just a big old boat. You stood and saw it in hopeless sections—a warped promenade, a crumbling boiler deck, a lot of old machinery, planking scummed and unscraped, paddlewheel housings with loose boards through which moss grew, and the birds had nests in the twin chimneys.

"It's the same boat, boss," said Prince George. "We looked at it last night from right this angle and everything."

"But you can't see so well at night."

"There's nothing wrong that some good, old-fashioned elbow grease—"

"And ninety thousand dollars."

"Yes, granted. You wouldn't even be given the chance at this if you didn't have the capital, and you know it. This girl, she'd be runnin' it herself, simply coining the money, getting rich, only she requires capital."

"Let's sit here. I see rats, mice, pelicans—it's only a question of time before the other animals come down off that thing, two by two."

"Noah had a good boat, too, Mist' Jarrett."

"But mighty old."

"Anyhow, it wouldn't do a bit of harm to go aboard and look. Don't forget Mr. Zach Thomas thinks this has real profitable possibilities. Mr. Zach Thomas, he ain't afraid of a little bit of paint and elbow grease."

"You're right." Indeed he was right. Mention of Zach made

all the difference. If Zach wanted that boat, there was a reason. "No, you wait here. I don't want anybody coaching me. I'm going to look at this by myself."

He walked down the dock and started up a cleated plank to the deck, and a gun cracked, putting a hole through his stovepipe hat. He retreated and took cover, thinking he had fallen into an ambush. It was exactly what Zach had promised him, only he hadn't expected it *here*.

"Mr. Jarrett! Jarrett!" It was the Angel. "I'm sorry, I was on the other side, I didn't know. Are you all right, Mr. Jarrett?"

"You damn near lost yourself an investor." It troubled him that the bullet had damaged the top hat. In all the years old Lantern had owned it, he had never had a hole put through it. It was a blond beaver velour, and Lantern had kept it in mint condition. "Who the hell shot at me?"

"The young lady, sir. She didn't *know*."

"She'll know when she gets a bill for this hat. That's a twelve-dollar hole she put in that hat. Do you realize they can't even fix a hat like this here? I'll have to send it to Massachusetts by express."

"I know she'll be most sorry about this. She saw the hat and thought it was that dress-up Zach Thomas coming around."

"Well, I wouldn't want to discourage her from shooting Zach."

He put the hat back on and showed himself. Nothing happened, and he walked up the plank, towering over the Angel.

"You her partner or something?" he asked.

"I used to perform on her father's boat. This very boat you're standing on! It was a showboat, the finest on the river. Long after it went out of service as a passenger boat, Mr. Richter operated it as a showboat. We played all the way from Cincinnati to New Orleans, and we braved the Gulf itself and sailed to Mobile and Pensacola and here to Galveston. That was before the war. I was a wrestler. I engaged in butting exhibitions."

"Butting?"

"I have the hardest head in the world," he said proudly. "I sometimes bet I could break coconuts with my head. People would at times pay up to twenty dollars to see it done, or they would take up a collection. Mr. Richter was my best friend. He was a brave man. He put this ship, the *Weymount Castle*, in the service of the Confederacy.

We fought in the battle of New Orleans and were sunk. But we raised it again during low water and tried to go on giving shows.

"He is dead now, and she turned to me for help. I was responsible for bringing the boat here. You see, I knew about Mr. Burden. Did you know he wrestled in the old days?" He spoke as if his present career as banker was a comedown. "Yes, indeed. Not that I ever contested with him. But he wrestled. That was why I came here, being sure he'd help. But all he did was buy our mortgage paper from the New Orleans bank and attempt to foreclose."

"The swine! I'm surprised you took my account over there."

"Oh, I knew I could count on him. I knew he'd be afraid to touch a deposited account."

"That doesn't explain how you—"

Jarrett stopped suddenly. A young woman was standing in the between-decks companionway. Her beauty startled him, and he was not a man who startled easily. It stopped him in his tracks and left him staring. And it wasn't what she wore, either. Her clothes couldn't be worse. Everything she had on was old and shrunken. She wore a man's shirt and it showed her bosom—just as a low-cut ballgown might do. She had no corset on, none at all, nothing to shove her breasts up, but they threatened to escape anyway. He had the almost uncontrollable impulse to reach in and take hold, to cup one of those lovely breasts, just as he might a kitten, a little bird, or anything else delectably smooth, and soft, and tender. She wore a skirt that was tight at the waist and ragged around the bottom, and he saw that she was barefooted. She had strong legs, smooth and brown, visible when the skirt swung to a few inches above the ankle. What was there about barefoot women that always affected him? Was it something that appealed to the primitive in him? Her eyes met his steadily. They were deep brown, but she was not of West Indian blood. She was German, Bavarian, maybe Italian. Richter—the south of Germany. There was a rifle in her hand, a lever-action gun with a brass receiver. It smelled of fresh powder.

"Maxine, for God's sakes!" said the Angel. "This is *him!*"

"Oh!" she said. Just the one syllable, exhaling, but it had a warm glow, a charm, a womanliness. She had the voice that women ought to have, and almost never did. She could speak and it was a caress. He wanted to hear her say more.

"I'm Joe Jarrett."

"You come here with money?"

God damn it, why did everyone have to talk about money? He was sick and tired of hearing about money.

"I don't want to talk about money. Money, what's that? Something, nothing. Here today, gone tomorrow. Easy come and easy go. 'He who steals my purse steals trash.' Et cetera. I never worried much about money. It's the human things that count in my book."

"You must be very wealthy if the human things count so much," she said.

"I have a few dollars. I came into a little cash unexpectedly."

"Would you like some tea?"

She turned without waiting for an answer and disappeared. With her barefoot walk she had the grace of a leopard. She was animal-smooth like a leopard, too. He followed her through a colonnaded hall with cloverleaf apertures looking into a long, narrow salon. Some theatrical flats of palms, bamboos, and jungle waterfalls indicated it had once been used as a small theatre, probably for a side show or a museum. The floor, he noticed, was worn and coated by brownish gums and waxes, but it was still solid. The walls, although painted over too many times, were in good shape.

"This is the grand promenade," said the Angel. "The panels are all removable for a view of the river, but it needs new screens."

Jarrett heard him, and he didn't hear him. He could not take his eyes off the girl. Her movements, so sure-footed and jungle-cat-smooth, fascinated him.

"My father's office!" she said.

The room was six-sided and filled with dilapidated furniture, but still it managed to maintain a semblance of its ancient charm.

"Sorry, Angel," he said, and closed the door.

"Leave him in."

"No. I've found out that two people can do a lot more business than three. If I'm going to put money into this wreck—I mean ship—"

"I don't like you. I don't like your attitude."

He was taken aback.

"No, I don't like you," she said again. "You will no more take over this boat because you have money than Zach Thomas could take it over."

"Who said anything about taking over? And as for my money—I haven't offered it yet."

"Why are you looking at me like that?"

He hadn't realized it, but he had been staring at her very

middle, the broad spread of her hips, the thrust of her pelvis, and the way her strong legs moved under the dress.

"I'm sorry. But I came from out west, where men are just plain honest. When we see a beautiful woman we look at her. We'd look at you plenty."

"Stare, then!"

"Now, ma'am—"

"All men are the same. They all are looking for the same thing. And then, good-bye. Men are worse than wolves. . . . Is this what you were looking at?"

He didn't realize what she was about until she had stripped her dress off. She stood naked before him—the dress was all she had had on. Her body was uniformly tan from head to foot, so she must have spent a good share of her time naked. He started towards her, and she backed away, taking up a Spanish seven-thong quirt. She swung it whizzing down and it would have cut his face in strips if he had not checked himself.

"Now you have seen what you were looking to see. Are you satisfied?"

"I wouldn't say— No, I—"

She laughed with contempt. Then languidly, watching him and yet ignoring him, tossing the quirt aside but still leaving it within reach, she found another dress, quite a good one, black silk with lace edgings, and put it on. She shook out her hair so that it fell in dark abundance to her shoulders, then she pulled it back with both hands and tied it with a red ribbon. She sat down and pulled on stockings and slippers.

"How much is the mortgage on this ark?" he asked.

"*Signed* mortgage? My husband, Mr. Messimo, lost money at the Four Winds. He lost at the Crystal Palace, at the Alcazar, and at the Sunny South. He liked to gamble, he lost, lost, lost."

"And signed I.O.U.'s."

"Yes."

"They're not collectible."

"Zachariah Thomas has a judgment."

"Then it's an illegal one. You can't collect gambling debts in this state. I know. They tried to collect some from me."

At last he had won a smile from her.

"Where is he?" he asked.

"Who?"

"Your husband."

"Dead. He went to Central America. The fever."

"Well, that's too bad." He tried to seem sorry. "So you're Mrs. Messimo. Or do you call yourself Richter?"

"Richter." But she rushed to Messimo's defense. "He was not a bad man. He was only not a strong man. He was very handsome. And he had—talents. He was born out of his time. He should have been a duke in medieval Florence. Ah, how he would have worn the sash and doublet! And the sword with the twinkling handle! What paintings he would have commissioned! What sculptors would have eaten at his table. What fêtes he would have given, what churches he would have endowed! He was a connoisseur without the price of admission to a gallery. A gourmet with ten cents for a bowl of stew. New Orleans' best-dressed man if he could only pay the tailor. He could sing, and play the pianoforte, and dance! You have never danced with a man until you have danced with Messimo! Like floating!"

"I never danced with a man at all."

"But he was a poor gambler, the only line of work that seemed open to his talents. I loved him." She said it in a manner direct and sincere. "I loved him, Mr. Jarrett. You who are so strong, and sure of yourself, and fast with a gun, and domineering, dominating, with hands to tear a world apart and boots to trample it into the dust—do you understand, I loved him?"

He did not believe her.

"I loved him in one way, and not in another," she said as if to herself. "He was fifteen years older. He had—other women."

"He must have been quite a man!"

"He was a gentleman!"

"And now, what? What are you looking for?"

"Money!"

"*My* money."

"I want to rebuild the *Weymount Castle*. I want to have the most beautiful gambling house in the world. Then some night a man will come aboard. He will be rich. Of the best family. He will ask me to marry him. *Comme il faut*—respectability! I want that. I want to ride with coachmen, and have men tip their hats to me." She cried, "Do you understand that? I want them to take off their hats, not start taking off their pants!"

"Maxine! Mrs. Messimo! My hat is off. My pants are on. I haven't unfastened a button. Let's look at this ship. What is this paneling—bloodwood, or mahogany? The floors are teak? Good Lord! Don't tell me you painted over this? Why, this is rosewood! Ma'am, with just a little elbow grease . . ."

II

As soon as he could decently do so, and after personally inspecting the currency Jarrett had deposited in the bank, Harvey Burden sent messages to Saigon and the other partners telling them the money was on deposit, and that he wished to see them, strictly in private, warning them not to come before ten P.M., and to use the rear entrance. This forestalled their pre-emptory arrivals earlier; it gave them some assurance in regard to their money. And this assurance Burden, freshly shaved, massaged, pressed, and starched, and speaking in his best resonance, was able at once to fortify.

"And that, gentlemen, is the story," he said in conclusion. "I'm sorry, but I can't answer your questions as to *what next*. Only let me say that the money is here, and I don't intend to let it get away. As to just what and how—well, it has to be legal. It has to stand inspection. I'm afraid you will have to leave this in my hands. Don't forget what our original purpose was. It was to rid ourselves of Zach Thomas. That purpose remains. It is unchanged. The money is still our best gambit in accomplishing it. We give a little in order to gain much. No great gain without risk, as the saying goes. We must never draw back from risk. Recall how in the darkest days of the war we met the enemy at our portals, met them strongly, and I call it to your attention that Galveston remained the one and only major seaport of the South that was not in Northern hands. Mr. Saigon does not hesitate to expose his heart to the bullet or the dueling sword when honor is at stake. No, he advances bravely, knowing that in his cool eye and steady hand lies the best assurance of safety. And now"—he looked at his watch—"I have an appointment which may make all the difference between the success and failure of our project. Leave as you came, please. I swear you to utter secrecy."

After they were gone and the bank building was quiet, he turned out the lamp and went along a hall and down some stairs to a tiny office, and there, with a light burning and the shades drawn, sat Matson.

"You were long enough," Matson said morosely.

110

"I am always long enough. But I get the job done. Can you say as much?"

"Matson didn't answer. He sat tilted back on the hind legs of a chair, his hat over his eyes, and only narrow slits of the whites showing. He was perfectly dead-faced. After he kills Thomas, Burden thought, I'll have to kill him. This was the room to do it in. When you met a gunman, the smaller the room the better. In a grapple, skills with guns did not count. In this small room he would crack Matson's neck, hold him until the life ran out of him, then he would unlock the window and go around by the alley to drag his body into his carriage.

He would have to give Ralph, his coachman, the evening off. He would drive Matson to the old Honduras docks and drop him off. There would be no need of anything else—perhaps some weights in his pockets. The fish would get him. You could make a scratch, just a scratch, around the neck and he would be decapitated before morning. The sea was a great thing if you knew how to use it. The broad, rolling, cleansing, purifying sea, in which the corruption of all lands were nothing.

"Well?" said Burden, coming back to the present.

"Well what?"

"You answer *me*, man! I gave you a job to do! Don't you realize that each day that passes, each hour and minute—"

"I'll kill him, only don't hurry me."

"I want that man dead, and I want him dead very soon. Remember that I will have more work for you if this goes right. You can have a great deal of money through me, but if anything happens to me, none at all. Do you realize that? With Zach dead, your risk ends."

Here was something that interested Matson. He waved at a fly, and opened his eyes so that the muddy centers were visible. "I won't have to run afterward?"

"Of course not, man, why should you? You must realize that this man is all that stands between me and having this town in my pocket."

He's tough and strong, thought Burden, and he will be quicker than he looks, but he has a long neck and a habit of stiffening in excitement. That will make it easier. All you have to do with a man like that is twist and snap; you don't have to crotch-ram him against a wall with your knee, and end by strangling him; nor is it necessary to lift him and drop him against a sharp surface like the edge of the desk. It was going to be a very great pleasure to kill Matson.

"We can go a long way together, Matson."

"Yah. Well, we understand each other."

111

"Indeed we do."

"You know what I always thought I'd like? To be in the hotel business."

"Then a hotel you shall own."

"Do you mean that?"

"I never say things I don't mean. A hotel you want, then a hotel you shall own."

"You'll stake me?"

"I want him killed tomorrow, and then—"

"Tomorrow!"

"Yes, tomorrow, my good man."

"You can't just walk out and pull a trigger—"

"And why can you not walk out and pull a trigger? Act, sir, when it is time to act, and act boldly. Procrastination is the thief of time. I am done with procrastination. You wish to be a hotel owner. Then you will find a way to accomplish this task *tomorrow*."

Matson sat with stony eyes, silent.

"So you will pull that trigger. And I will tell you where to pull that trigger. Each day he has late breakfast at Orlando's. Two in the afternoon—a gambler's breakfast. He goes there with that woman. The lady barber."

"I'm to walk into Orlando's restaurant and kill him?"

"You are. He will die in style. With his red blood spilling over the whitest of tablecloths. Here is a key, which will let you in the rear door. The stairway is never used. It happens, by good fortune, that this bank is the owner of Orlando's—that's not generally known. We were forced to foreclose. In leasing it, we of course retained a set of keys.

"Climb the stairs, go in the old dining balcony. It is never used during the summer. There are some draperies—wait behind them. Shoot him—and make sure to do it with one shot. Like the skilled forester who always lights his fire with a single match. In the excitement you will have no trouble leaving by the rear way. Walk, man—walk, don't run. Stay out of sight. Just sit, sit somewhere quietly. By all means, do not come here. Not until night. Here, this same room, rear entrance, at this same hour."

He looked at his watch. "It is now 11:18. Tomorrow, 11:18 P.M., come to this same room and there will be one hundred crisp ten-dollar bills waiting for you. And we will talk further of the hotel. You will find I am not a niggardly man when I deal with *success*."

III

When Blackie Matson left the bank, using the alleyway at the rear, his dark garb and deeply tanned, sallow complexion blending with the tree shadows, he did not go directly to the cheap hotel where he had put up, but went around to the Congress and sat on one of the rattan settees with a view of the front drive, in hopes of seeing Jarrett. He did not want to ask for him at the desk, but it occurred to him that it might be possible to collect for Zach Thomas' corpse twice. He was in luck, for he had been there scarcely half an hour when, with a grating of wheels on the shell drive, Prince George drove up with Jarrett as passenger.

"Tomorrow, usual time, Major?"

"A trifle later, if you please. . . . Good night."

"Good night, Major."

"Major!" said Matson as Jarrett entered.

"Oh, *you*." He looked on Matson as he might look on a reptile, with loathing and with a little fear, but Matson didn't mind. He did not care in the slightest what anyone thought of him, only what they could do to him, or for him. "I heard you were around," said Jarrett.

"Who told you I was around?"

Actually nobody had told him, but he knew that Matson would be. "I have my sources," he answered.

"I want my share of that money."

"You can want and be damned."

Matson did not expect any of it, but he thought it no harm to try. "You double-crossed me," he said.

"You can't double-cross men of your stamp any more than you can cheat a crooked dealer."

Matson looked at him, but showed nothing. The mosquitoes were bad and Jarrett kept swatting at them, but they merely lit on Matson and flew away.

"What if I did you a favor, a real big favor?" Matson said. "I'm broke. I have to have money to get out of town. I could kill Zach Thomas for you and get out of town if you paid me. I need a thousand dollars."

"All the world needs a thousand dollars. If you want

money, why don't you talk to some of those big merchant outfits you told about in Floral City? According to you, they were just busting themselves to hire you. Go back to detecting. Get back on as a wagon freight guard. That'd take you out of town."

"I'll do it for five hundred."

It was far too little for Zach Thomas. "If I gave it to you I'd never see you again. And Zach would still be around."

"Half now, and half afterward. Two-fifty now, and I'll collect the other two-fifty tomorrow night right here after he's dead."

"How about you collecting all five hundred of it here tomorrow night after he's dead?"

This was obviously a ridiculous proposition after the way Jarrett had served him in the matter of the stagecoach, but Matson, after some ill-tempered words, agreed.

"All right. I'll show I hold no hard feelings. I'll trust you again. But you better have that five hundred!"

"I'll have the five hundred, but you won't have any Zach Thomas."

"He'll be dead by half-past two tomorrow!"

Jarrett laughed.

"He'll be dead by half-past two tomorrow, double or nothing!" Matson said.

"You're betting me on that, double or nothing?"

"Yes! How about it? Double or nothing."

"That'd be the thousand dollars again."

"Yes—or aren't you that much of a gambler?"

"I'm a gambler. But I'm putting up all the money."

"And I'm putting up my life."

"All right, two-thirty tomorrow afternoon, and I pay you double or nothing."

Why, that son of a bitch really means it, thought Jarrett as he watched Matson go out to the street. Up until his leaving, he thought Matson was trying to draw him into some crude confidence game and get part of the hundred thousand away from him. But apparently he intended to kill Zach Thomas, and by two-thirty tomorrow.

"One thing is certain," Jarrett said later to the darkness above his bed, "he wouldn't contract for it at a special time with no money down. Somebody else hired him. Me, I'm to pay a sort of a bonus."

He slept poorly. He wondered if he was getting a touch of malaria. He resolved to start drinking quinine water in his highballs.

He would have to do something about Zach, because, much as he disliked the man, and had contempt for him as a tinhorn gambler grown out of size, he wasn't going to have Matson kill him. He got up and saw it was barely seven o'clock. He had never known a gambler, big or little, who got up before noon. He tried to sleep again, but it was too hot; the pavements were aclatter with wheels; men shouted, and the boats kept blasting their whistles.

He went below and had breakfast. Like a fool, he had told George to be late. He drank coffee and read the newspapers. At last George arrived.

"Why, yes, I do know something of Mr. Zach's morning habits," George said. "I drive him from time to time, or did. Then he bought that swell new carriage with the mirror ebony and liveried a coachman. Used to be he'd go over to Madame Elya's for a shave at noon—and come out looking so pink and smooth! Then he'd have him a dip in the surf, and repast at Orlando's. You'll have to dine there. It's famed all over for its crab Napoleon. They serve it with the white brandy lit up flaming. Also—"

"Does he happen to enter Orlando's at about two-thirty?"

"At two, prompt. That's his breakfast time."

Jarrett had a morning to spend, and he kept watch of the area between Madame Elya's and Orlando's. Finally Zach's carriage appeared, but he was not in it. It drew up in front of the restaurant, with its ugly iron marquee and iron filigree balconies, and a footman in livery got down to hold a sun parasol, while the passenger, a woman, was shown to the door. She was blonde and beautiful.

"Who in God's world is that?"

"Miss Elya!"

She turned and looked at Jarrett, and he lifted his hat. She smiled and languidly turned to the door. The door was still swinging a little when he reached it, and he could smell her perfume, but he found himself alone in a foyer with a great deal of fumed paneling, and he had to pause to let his eyes grow accustomed to the darkness.

IV

"Monsieur?" said a trained and subtle voice beside him.

"Oh, hello." The man wore a turned-down collar and a frock coat, and he had a small, waxed mustache. He was the headwaiter, or the host, and he held a menu in his hand.

"Has Madame Elya arrived?"

"She is expecting you?"

"Of course."

"Unfortunately—she said nothing."

"*I'm* saying something."

"She's with Mr. Thomas."

"That's all right. He's one of my dearest acquaintances."

"I regret, monsieur . . ."

He relented at the sight of five dollars and said, "I will deliver your card." Jarrett followed him.

"Your hat, sir," said another man.

"The hat stays with me."

"I insist on the hat." The man looked like a bouncer. Jarrett gave him a dollar.

The room was crowded with tables and there were many buffets, colonnades, and private nooks. The air was heavy with an odor of shellfish, onion, and brandy. Several prosperous-looking men were at a round table where a Negro operated an ornate brass double-deck brazier. It was full of shellfish that sizzled in butter, and he kept shaking drops of this and that from a number of cut-glass decanters.

In circling the round table Jarrett lost sight of the headwaiter, but a moment later he heard his voice close by, beyond a colonnade. He seemed to be very cautious in approaching Zach with the card, and Zach said, "Who is it? Him? No, I don't want to spoil my appetite."

"So sorry! A thousand pardons for disturbing you."

"That's all right, Antoine. My advice is to toss this person out."

Antoine started back for the door. Jarrett kept out of sight by sliding into a booth, deep and luxuriously leather-lined. He could hear Zach through the grillwork that topped the wall separating them. And by rising a little he could see the wagging plumes of Elya's bonnet.

"Who was it, darling?" she asked.

"One of my riffraff acquaintances. Confidence man, cheap grafter. He scored a small triumph over me in a financial matter and now he's here trying out the fast track. Believe me, he has plenty of early foot, but he won't go the distance."

"Don't talk racetrack, please. What do you mean, trying the fast track?"

"I think he intends going into competition with me."

"Casino?"

"Gambling, darling."

"Oh, but he couldn't. He wouldn't dare."

"Strange to say, he does."

"But didn't you explain to him——"

"Some people heed one argument, and some another. I have an idea he'll heed the kind that weighs 250 grains, and measures forty-four calibre."

"Ah, you always talk about shooting people, Zach. In this one way you are not like a gentleman. Shooting people has gone out of fashion."

"Not in Texas."

"Dear Zach!"

"Your hand is so smooth."

"And yours so brown and strong."

Antoine came back. He was walking toward Zach's booth, but he stopped suddenly when he saw Jarrett. He stood very quietly while Jarrett glared at him and allowed his coat to open, revealing the silver shine of the gun. Antoine retreated. He stayed by the door, watching, and the bouncer was also watching.

Zach was talking. Across from Jarrett was a dark panel that had been finished in lacquer and rubbed down to particular brilliance, and in it he could see Elya. Her face was turned towards it. He realized that she could see him, just as he could see her. He smiled and she smiled faintly in response.

Zach had lowered his voice, but Jarrett heard his own name —nothing more, just the name. He listened closely.

"But how would you suggest I go about it?" Elya asked.

"How did you go about it with *me?*" asked Zach, his words plain now.

"But how would I meet him? He hasn't even been around for a shave."

"Give him time, darling. He's after everything I'm after,

117

and so he'll be after you. Now, I'm not asking you to be a spy. It's just that I want to know when that certain point has been reached. I want to know when he has invested his all in that boat—and when that moment comes, as we know it will, boom!" He struck his hand on the table. "Then I will rescue him from his difficulties."

"But what if there are no difficulties?"

"I will *make* the difficulties."

"Dear Zach!"

"It's like you had an orchard—do you pick the fruit green, or do you wait for the harvest?"

"I believe," she said, "there is someone else involved."

"Who? Oh, yes—that woman. Messimo's wife."

"You are perhaps to charm her while I charm Jarrett?"

"Listen, she took a shot at me. I paid her the respect of dressing specially for the occasion, and still she shot at me. She's not my kind. She looks like a mare—those great big hind legs of hers—there's nothing feminine about 'em. Why, she could put a scissors hold on you, and—"

"Zach, please! At least not in Orlando's."

"I was just telling you how it is. I just want you to know that anything I do down there is strictly business. And anything you do with Jarrett had better be strictly business. But I wouldn't mind you charming him."

"He is *very* handsome?"

"Oh, my God! Jarrett? To begin with, he has a face like an empty satchel. His jowls, they sag. His eyes are bagged, too. Bagged and watery. He's led a hard life. Jails, cheap hotels, cheap whisky. And in those scarecrow clothes!"

"I heard he was most exquisitely dressed."

"He must have got that costume he wears from a bankrupt theatrical company. People just don't wear such clothes except on the stage. . . ."

Jarrett noticed that Elya was no longer watching the panel. Her eyes were on something overhead and to the far side. There, a number of balconies had been draped off. He assumed they were rooms for private parties. Two narrow staircases twisted toward them, but by the arrangement of tables it was apparent the stairs were never used. A couple of the draperies now swung gently, as if a door had been opened to a breeze. Jarrett, who was in Orlando's for the first time, saw nothing peculiar about it, but it was apparent that Elya did. A tremor of alarm passed through him, an instinctive awareness, the feel of danger, and he thought of Matson. Up until now he had assumed Matson would ambush Zach outside. At about two-thirty, when he came through the door. But Zach wouldn't be out by two-thirty. It would be three, or later, because Orlando's was not a short-order bolt-food-and-run type of place.

Was Matson really up there? It was so brazen he almost admired him. Admire wasn't the word, but Matson did rise a trifle in his estimation. From copperhead to cobra, or gila monster to rattlesnake.

Only one of the draperies was now moving, and so imperceptibly it might almost have been his imagination. Some polished brass attachments glinted in the light. He judged the height of a man, the height of his chest, its width, and where a bullet would center. He was tempted to draw, aim, and . . . Then he thought, good Lord, it might be a waiter, a guest, a child—he had no proof it was Matson. Only a gun-itch, a feel, a hunch. You couldn't blaze away just on hunches. Not in a fine restaurant like Orlando's.

Then two things—or three things—happened. He was never sure afterward. He saw the gun and caught an unmistakable shadow of Matson against some far source of light; he heard Elya scream. Then, although there was no connection at all, at that same quarter-second a glass or a pitcher was broken. And Jarrett stood and drew, and fired.

Zach Thomas cursed, and twisted his sinewy form out of the booth. There was a gun in his hand. Elya seemed to have grabbed him, pulled him to cover, but he wrenched himself from her grasp. The gunshot smashing across the room with impact and echo was confusing to the other occupants, who were up and looking every way but the right one. The crash of glass, although preceding it, seemed connected, and most of the people thought someone had shot a pitcher.

Then Matson came into view, clutching the draperies. He was hanging on with one hand and holding his gun with the other. With a doubled arm he held tight, while swinging on buckling legs over a low iron balcony rail. He fired, and the bullet, glancing from the ceiling, tore a gash and scattered slivers and gilt plaster. Then his hand slipped and he fell head-first to the floor. It was a deeply carpeted floor, and he seemed to hit it with the impact of a falling beef.

"Who the devil?" said Zach.

"That's Mr. Matson," said Jarrett, beside him.

"Who?"

"Matson. He had a gun on you. I just saved your life."

"*You're* pointing a gun at me."

"Yes, and you've got one on me."

"You put yours down, and I'll put mine down."

"I'll take both guns," said Elya.

119

Everyone in the room was talking. There was a great deal of shoving, chairs were overturned, a force of three waiters, armed, came from the kitchen and added to the excitement. The manager came in. Everyone called him Mr. Tedesco. He looked at the dead man and rushed around the room apologizing. Especially, he came to apologize to Zach Thomas.

"This is dreadful. What was he doing? Did you kill him?"

"Mr. Jarrett did that."

"Who?"

"Mr. Jarrett. This man here."

"But why?"

"May I ask you, Mr. Tedesco, what he was doing on that balcony? Did you give him access?"

"No, no! Most definitely not. I can't imagine how he got there. The doors are locked—always locked. He must have gone through a window."

"I hope for your sake that's true."

A crowd was gathered around the dead man. He looked broken and out of joint. He had somehow landed so his belly was flat on the floor, and still his face was turned up. His eyes and mouth were open. It almost seemed that he was about to say something, but he was beyond speaking. Even if the bullet had not finished him, the fall would have.

"This is getting to be a hell of a place," a man said to the woman with him. "You never saw this sort of thing when the old Orlando was here."

"I still don't know what happened."

"Why, this man was on the balcony, and Zach Thomas shot him."

"No, I did not shoot him," said Zach. He turned to Jarrett, "Say, I remember this fellow. He's the one you had cached across the street in Floral City."

"I had cached?" said Jarrett.

"Yes. You had him cached there. And cached along the stage road. And cached here. It seems you always have him cached somewhere."

"You'll notice he's cached for good now—and that's a hell of a way to talk to a man who just saved your hide."

Zach looked at him and laughed. "Saved my hide again! I wish you'd stop doing me these favors, Jarrett."

"But he had a gun!" exclaimed Elya.

"Stay out of it, darling. This is my line of thing."

"Let's sit down and have a drink," said Jarrett. "I'm sure that with a little thought—"

"Waiter!"

"I'm sure with a little thought you'll piece something bet-

120

ter together. For instance, how did he get there? I couldn't put him there—I've never been in this place before. And I'll bet Tedesco didn't. So who did?"

"You did. You're quick-witted—you're sharp. For instance, who is the one man who could connect you with the robbery? Him. So, why not get rid of him and put Zach Thomas in your debt at one blow? Good! I admire that sort of thinking and acting. It's got nerve and finesse. Nerve, did I say? Effrontery, that is the word. Boldness! And besides, if it fails, if everything goes wrong, if you don't stop him—well, everything doesn't go wrong. Who is it that's dead? Not Jarrett. Zach Thomas!

"Or maybe it did go wrong—maybe he was supposed to kill me, and you him. What a fine accomplishment that would have been! You would, at one blow, one shot, be rid of the two men who could harm you most. Only, Elya screamed, and that saved me. You were afraid of frightening the man off, so you said, 'Half a cake!' and killed him."

"Zach, it wasn't that way at all."

"He just *happened* to be up there, and you *happened* to be here for the first time, like that. Click-click-click! Just an accident. But click, click, click!"

"Will you take me home?" said Elya. "Somehow, I have no appetite."

"Gladly!" volunteered Jarrett.

"No," Zach said. "You must stay and supervise the removal of your colleague. Good day, Jarrett. And don't push your cards too far. They might turn up deuces."

Part Four

I

For a man who sat so big and solid in a chair, Harvey Burden was a poor man at waiting. All morning he had busied himself with routine. Time passed slowly. He looked at the clock a dozen times between ten and eleven.

Zach was up by then, he knew, and in his robe. He would have his bookkeeper in, counting the gambling take for last night. It wouldn't be big, for it was a poor time of year, and he would be out of sorts. He would dress and go to Madame Elya's for his shave, and afterward drive out to the beach. Sometimes he bathed there, but sometimes he merely sat. Sometimes he swam, and Burden would wish the barracuda would get him, but it never happened—no such luck. The barracuda were very overrated fish. Then Zach would get back in the carriage and be driven to Orlando's. Or he would get Madame Elya and go to Orlando's with her. The routine varied a little, due to the whims of Madame Elya, but Zach always had his breakfast at two P.M.

When Burden could think of no better way to fill his time, he called a series of conferences and browbeat the employees. He liked to keep men on the staff who cheated in small sums, short-changed the minor depositors, stole stamps and envelopes, and in other ways gave him things to hold over their heads so that he could remind them it was only his charity and consideration for their families that kept them from being in jail that very minute. He liked to see men pale and fidget in his presence. At such times he would sit erect in his chair, solidly seated, with his stomach like a sack of grain hanging between his legs, and would talk in a strong, stern voice.

Today, however, his mind kept wandering in conference. He would forget what he was taking a man to task for, and he imagined he was being looked at strangely. This alarmed him, for he knew he must not reveal by word or manner that this day was in the least different from any other day. By a quarter past eleven he felt it safest to shut himself up alone. He paced the office, looking from the window a dozen times, until it occurred to him that in his pacing his weight could be heard creak-creaking the floor if any of the employees were in the ground-level basement below. It left him nothing to do but sit and wait, and wipe the sweat away.

What the devil is wrong with me, he thought. Once Zach Thomas is dead, who can harm me? What do I care what they say then? If only Matson doesn't bungle it! He had the nerve, he would not tremble when the time came, that he could be sure of; but Matson lacked the quickness of imagination that would allow him to improvise, make new plans if necessary, move with the unexpected. He couldn't think on his feet.

That's how they were different—himself and Matson. Both were ruthless and would stop at nothing, but Burden could think on his feet. He looked slow-witted, his underlip tended to hang down, due to his old jaw injury, and he knew it made him look somewhat stupid. He attempted to counteract his appearance with an air of pomposity, but he knew it was sometimes to his advantage if people believed him less quick-witted than he was. Because, he thought, I am very quick-witted indeed! The key to Orlando's rear entrance, for example. It was not the bank's key—the bank had never had a key. Under the old management, several keys to the rear upstairs had been handed out to leading gentlemen of the town so that they could come and go to private parties without being observed. He would wager he was the only one who still had his key, or even remembered that such keys existed. Certainly he never anticipated this particular thing; he had not made it Zach's habit to visit Orlando's at two o'clock each day . . . but he had the key.

It was then twenty-two minutes before twelve o'clock. The hands of the clock seemed to be stuck fast. He listened to make sure it was running. . . . He would see to it that Zach had a grand funeral. He wondered if he had relatives somewhere? It would be a fine thing, wouldn't it, if the relatives showed up before he could rush the estate through probate, and demand an accounting? It would make it very difficult and complicated. They were involved, the two of them, in a maze of cotton dealings, with several thousand bales under bond, with a good portion of the new crop under option, and a total of almost a quarter-million in short sales. It had been a bad overextension for both of them. What with the New Orleans market dropping steadily . . . Yes, he would give

123

Zach a fine funeral. I'll bear the pall myself, he thought; it is but meet that I take charge and became chief friend and mourner. I will have him laid away in a wilderness of flowers.

To kill time, he jotted down a few words of eulogy he would himself deliver at the grave.

> Life is but a short and
> fragile hour which separates
> the gulf of two eternities.
> Beyond us, like the curtain of
> the night, spreads the land
> through which no man may see,
> but our hopes are there . . .

His mind wandered, and he laid down the pencil. He paced the room again without thinking, got a drink of tepid water, and came back to his desk. His eye fell on the eulogy he had begun, and he wrote:

> Saddened, indeed, by the untimely
> taking off in the very prime of
> life of our dear friend with whom
> we spent so many happy hours, we
> are none the less sustained by
> the unfaltering trust that that
> which lies ahead is not heartache
> and travail; indeed, with the poet let us
> say, "After life's fitful fever he
> sleeps well." Well done, thou good
> and faithful servant . . .

He wadded up the paper. I must be crazy, writing a eulogy, he thought. What if someone saw it? He got it out of the wastebasket and tore it into tiny pieces.

It was now a quarter past twelve. At an earlier, easier time it had been the bank custom to close until after siesta, but with the Yankees and all the other newcomers, and the telegraph stock and draft transactions, the former mid-siesta had become the most hectic part of the day. He stretched out on a couch and tried to sleep. He was tired, beaten-out tired, but every nerve in his body seemed set on tiny triggers. . . .

"What is it?" he asked, springing up.

"I'm sorry, Mr. Burden," said Dwight Franklyn, "but Mr. Saigon is here to see you."

"No, no, absolutely not. Tell him I'm closeted with—no, tell him I'm out. Say I went out on business and will be back at three o'clock."

"I don't know, sir—"

"*I tell you—*" Burden checked his voice. "I tell you I'm not in. Is that a clear and decisive piece of information, or isn't it?"

"Yes, Mr. Burden."

"Then relay it to Mr. Saigon."

He was getting very sick of Claude Saigon. A man killed four or five of his rivals in duels and he developed what might be called a duelist's state of mind. He got to assuming that the duelist's code could be introduced into business practices, as if a man dealt out of his money through accident could act like an aggrieved lover. Well, business was no glove in the face. He would have to let Saigon know that.

He looked at himself in the mirror and thought that the man who could handle a Zach Thomas certainly would not retreat before a Claude Saigon. But one at a time, one at a time . . .

He imagined he heard pistol shots. Two o'clock passed, two-thirty. It was nearly three o'clock when there were hurrying footsteps to his office.

"Yes?" he said. "Come in!"

It was a little old man delivering a telegram. Burden ripped it open with his heavy fingers, strong fingers that were unable to overcome trembling, or to cope with such a light task as tearing open an envelope. It was a wire from Moncrief & Dill asking for added margin on cotton.

"Wait! I have an answer." He scribbled answers to Moncrief, and to Bischoff at the Cotton Exchange Bank, breaking the lead of three pencils, one after another, cursing under his breath, and hurling the pencils aside.

"There. Get those on the wire *immediately*. What news down the street?" The man looked at him in surprise. "Come, come, man, didn't I hear about a shooting down the street?"

It was nothing for the messenger to look so damned surprised about. There was almost always a shooting of some sort, real or reported—the gamblers, the sailors, the whores and pimps, and the swashbucklers. Even Mrs. Brundick, a woman of good family, had shot a rival, a Mrs. Adkins, over some man, neither one's husband. Every day or two saw a shooting in Galveston.

"I heard there was a shooting at Orlando's," said the messenger. "I heard Zach Thomas killed a man, but then I heard somebody else killed him."

"Killed Zach? Come, man, did somebody kill Zach? Answer me! Don't you realize he's an associate? One of my very dearest friends?"

"No, Zach didn't get killed. I said—"

"I heard what you said!" He got control of himself. "Zach didn't get killed?"

"No. He was standing out in front by his carriage when I came by. It was some other fellow—I heard his name was Matkins."

"Matson? Matson? Are you sure that wasn't his name? But he's dead?"

"Yes, I guess so." The man waited, not wanting to say the wrong thing, and unable to understand Burden's anger. "Is that all?"

"Yes, of course. Get out of here."

He felt as if he had received a heavy physical blow. He had a hard time focusing his eyes—the room seemed jarred off center. He had to be alone, for he needed a few minutes to steady himself. After sitting down and breathing more calmly, he got up for a drink of whisky. But a voice inside him seemed to cry out, "No! No liquor!" Now he had to have all his faculties. He sat down again and tried to think, to concentrate.

Obviously the whole thing hinged on how much Zach Thomas knew. Did he have the slightest inkling, the very slightest, that Matson worked for him? Who knew besides himself? Franklyn, certainly, for he had brought Matson to the office and had had a hand in issuing him his pay. Who else? There were so many snoopers around a bank. Underpaid little men with their eyes and ears at the keyholes. The others, his partners in the hundred-thousand-dollar thing, what of them? They talked behind his back, plotted, carried tales, had secret meetings.

He had recovered now—everything was steady. He took the pistol from his desk, looked at the blue ends of bullets, at the brass percussion caps. He put the pistol in his pants band and drew his coat over it. Then he went to the mezzanine, where he could look down on the tellers. A large man in a ship's officer's cap was talking about the killing. He had just come from Orlando's, and was drawing money against a South American draft.

"Who was he?" someone asked. "Why'd he want to kill Zach?"

"Why does everybody want to kill Zach?" the man said, laughing. "Because we all lost money to him. But I'm not sure what the man wanted. All I know is he got shot and went head-first over the rail. He never said a word. That other fellow, Jarrett his name was, *he* said the fellow wanted to kill Zach. Personally, I think it was some kind of a private feud between Jarrett and the dead man."

Burden went back to his office. Thank God, Jarrett had made a clean kill of it. He put the pistol back in the drawer. Now at last he could have a dram of liquor. Only a dram, however.

When he heard someone at the door he said, "Come in, Dwight," without turning.

"Burden!"

He spun around. It was Claude Saigon. He was carrying his knotty walking stick. It always indicated something about Saigon's humor when he carried that particular stick. It represented a cudgel to him, Burden supposed. However, he was feeling too relieved after a worse scare to let Saigon trouble him.

"Drink, Claude?"

"No, I want no drink!"

"Now, that's no way to refuse, is it?"

"Allow me to judge the proper way to refuse! I'm not here to drink with you, or to exchange pleasantries with you. I've been doing a lot of hard thinking. The market closed down another fourth today, do you know that?"

"No, I haven't seen the wire." He hadn't, but the telegram from Moncrief was sufficient hint that the trend was continuing.

"It's down, and I have to have money."

"Well, Claude, you came to a bank. Money is our business."

"I'm not borrowing money from you when you have more than sixteen thousand dollars of my cash on deposit under the name of a highwayman and a murderer. However, I'll give you your choice. You can pay me my cash, or you can liquidate your cotton futures at this time. Without discount."

"Claude, you know better than that."

"My money—this instant! This instant, Burden!"

"Since when have we called each other by our last names? Claude, we've been friends—"

"I'm not leaving without the money."

"You quite certainly are leaving without the money. You'll get paid when the others get paid, and as for the futures—"

Saigon struck him a raking backhand blow across the face. It was so unexpected he had no time to move, scarcely to blink.

127

Then Saigon stepped back, and his anger brought a trembling twitch to his eyes.

"I expect your seconds, Burden!"

"No, I'm not dueling with you, Claude."

"You Yankee coward!"

"No money, Claude. And no pistols at sunrise under the oak."

"I'll repeat this insult in public! And then you will be forced to accept, or live without honor."

"Don't be a fool. This is a business matter. Nobody's honor is involved."

"Very well. I wanted to settle this as a gentleman might. But you force me, sir! You force me to lodge suit against you for my money, my sixteen thousand. If the circumstances of that must come out in open court, then it must. You will hear from my lawyer!"

He meant it, there was no doubt about it. He turned toward the door, and Burden, knowing he must, acted. With a long stride he reached Saigon. Seizing him by the arms, he dragged him backward. Saigon spun and tried to drive the knob end of his walking stick to his attacker's head. But he was engaged in a duel of a different kind, and one in which he was not master. Burden surprised him by releasing him entirely. The stick, missing, carried Saigon off balance. Then, timing himself with a precision measurable in twentieth parts of seconds, Burden kicked Saigon's legs from under him, grabbed one arm, pinned the other with a knee, and, opening coat and shirt, pressed the man's face deep into his own abdomen.

Saigon writhed and twisted. His feet beat a frenzied tattoo on the floor. He was able to force his breath out under a bubbly pressure, but the more violently he tried to inhale the further he drew in the soft, white flesh of his attacker. Burden held him, but he did not use all his strength—he did not wish to leave bruises.

"Now, now!" he panted. "Now, Claude! There. There."

He was over the peak. Saigon's movements became clawing and futile. They weakened, and after a short while of jerking, of feeble, pointless reflexes, he went limp.

It was all over. Still, Burden did not let go. He kept the face buried in his fat abdomen. He decided to take a half-minute more and make sure. He counted slowly to thirty. Then, for a certainty, Saigon was dead.

Burden tried to move back, but Saigon's teeth were clenched on a fold of fat and skin. He used his thumb to work it free, and laid Saigon gently on his back. He was

128

purplish, eyes still open, teeth showing, but very still. Still as death. Of course . . .

Burden stood back, breathing deeply and wiping the sweat from his face. The marks of Saigon's face were planted in red and white on his belly, and all of his teeth marks, but there was no blood. Human bites are dangerous purveyors of blood poison, but his skin was not broken. On the dead man there was no mark at all. His face was discolored only as that of one who might have suffered a seizure. The impression of Burden's fingers lay around one arm, but it could easily be explained. Catching Saigon by the arm would be the most natural thing in the world.

When he felt that his breathing was even and his pulse had returned to normal, he rushed out and called: "Catling!"

Catling was his general-purpose man, and guard. "Catling, will you rush over and get Dr. Griffin? Immediately! Poor Claude! He's had another of his seizures."

When he was gone, Harvey Burden washed his hands carefully, using perfumed soap. Then he combed his hair, slicking it flat to his head. He was rather handsome, when one came to think of it. He looked at himself in the mirror, thinking, yes, in a purely masculine way, he was good-looking. Strangely, he felt better, too. It was a matter of doing something. Of recognizing a problem and acting on it. It was the difference between his early success and his later failure— the matter of *doing*. He intended in the future to be less considerate, less socially amenable, and *do* things. When a man advanced boldly and met his problems, it was amazing how they faded away.

"You fought a duel with *my* choice of weapons, Claude," he said, addressing the purple face, the wide eyes, the sagging mouth. The code duello, after all, was recognized on the Cincinnati docks. It might not have the style, and the formality, but it had the *finality*—the quietus.

I'll be a pall bearer, of course, he thought. I will sob openly at the funeral, it is the least I can do for him.

"He had these attacks before?" asked the doctor, standing with his stethoscope swinging.

"Well, no. Not, that is— He was a proud man, sir! Very proud. It was only—well, the way his face darkened and he held his breast. It concerned us, Doctor. But he always said it was nothing."

"Yes. The heat and the stairs must have been too much for him."

"Poor fellow. He was my first, my best friend. Well, that

129

is the way the cards fall. Poor Claude! But it was an easy death. Painless—and at least quick, I can assure you. One moment here, and then gone. Life! . . . 'Life is but a short and fragile hour which separates the gulf of two eternities.'"

"He has a family, doesn't he?"

"His poor wife! Thank God he entrusted me with his business affairs. At least I can remove some of those worries from her poor shoulders."

"Will you send a message?"

"I will go in person—my sad duty. You will send them your bill. That is, to his estate."

II

Lucy Saigon, dabbing at her eyes and blowing her little pointed nose, was grateful to have Burden take over her husband's business affairs. She knew he was having trouble, but she had never inquired into its nature or extent, and would have been put in her place if she had. A true Southern belle, although some years beyond her prime, she did not consider business a wife's domain, and limited herself to complaining about the amounts she received for dressmakers, trips, and the household expenses, and upbraiding her husband about the octoroon girl he maintained down the island. She anticipated a rise rather than a fall in her finances now that Claude's race was run.

"There was a great deal of involvement in Claude's affairs, but trust me to cut through the Gordian knot," Burden said. "Rest assured, no verbal agreements will be honored. I will pay only those commitments which are documentarially bona fide."

"Of course," she said, mustering a smile, "I wouldn't want any gentleman being crooked fo' little silly me!"

"My dear Lucy, the word 'crooked' does not exist in the banker's vocabulary. We prefer the terms, legal and illegal. Everything I do on Claude's behalf and yours will have a strict legality."

"Oh, you're so big and strong!" she said, taking hold of his hand. "I don't know how to show my gratitude."

If she were a few years younger Burden would have told

her how, but he dismissed such thoughts from his mind. There must be no gossip, absolutely none. "Just you leave everything to me," he said. "Don't you worry your pretty little head about a thing."

His involvement with Saigon had commenced several months ago when he took an option on a good quantity of his stored cotton. There had been a cash payment, and a handshake on the rest, it being Saigon's old-fashioned way to conduct much of his business verbally, maintaining that a man's word was his bond. In his case it had its advantages. He knew his reputation for honor, proved with both pistols and blades, and this served to keep his associates in line. The possibility of dying perhaps never occurred to him. He conducted himself like a man who expected to live forever. Such was not his lot, however; and now Burden felt a lessening of tension in his own business affairs. To put it bluntly, he could now wriggle out of his deal with Saigon and take over their cotton without paying a cent.

His cotton involvement went far beyond this, however. Several months ago, when he became convinced that heavy rains and floods were due to cut deeply into the year's crops and cause a major rise in the market, he had purchased some 120-day cotton paper, and had talked Zach into joining him on a fifty-fifty basis. Zach, he believed, was not going to live long (he had already commenced making plans for his demise), and it was his hope that the profits, Zach's as well as his own, could be diverted into his own account.

The floods materialized, but they were less destructive than he had anticipated. The Western crops were at least average, while Mississippi had the biggest yields since before the war. Then the English demand turned to the longer staples, a further depressant, and the Northern bankers, to protect their loans, were in the process of liquidating the greenbacks and squeezing other water from the financial supply, with the result that all the markets, except railroads, were going down, the wheat and cotton markets most of all.

As this went on, Burden was forced to do quite a bit of maneuvering, but as there was always a lapse of several days between the issuance of paper and its liquidation, particularly when the deals were spread between Texas and Louisiana, and even Boston, he was always in possession of enough perfectly good credits to save himself. His position, he had often thought with amusement, was like that of the very swift house painter who dropped his bucket from the top floor and had to race down in time to catch it. He was indeed good at this sort of thing; like a fencer sure of his prowess, he did not mind the risk involved, but rather enjoyed it. However, as the market continued to fall, his maneuvering had to become more complex and adroit, so that sometimes he was only morning and night between serious overdraft, and he seemed like a painter not only racing down to catch one bucket, but juggling two others as he ran back up again.

Zach had been sharp enough to realize that Burden had overextended himself and was using some unorthodox banking procedures to keep going; it was that which lay behind his remark about "dipping into the till." However, it was crude, and tended to undergrade Burden's talent. He would never think of being short on the books, yet yesterday it had almost happened. The books had closed all right, but he had had to enter some non-existent Memphis collateral to accomplish it. Memphis was always a full twenty-four hours behind New Orleans, allowing him to buy a day in this manner, but he was in trouble. Then Saigon fell into his hands like an answer to prayer.

He did not delay. Before nightfall he had a tug and barge at work moving cotton from one warehouse to another. He had had a great deal of experience in this sort of thing, creating complex situations to free embargoed cotton during the war. While the transfers were taking place, he had himself rowed to a huge old bilge-keg sidewheel ocean vessel that was anchored out among the bars to save dock rent. It was the *Spindrift*, Jos. T. Hiskey, owner and master.

When ashore, Hiskey was frequently mistaken for the Rev. Lenhart Love of the First Methodist Church. The similarity was the merest coincidence. Hiskey, despite his sacerdotal mien, was a thoroughly dishonest man, and he did not blink an eye when Burden, puffing and sweating from his trip up the ladder and down the hot companionway, suggested that he scuttle his boat with full cargo. Hiskey had his boat insured for all it was worth; and this, with Burden's cash payment, would allow him to show the first sizable profit from the *Spindrift* through the nine years of his ownership. Burden owned a large quantity of cotton which he had salvaged from six feet of water beneath a collapsed warehouse after the tornado of four years before; and this, rebranded and falsely billed as last season's No. 1 strict good middling, would form the *Spindrift*'s cargo.

Everything went well. Burden secured insurance from an underwriter who had handled much of his business in the past. The *Spindrift* put its cargo aboard and sailed without incident. By now two days and nights had passed, and

Burden had not been to bed, although he had caught a few hours' sleep while seated in his carriage. He was returning from the docks when the undertaker's man came around to remind him of the funeral.

"Ah, yes, my sad duties!" Burden said. ("Mr. Burden is certainly taking it hard," the undertaker's man reported. "He looked simply haggard.")

He went to his office and had food sent up from Orlando's. Food always made him feel better. While he ate squab with dressing, shrimp Louis, asparagus, and pastries, topping it all off with strawberries glacé Benedictine, he was worked on by a barber, valet, and shine boy. He emerged refreshed, and had his cordial while riding in his carriage.

The Saigon home was a mile drive, and he reached it just in time to take his place as bearer of the catafalque before the family arrived. There was the service, then the long trip to the cemetery in which he rode in the second carriage wearing crêpe collar and medallion. Here was another ordeal, but he bore up well, and even managed to doze with his eyes open when the undertaker thoughtfully provided him with a chair.

He still could not rest, however. After the formality of leaving his card with the Saigon gateman, he returned to town and sent for Zach Thomas. He was seated at his desk with a bottle of 7-star opened when Zach arrived.

"I hope it's something pretty damned important," said Zach, who did not like to be summoned. "I see you got out the best brandy."

Burden, looking very serious, said, "I wanted to talk to you about poor Claude."

"Yes, poor Claude. He was an arrogant and unreasonable son of a bitch. The town is going to miss him."

"Now, now, Zach! The dead, you know. He died right in this office. Right there in that spot he breathed his very last."

"You ought to erect a marker."

"You didn't hear—the details?"

"Only that he keeled over. Don't tell me that you helped him on? There were no marks or contusions? No finger marks around the throat? No tooth marks in the jugular?"

"Ha-ha! But seriously, I think it's only fair to tell you how he happened to have his seizure. The fact is, he was deeply tied up in the futures, as deeply as we are, but, I'm afraid, without our resources. Then, alas, he came up here that afternoon wanting to borrow from me, and I just couldn't let him have the money. He wanted to put up some last year's bales he was supposed to have in storage, and,

133

good God, do you know that I can't even find the stuff in storage? I don't know what happened to it, but a search of his invoices may reveal something."

"I knew he had some short dealings, but how does that involve me?"

"Well, after all, our position is somewhat the same, isn't it?"

"I don't think it's the same at all. We've obligated ourselves to purchase certain ginnings when they come in, and we're going to have to raise the money. I'm having it very tight. I only run a *faro* bank. Regular bank business is always good. If they don't pay, you take over."

"Yes, foreclose, and then what? Use your head, man. How well would any business prosper without customers? No, we in banking go to all lengths to help our customers maintain a solvent position, for therein lies our only hope of continued profit. Surely you don't think there's any profit to be made in checks and vaults and savings accounts to be lent out at six to eight per cent? Why, there wouldn't be enough profit in it to pay our tellers."

"*We* operate on a hell of a lot less than eight per cent," said Zach. "Roulette is about five, chuck-a-luck five and a half, and faro is a sneaking four. And we have more risks. You can never tell when some sea captain will come in and start doubling up on the thirty-five-for-one and walk off with all the money in the joint. The only way they could do that here would be with a gun, and believe me, you have your money cached away in so many drawers and pigeonholes they'd go crazy finding it."

"But we collect our percentage only *once a year*, while yours is effective with each turn of the wheel. We have to lend out money over and over. Credit, man! Every dollar has to create ten more in credits, or we make no profit. You, a director, should—"

"Is that what you got me up here for? To tell me why I'm making no money on the stock I own in this bank? Believe me, if I could sell, and then get off the gaff on that futures deal—"

"The market could still go up, Zach."

"You seem a hell of a lot happier about this whole sour mess today than you did a little while ago. What happened? Did Saigon leave you some money in his will?"

"I fear there was little to leave. Poor Lucy! Everything—home, farm, horses, carriages, dock, warehouse—everything is likely to go in the final accounting. I'm going to do what I can. I offered her my services. Maybe I can save a little from the debacle."

Zach was waiting.

"Fortunately," Burden went on, "he kept few records. Nothing much in writing. I mean, all his handshake obligations will simply be tossed out in a court of law. If I am made his executor—and I offered my services free to his widow—that will be my policy. I will certainly honor nothing that isn't signed, sealed, and witnessed."

"I had no cotton dealings with him, if that's what you're getting around to. I had nothing but trouble with him. He came in the casino once and beat on the roulette table with that knobby cane of his. If it'd been anybody else I'd have—"

"Well, he's at peace now. After life's fitful fever he sleeps well. What I was getting to is this: He had some cotton here and cotton there, and it happens that he had a *considerable quantity* of last year's storage in that old Carmichael warehouse." He tossed over some papers. "Now, I'm not going into the complexities of the transaction—they're pretty involved; but in order for me to get out from under, and to provide a little ready cash to the widow, and knowing that in you I am dealing with a man of the utmost discretion—"

"A crook."

"Now, now, Zach! Just bear in mind this is for a good cause. It's for her, the little widow, and for me, and for you. We will all benefit, and if there are losers they will be the holders of paper in faraway New Orleans, et cetera. Are you listening?"

"I'm listening."

"It was necessary for me to get a shipload of our cotton out of town. Obviously I'll be unable to sell it if I'm also acting as executor. I have a few days in which to act—before the product reaches consignee in Boston. I'm willing to transfer this to you, Zach, and at a figure all out of keeping with its quality. In fact, I'm letting you have this at exactly three-fourths of the market. This will allow you to assume my half of our futures dealing and pay all of your loss for that transaction, and fully half of your own. Nor is this all. I have two hundred and forty bales of another consignment left in storage, and I ask you to take them over. With them I will lease, for a dollar per year, the warehouse and docks."

"Hold on! Where do I inspect this shipload of cotton?"

"Zach, I thought you got my point. It is now on the Gulf, steaming toward Boston."

"I take your word for this?"

"And the bill of lading."

"Let's see it?"

Burden tossed over the certificates.

"The *Sprindrift*?"

"It's a sound ship, only slow. That was an advantage. A longer time in transit would allow me, you understand—"

"I understand. I understand this man Hiskey is a free-booter who almost had his license revoked."

"They all engage in swashbuckling during the dead season. Besides, I wanted a man who could be discreet."

"He'll come back here and blackmail you."

"Oh, Zach! That's assuming he has something to blackmail me about."

"Half!"

"What?"

"I say I'll pay half."

"No, Zach. I can't do it. Sorry." He stood up. He was willing to pay Zach half, but he was quite certain it would not be necessary. He still had, as the gamblers said, an ace. Zach did not move. He sat, staring at Burden. Those damned gimlet eyes! Burden paced and sweat, and poured another brandy. But he did not touch it. He wanted his faculties alert, all of them.

"Damned sorry, Zach, I wanted to see you have this."

"I'd be a fool to accept that weight and grade on his signature."

"Oh, if that's what's troubling you, here's the insurance." He tossed over the policies. "Standard marine, F.O.B. and beyond. This follows the product and doesn't terminate at each exchange. All I do is sign the endorsement, then you sign it and mail to the head office in New Orleans. There's the agent's signature and the co-signature. Grade and amounts certified. It's all in order, but I can send and get Harry Van Buren. I'd rather not upset him, but I can do it if it would make you feel better. Even should the cotton sink beneath the waves, you'd be clear. You, Zach, may well be the only speculator in this port who has made a sound dollar on cotton this season."

It was plain Zach was still suspicious. It was the natural wariness of a gambler for a deal that is a little too pat and good. You always look for the sleeper. Beware of aces in another man's game.

"How about that other cotton and the warehouse?"

"I'll have to ask you to take that at the full market, but I'll pay brokerage. This has nothing to do with the estate. I just need the money."

"I'm going to have a hell of a time raising the money, too."

"Taking over my half of the futures will liquidate most of it. And your note—we'll handle it through the bank. It can be secured by your property, the Four Winds, the Casino. Goodness gracious, Zach, your signature is certainly good in this town."

"Why do you want to lease that warehouse for a dollar a year?"

"Ah, yes." He acted like a man who had been found out, aware all the time that he *would* be found out, that this fellow Zach was really too much for him. "I'll tell you why I'm so anxious. It's that ship down there, the *Weymount Castle*. What happens when they finish pouring their money into her and the crowds commence coming aboard? Why, the only entrance is across that Western Company dock, and what chance would anybody have to conduct an orderly shipping and receiving business? None at all. I'd have to get injunctions and start court actions, et cetera, to make them move, and you know as well as I do there's no place that boat *could* move. It's not seaworthy. It had to be towed the last hundred miles on its way around from New Orleans.

"I'm not asking that you buy the dock. I'm only—well, the devil with it! Forget that part of it. No, I won't ask you. Come to think of it, holding the mortgage, I couldn't. I could sell you the mortgage. But I'll foreclose. That's what I'll do. I'll foreclose and advertise it for sale."

"Wait! Not so fast, Harvey. You mean you are offering me the old Western warehouse and dock, and that dock forms the one and only entrance to Jarrett's gambling ship?"

"Yes, indeed. Therein lies the trouble. You can imagine the congestion, the brawling, the—"

"It would be terrible, wouldn't it?"

"Frankly, I don't want to fight that man Jarrett. He could be a very unpleasant fellow in a fight. Yes, indeed. I'm afraid he'd—well, resort to extra-legal means. Then also"— and he laughed bitterly—"he's one of my largest depositors."

"Harvey, I'm glad you called me in. And I agree that it requires a man like me to deal with a man like Jarrett. I've made up my mind, and the answer is *yes*. I'm going to require some financing, but I'll sign the required liens. You take care of all that. I just mail this insurance certificate, you say? It requires notarization?"

"Dwight!" Burden said, opening the door. "Will you come and bring your seal?" He was in a buoyant, hand-rubbing humor. "The great seal of notarization!"

"I want the papers drawn up right away—the docks—"

"And, Dwight, will you get out that Western warehouse mortgage? That's the Western Steam Transportation Company, New Orleans."

"Harvey, you old rascal, you had this up your sleeve all the time! Just standing there, chuckling! And waiting to drop it like a firecracker in the middle of this desk."

"Ha-ha, Zach! Well, we do have our ways!"

"But not a word about this. I don't want it to get out. I want that tall-hatted Jarrett to have all the chance in the world to lavish his money."

"Right! Don't go near the place. Except, of course, to inspect the cotton. You can't be buying cotton without—"

"Why, Harvey, what are you talking about? There's the *papers*. And it will be insured, just like that on the *Spindrift*."

"Yes, but—"

"But me no buts, Harvey. Don't you think I can trust you in this, old friend? I won't go near the warehouse, or allow a representative to. You have to walk quietly when you stalk the wild cock, Harvey. But at the proper time—" His hand, stealing across the desk, darted and closed on an imaginary chicken neck and twisted. "Then this, and *this*, and THIS!"

You could almost imagine that Jarrett was a chicken, and that he was kicking.

III

It was midnight on the dock, and the last sound had stopped. Only, distantly, one could now and then hear the bass moan of a whistle. On the old palace boat, the *Weymount Castle*, a single light was burning. It was a student lamp with a circular wick burning turpentine. The turpentine gave a high whiteness, but it tended to smoke the chimney; and now, after hours of burning, a good deal of its light was reflected from the ceiling, and the man, working over ledgers, bills, and scratch paper had to bend over farther and farther to see.

The man was Jarrett. He had discarded his coat, collar,

and tie, his gun and harness, and sweat worthy of Burden himself soaked his shirt under the arms.

"You have worked since nightfall," Maxine said, coming and looking in on him for the half-dozenth time. "You will ruin your eyes like you told about in Colorado."

He kept adding but the columns came out wrong. He added the figures again and sat back.

"What?" he said.

"You ruined your eyes with book work in Colorado, remember?"

"I lied to you, darling. It was cards and keno. I had to read those little numbers that fell out of the goose."

"Anyway, let me clean the lamp chimney."

"Don't touch it. It'll burn your fingers off."

"You worry so about me!"

"Yes, I do," he said, but he was preoccupied with other things.

"You know, money doesn't go as far as you'd think. Look here—rough labor, a dollar and a half a day! These fellows used to be slaves. Well, they're still slaves. Do you think they get this one-fifty? Not on your life. I have to pay it to this agent, Hopkins. I'd make him hop if I had my way, but you have to deal through him. Believe me, I have trouble enough without trying to reform the docks. Those poor devils get maybe seventy-five cents. If they raise a cry, no more work.

"And look here. Do you know what I have to pay this cabinet maker? Four-fifty, and he works ten hours. Believe me, when that tenth hour is done, he's gone. He stops right in the middle of a shaving. Four dollars and fifty cents for ten hours, can you imagine that? I tell you the war has ruined things. You could have hired this same fellow for two dollars before the war, and he'd have given me a good, solid twelve-hour shift. The country is going to hell, darling. I tell you, they see a man with money and they're all there trying to put the shag on him."

"They are doing a beautiful job. Such floors, when the grease and varnish are off!"

"And supplies! I was supposed to be getting all this wholesale. I was supposed to get jobbers' rate, ship chandlers' rate. Look at this! Doorknobs, a hundred and forty-five dollars! That's better than a dollar a knob! Who ordered doorknobs? I ordered no doorknobs. I can go over town and buy them for a dime."

"I ordered the doorknobs. Mr. Dickenson said that with the brass fixtures we needed cut-crystal knobs."

"But a gross!"

"One to every door. You yourself said we should spare no expense."

She had come from her bed, apparently driven out by the warm, muggy night, and was garbed only in a thin gown of some sort. But Jarrett's eyeballs were hurting him, and he sat with his eyes closed and rubbed his forehead with the tips of his fingers.

"What's this?" he said, continuing after a moment. "I don't know whether I'm seeing right. One gross lavender smelling salts, five hundred dollars!"

"But they are in the cut-glass dispensers. We decided to give one as a favor to each lady on the opening night, don't you remember?"

"Five hundred dollars for smelling salts! Do you think I have my own printing press over town where I make my money, like those Spanish-American presidents who come here? I don't, Max. Every time I write a check I have to make sure there's money in the bank to cover it. At these prices who can afford to smell? It's cheaper to drink."

"Dear Joe!"

"Do me a favor, will you? Get me some coffee. Strong and black."

"How do you like what I am wearing? I went over to Madame Elya's salon—"

"Don't you know Zach Thomas owns that joint? Isn't it bad enough to spend my dough, without going to a competitor?"

"Damn you!" she said, picking up a cup and hurling it. "Here is your coffee!"

The cup smashed and cold coffee was spattered across a wall.

"I'm sorry," he said. "It was just a joke."

"Then you do like the negligee?"

"Is that what you call it? Darling, do you remember when you peeled off stark naked for me that first afternoon? Well, you shouldn't have done it—it left me no surprises."

"I have plenty of surprises."

He stood up and said, "I was only joking. But you don't need those expensive thin silk things—you're more beautiful without them."

"Oh, Joe, what is going to happen to us?"

"First of all, we have to open this boat. We've got to cut down on the expenses. We have to get more work out of the men. We've got to make money. I'm past thirty years old and I've done a lot of knocking around, and no money, nothing. Not until right now. Well, I hit a streak of luck. The fates dangled a big bagful of money right before my eyes. So I acted, and I struck hard, and I got it. But I didn't come down here to toss it away on cards and liquor and women. I came down here to be a success in the business world. Zach Thomas over there thinks I want to take the town over from him. I don't care about Zach. I'll let him live if he lets me live. Do you get what I'm talking about? I mean I want to make something of my life. I want to make a stake and get a fine home, a carriage, the works. I want position."

"A home?" she said.

"I know what's in your mind. You have that look in your eye. You're looking at me as husband material. I'd be very poor husband material."

"I am not asking you to marry me. I only came up here because it was too damned hot to sleep."

"No more coffee cups, Max."

"I don't need coffee cups!"

"Get me a brandy."

"Get your own brandy. And I wouldn't marry you if you were the last man alive."

"If I was the last man alive, honey, I wouldn't be in the market for any monogamy. It wouldn't be fair. If I was the last man alive I'd take it as my duty to have at least three hundred and sixty-five wives a year. They'd have contests to decide who they'd be. Every night I'd have the winner from a different state, and then the girls from the territories would have their chance, and from England, France, Mexico, and so on. You'd be the winner from Texas, darling. I might give you two nights a year, but there'd be all the runner-ups to think about—"

He stopped suddenly. He had heard—felt—the presence of someone on the deck outside. Instinctively, he stepped away from the light and looked for his pistol.

"Me!" said the Angel.

He came quietly, barefoot, a rifle making a blue, moonlight shine in his hands.

"You gave me quite a start."

"Come out and listen to something."

Jarrett put on his gun, and followed the Angel around the hurricane deck, through stacks of lumber and past a furniture refinishing bench, down the stairs to the boiler deck. There, in the shadows from the dock, the Angel paused, and

141

signaled for him to listen. There was nothing for quite a while, but then came a sound vaguely like thunder.

"Hear it?"

"Yes."

"What do you make of it?"

The water below vibrated peculiarly, and he thought for a while it might be something like an earthquake out in the Gulf. One time when the Mexican volcano at Xhilopac exploded, there were tremblings and portents, followed by a swell that lifted some of the small boats over the docks and did quite a lot of damage; but the thunder accompanying that had been steady, and this came and went, and was obviously much closer.

He kept watching the water. The moon glistened along its surface. The little waves bounded outward from the piles, so the vibration must originate somewhere along the length of the dock itself. It had to be inside one of the dark and shuttered warehouses. The sound was like that of heavily weighted wheels, or barrels rolling.

"How about those warehouses? Are they all sealed under bond?"

"I think so. It's mostly dead storage. You can smell some of that cotton for mildew. I understand you can buy it at ten dollars a bale for waste packing."

"Has anybody been in?"

"Not from this side. There's a canal on the back. And a wagon lane."

"I'm worried about that warehouse. It's been losing money. It's just the sort of thing that might catch on fire for the insurance. And there we'd be, stranded, burning."

"I think you're worrying without need. This boat may not be ready for any ocean voyage, but we could float it into the bay."

Jarrett walked across the docks. The noise had stopped, and the vibration too, as far as he could tell, but he could hear the lighter tones of voices, and the slow, tortured creak of a board being drawn.

The Angel had remained behind. Jarrett could not even see him in the shadow. He himself would be as well concealed were it not for his white shirt. He walked along the front of the building, past shuttered windows and paint-peeling signs, past the places that once had been rented to pawn shops, tattooing parlors, barber shops, lunch counters, commission offices, cordage companies, insurance agents. All, all of another time. He remembered the section from his boyhood, one of the best on the island, at least the busiest. Tomorrow he would check the ownership.

The boat was going to attract a high-class custom and he might fix things up a little. At least he had to do something about the dock, which had cracked planks and open holes that a person could run his leg through. Besides, once he became an attraction, property values would skyrocket. Other places would open nearby, and he didn't want them to be the sort of joints he'd be ashamed of, and maybe have to run out of business. If he overlooked the real-estate angle, he was passing up one of the main sources of profit. But it would take money. He saw the need for borrowing. "Never borrow and never lend," they said. Oh ye poor in spirit! It was groveling talk, poor man's talk, like the old Reverend and his "He who hides farthings shillings will find." But what of the dollars, double eagles, and pounds sterling? Did the Rothschilds, the Astors, the Belmonts make it by hiding their farthings? No, they did it by getting the other man's dollars, dimes, and farthings, paying three per cent, and getting back fifty or a hundred. Yes, he would move in on Galveston real estate. Increase the values by development. Make your own wave and ride on it. Build, grow, expand!

The warehouses and docks formed a wedge on pilings between the bay and a lagoon. The far end of this was occupied by a dredging firm with a large accumulation of steam equipment, some floating on barges, a great deal more in various stages of dismemberment on the dock. Here there was a post light and a watchman's shanty.

No one seemed to be occupying the shanty. He passed it and turned the corner, reaching a catwalk, and then a wagon passage that ran down the backs of the buildings, giving access to the town. There was a succession of awnings, and it was very dark under them, but through loose slats he got an occasional glimpse of the sky. The moon was out, passing now and then behind clouds. He walked quietly. A carriage and horses farther along were shaped in silhouette, and he could smell the horses. The carriage gleamed with lacquered wood, and he thought of Zach Thomas. It was not Zach's, however—it was older, more conservative in style.

A man's voice startled him. It seemed almost at his elbow.

"Yes, I did," the man said. "I went to make sure."

He was talking to someone in the carriage forty yards away, but his voice was held in by the awnings.

"You couldn't have looked very well," came the reply, and that voice was Harvey Burden's. Now he could make out

143

Burden's massive shape. "There was a shadow under the light."

"Probably the watchman's."

"Why isn't he asleep? When I hire a watchman he's always asleep."

"I don't know, Mr. Burden—"

"You damned fool, don't say my name! If I wanted advertising I'd buy space in the *News*. Go back in and help them."

The man obeyed, leaving Burden in the carriage. He was smoking a cigar. The odor came to Jarrett, mixed with the pungent smells of the dock and the lagoon, the fermenting wood, the flowers. Occasionally Burden moved, and his weight caused the carriage to creak. Inside the rolling sounds continued—they must be moving cotton. Finally it stopped, and a man came through one of the wide doors.

"Two hundred and six bales," he said. "A hell of a job with that old-fashioned winch."

"When I was your age we handled them without equipment, just our backs, our hands, and a toe dolly. All right, don't stand here. Get the wall back, and mind you, no hammering."

"It can't be done without hammering."

"Muffle it, man, muffle it."

"With what?"

"With your thumb over the nails—I don't care how. It's your job, do it. I'm paying enough."

The man went back, and a sound of careful pounding followed. Then it became quiet, and the quiet lasted for a long time. But at last the men came out; there was low laughter, and a smell of whisky. The carriage left, everyone left, the dock was silent.

Jarrett then tried to find a way into the warehouse, but everything was boarded tight, locked, double locked, padlocked. A loose awning board allowed moonlight through to a notice tacked on one of the doors.

This warehouse has been sealed in Bond under the laws of Texas not to be opened by unauthorized persons, and any person whatsoever without permit 223A or 223B and accompanied by certified officials. (Signed) And it was stamped and signed, but he couldn't make out the signature.

He went back to the boat, and to the stateroom he had fixed up as quarters when he moved from the hotel. It was almost daylight when he got to sleep.

He got up about ten and went to the bank to look for Burden, but he was not to be found. His inquiry concerning

144

the status of the warehouses, which were, like the dock, known as the Old Western, was less than satisfactory. Although the courthouse had records of its attachment from the Western Steam Transportation Co. by the Merchants & Planters Bank, nobody there would talk about it.

It worried him, and Maxine noticed it. "No, it's not the bills," he said, "not the lavender smelling salts, nothing like that. And if Burden wants to move cargo in bond-sealed storage through dismantled walls, that's his private matter. But why won't he talk to me when I'm willing to pay good money to lease a defunct dock? That's not like a banker. Particularly it's not like that banker."

"Perhaps he was really gone from the city."

"No, he was in there. I could hear the creak-creak of his three hundred pounds as he walked around. Money or no money, he didn't want to see me."

Later he said, "I've been thinking, and there's just one man in this city Burden would be afraid of. Zach Thomas. Somehow or other, Zach is involved. And where Zach is involved, I've got a notion that we're involved too."

"But Zach could have interfered with us a hundred times. And so far he has not lifted a finger."

"There's another thing I don't like. It's not Zach's way to sit still while we outbid him for the fancy trade. I'd feel better if he *was* lifting a finger."

IV

When the sidewheeler *Spindrift* was ten days overdue in Boston, and no word heard of her since rounding Key West, where she took on a quantity of fresh meat and vegetables, the U.S. Lighthouse and Cutter Service was notified. Later a cork life preserver with the *Spindrift's* stencil was picked up by a crabber off St. Helena Sound, and bits of wreckage reported. The Service then talked of instituting a search, and a headline reading ALL FEARED LOST appeared in Charleston.

All were not lost, however. Captain Hiskey had turned up in Port St. Helens with six crewmen, telling about a fire and boiler explosion, heroic rescue work, four days in an open boat, and a week or more working their way along the islands that formed a desolate, sandy barrier to the Carolina Coast.

The appearance of Hiskey and his survivors seemed to belie an ordeal—they were well fed and noisily drunk when discovered in Port St. Helens—but there were no owners to lodge a complaint, the insurance companies had not been heard from, and the port authorities did nothing.

Later the engineer, Bronson Monk, was picked up in Charleston after smashing some furniture in the Petty House, where he claimed to have been swindled of $800 at dice. When it occurred to someone that $800 was a great deal of money for a man who had just had his ship sunk from under him, an inquiry was started. In the meantime, however, Monk had been given a floater out of town, Hiskey and the others similarly dropped from sight, and the inquiry died almost before it had started. Hiskey's insurer was unhappy, and delayed payment, but the other quickly settled. Its cotton paper was highly profitable and it did not wish to jeopardize business through procrastination. Texans, while seldom objecting to exorbitant premiums, became outraged at contested claims, and had been known to call on underwriters with pistols. Besides, this cargo had been originally drawn for one of the most honored banking firms on the Gulf.

In Galveston the *Spindrift*'s loss was reported by the papers, but by the time the search for Hiskey, Monk, and the others commenced, it became known that Zach Thomas was owner of the cotton, and succeeding stories were never printed. Zach was a favorite of the papers, fêting the staffs from editor down at parties twice a year, giving them cases of liquor on holidays, and lavishly subsidizing their advertising columns.

So the weeks passed, and autumn arrived with a diminishment of heat. It was coming on to the gayer time of the year. People looked to have more money, what with cotton pouring in along the dusty roads from the backcountry. No more was heard of the *Spindrift*. Another vessel, the *Weymount Castle*, renamed *La Maison Rouge*, was then in the public eye. It had emerged in glittering gilt and ivory with a scarlet pilot house and twin chimneys, practically ready for business, and nobody visited the city without going to gawk at it.

One morning, three days before the scheduled opening, Jarrett was busy with a spirit level on the roulette tables, while a pair of mechanics followed him around ready to make the required adjustments in the leveling mechanisms.

Harry Pate, the watchman on duty, came to Jarrett in an obvious state of excitement. "You got a visitor!" he said.

"Does he have a pass? I issued passes to every man hired on this job, and—"

"Well, you might change your mind about *this* visitor. It's Zach Thomas."

He had been expecting him for some time—Zach, or his rough-tough wrecking crew. Zach had, in fact, placed a couple of spies on the boat; this information came to him via Prince George, but they were the best workmen he had, so he said nothing, knowing if he got rid of them Zach would hire more.

"Zach, come in," he said cordially, going down to meet him. "I was wondering when you'd have a look at your competition."

"I've been keeping tab."

"Yes, I know. Pete Frame and that bowlegged Mancini. I was saying to the Angel just yesterday how those spies of Zach's were the best workers we have. How they do pitch in! It was nice of you to pick such good ones to send us."

Zach fixed him with his gaze and said, "You're a smart fellow, Joe."

"No, I've just learned to anticipate."

"You're smart, but not real smart. A real smart man also expects his competition to be a little smart. I'm real smart. I never underrate my competition. I try not to overrate 'em either. In fact, I try to get 'em pegged just right. That's why I've right now got you nailed to the wall."

Zach was holding his hat in his hands, and Jarrett thought for an instant he had stolen his own trick—or Lantern's trick—and had a derringer in the crown. But the hat was a Panama weave, and not of pistol-carrying consistency. Besides, Zach's hands were clear.

Zach knew what Jarrett was thinking, and he smiled. "Not that way nailed to the wall. I wouldn't want to do it and mar up the woodwork—it's too fine. I'm going to enjoy running this place. The first thing I'll do after taking over is fit out the engine and get the bottom scraped. Then I'd like to start out on a great, glittering tour to lift the gambling dollars in Havana and New Orleans, and maybe sail all the way to Charleston."

"And how do you plan to take over?"

"You're going to offer it to me. You're going to say, 'Zach, I'm an awful broke fellow. I spent every dollar I lifted off that coach, and now I haven't got a cent coming in, so why don't you come in as half partner for—well, say ten thousand

147

dollars?' And I'm going to say, 'Jarrett, I'd like about seventy-five per cent, but all I see clear of paying is five thousand dollars. However, if you stay friendly I'll see you get a job. And the young woman, also. I'd pay a hundred a week, plus a fair percentage, say, five per cent of the profits.' That's what I'll say to you, Jarrett."

"And I'll tell you, sir, to go jump in the lagoon, the one with the bull alligators in it."

"I wouldn't want to tell you to move your boat."

"You mean you own an option on the dock?"

"I do."

"And I'm paying rent on the dock, and you're stuck with me as a tenant."

"Granted. I can't make you move. In fact, if you got this hulk too far off the mud it'd sink, the shape it's in. But I'll tell you what I don't need to do. I don't need to furnish your customers with a promenade. No, indeed. In fact, this dock is going to be torn up and relaid, commencing day after tomorrow at twelve o'clock noon. So if you want to bring in the cream of this port's society for your grand and gala opening, it'll have to be by rowboat. They ain't going to like that, Jarrett."

"No, by God, you'll tear up no dock!"

"Jarrett, the veins on your forehead are standing out."

"You can't do it. The law won't let you do it."

"Well, that's a question. I've had some experience with the law. I've tied up a lot of money with the law in this town. And one thing I've learned is never to say what the law will do and what it won't do. So I'll tear up the dock. You bring action. I'll defend. We'll get it on the calendar. That calendar is a mite crowded, but maybe we can settle it in a year or two. I don't mind waiting. Not a bit."

As soon as Zach had left, Jarrett hurried to the bank, checked his cash account, and found that he had little more than eight thousand left. He debated whether to go out to the Lanternlight to borrow back some of the "interest" he had paid to Miss Ermaline, and decided against it. Instead, he climbed the steps to Burden's office and was stopped by a tall, walrus-mustached guard named Catling, who said the president was busy.

Jarrett said, "I'm busy, too, and that's why I'd rather not waste any time," and, using a shoulder and knee to practiced effect, he sent the man staggering and walked in.

"Hello, Harvey."

Burden sat hunched and massive, glaring at him.

"Harvey, I want to buy that Western dock."

"You'll have to see Mr. Thomas."

"No, I'm seeing you, because you own it. Well, I happen to know you don't *own* it either, you've merely attached it, which is a different thing. If I raise the mortgage money you have to honor the payment."

"Sir, no highwayman, gambler, and soldier of fortune is shoving his way into my office telling me what I have to do and don't have to do. The rights of this bank are well founded, I can assure you, in the documents."

"What if I told you I had secured a warranty deed to that dock and warehouse? What if I told you I will take possession under that deed? What if I was to tell you I was the new chairman of the board of Western Steam Transportation?"

It was all bluff, but it jarred Burden, so that he flushed mottled and rose to his feet.

"The mortgage on that property was executed long ago."

"But you haven't got the deed. And a bank without a deed is a bank with an unquiet title." He did not really know what sort of title the bank had, nor was he sure of the legal position, but Burden was not, either. "And if I come here with money to liquidate that loan you have no position under the law to refuse it."

"Don't tell me my position."

"You refuse the money then?"

"I neither refuse nor accept. I have to examine this more closely. Do you think I have every mortgage and note here at my fingertips? I will have to have the papers brought forth and examined by my attorneys."

"I'm afraid you don't have the privilege of that procrastination. You are open for business. I am here to do business. As far as I am concerned, you have refused my legal payment. Therefore I intend to take over the properties, both dock and warehouse."

"Sir, if you should make so bold as to enter—" He checked himself. He stood opening and closing his mouth like a great fish, but he controlled his temper. It was obvious that he had almost said more than he intended.

"What was that?"

"I said— Good Lord, man, what is your hurry? Is anyone interfering with you? You surely have no use for that fallen-down heap of boards called the Western Company warehouse. And as for the dock, you are there already."

"And I don't intend to have it torn up."

"Oh, so that's it! So Zach has been around. I'm afraid you have been made victim of one of Zach's little jokes. Yes, ha-ha! Pay no heed to it. Anyway, if he should get there

149

with hammer and wrecking bar, talk to him as you have talked to me. I'm certain it will still his violence."

V

He had scared the very devil out of Burden, and it encouraged him to go further. There was something very suspicious about the warehouses, and it could remain that way as far as Jarrett cared. In other words, he had too much trouble of his own to go digging up any of Burden's just through curiosity. However, it had become plain that Burden's secret could be used. Call it checks and balances. Call it moral persuasion. Call it blackmail.

As soon as darkness came, Jarrett went out on the dock. There was a lot of activity around the dredge headquarters, so he waited. Finally everyone was gone except the watchman, whose name was Jay Hockersmith. They were old friends by this time. Almost every day the watchman stopped and told Jarrett what a mistake he was making gaudying the ship for a gambling place instead of putting it out on the waves.

"Hello, Jay," said Jarrett now, looking in on him through the window of his shanty, where he sat reading, puffing a pipe, and swatting at mosquitoes. "Say, I should tell you, I'm buying those warehouses. I was wondering if you'd keep your eye out for me?"

"Well, I got my hands full—"

"It would pay you two wages instead of one."

"Of course, if you put it that way—"

"I do put it that way!"

"I get a dollar a day, seven a week." It was apparent that Jay considered it top salary.

"I'll pay it. And ten days in advance, starting today."

"That was done quick!" Hockersmith said, taking the ten dollars.

"By the way, there hasn't been anybody in there lately? In my warehouses?"

"There has, yes, sir! They're bonded shut, sealed, and the signs up, but people have been in there."

"Who?"

150

"I can't rightly say."

"You don't know what they've been doing?"

"No, they been pretty foxy about it, and I didn't feel it was any of my business. You get to fooling in things none of your business, and—"

"You're right, Jay—absolutely right. Well, keep watch!"

"I will, starting now."

Jarrett walked down the wagon way, beneath the awnings. He tried the doors, one after another. All of them seemed tight. He came back and managed to get in through an old office by inserting a flat strip of metal, a burglar's latch-opener, in the door. He found himself in a room smelling of dusty burlap and rats. Tables, chairs, tools, boards, baskets, and bundles of papers were stacked around. An array of old stencils hung on nails along one wall. By moonlight coming through a smoky four-set of windowpanes he could read some of the stencils—firms in Boston, New York, London, a who-was of the cotton firms before the war. He unbolted a door leading to the main shed, but it would not open. That part of the floor, resting on piles over water, had sunk so that the door dug into it, and you would need a pry-iron.

There was no other door, but a counter slot could be opened. It had not moved in years. This was a place where warehousemen had once waited for stencils, bills, and receipts. Dust was thick over everything, and the litter of abandon—the dirt, spider, bat and rat litter, and the microscopic refuse of the sea winds.

He slid through, feet first, wishing he had changed to other clothes. His gun dragged, making a thud as it passed over the edge. He stood still and listened. Something had moved in the darkness.

He walked ahead, groping. The darkness was huge. He could see streaks of light, and some distant windows. He bumped waist-high against an old crate. It squeaked, and he cursed it.

"Johnny?" a voice said, and it was so close he recoiled. The man was right there, so near he could sense his breath and warmth. The man had come through a door from somewhere.

"Yah," Jarrett said.

Obviously not recognizing the voice, the man spoke again. "Johnny?"

"I'm Johnny Anderson—who in hell are you?"

"I don't—" The voice stopped, and the man was moving. Jarrett played safe by moving also. I'll fire at the flash, he

151

thought. I'll fire to the right of it, and that way, unless he's left-handed, I'll get him.

"God damn you," said Jarrett in a rough tone, "I was sent here by Harvey Burden. If it's all right with him, it ought to be all right with you."

The thing that troubled him was that he didn't have the least idea who the man was. He didn't know whether he was old or young, large or small, married with a family, or single and able to die without responsibilities. He didn't want to kill a married man. He didn't want to leave all those children without a father, not even a wretched one. He didn't try to explain this feeling, it was just something he had—something taught him by old Enoch Lantern.

"We might as well get acquainted," said Jarrett in a cheerful tone. "It looks like Burden will have us working together for a time. Why don't you show me where things are? Then, I'll tell you what—I'll slip over to Aunt Pity's and get a bottle of whisky."

Just to play safe, he kept changing position a trifle while he talked. The man did not answer. "Hey!" Jarrett said.

The gun exploded with a flash and a streak of burning powder. It came from a totally unexpected direction. The man had been waiting, and at Jarrett's "Hey!" he had fired. The lead fanned past him and struck boards with a whip sound. Buckshot. Pellets of powder still burned with freckles of light, buried in the dusty old boards.

Jarrett was on the floor and moving. A second charge passed over him. He thought the man was armed with a sawed-off double, and if so he'd have to reload. The mistake almost cost Jarrett his life. He commenced firing, and more shots came in quick succession. He was at a disadvantage, long-range pistol against scatter-gun, so he went crawling for cover, through flying splinters and dust stirred up from the floor, collided with a pile of boards and fell over it, and there he lay on his belly while the shot rattled above.

It was not a full charge of buck, he decided. Not ten gauge. It was probably a revolver, one of those old fifty-bores turned out by the armory at Montgomery during the war by hurried, ill-equipped gunsmiths, and without rifling. They were no good for anything except buck, or three-ball head-and-tail, but a deadly vicious gun at short range, a squaw gun.

He kept moving. There was no more shooting. The man was putting more paper cartridges into the cylinders and fixing the caps—Jarrett couldn't see a thing but he could picture him doing it. He could smell powder, sulphury and raw. And there was another strong smell, that of mildew. The end of the warehouse was stacked with baled cotton, and he could smell it. He climbed in darkness over the bales, groped, nearly fell, and reached a window. He could have smashed his way out, but he did not dare silhouette himself against it.

He went back around the room, trying to figure his exact position in regard to the outside, and suddenly the man was in front of him. They bumped, and Jarrett, with the advantage of surprise, slugged him to the floor.

The man grunted as the breath was knocked out of him. Jarrett dropped on him with both knees. He could have killed him with a blow from his gun butt.

"Please, mister!"

"Who are you?"

"Ed Smith. I'm just watchin' the place."

"You tried to kill me."

"You broke in. I'm just doing my job."

Jarrett got up, keeping the man controlled by a hammerlock. He hit his scatter gun with his toe, and picked it up. It weighed about five pounds.

"Hey!" a voice was calling outside. It was Hockersmith. "Hey, in there!"

"It's all right," said Jarrett.

"You sure?"

"I said it's all right." He asked Smith, "Who hired you?" Smith did not want to answer.

"Burden?"

"I guess so."

"What do you mean, *guess* so?"

"Well, Catling hired me."

"Oh, that son of a bitch. Why are you guarding this mildewed cotton?"

"I don't know."

"I'm letting you live, Ed. But I don't have to go on letting you live."

"All I know is, they got this stuff up from the bay from under a warehouse that blew down. They hoisted it out, and it was supposed to be worth four cents a pound for paper rag, or waste, or something. But nobody ever bought any of it. It's just been around here."

"What did he do, load the *Spindrift* with it and have Hiskey scuttle it for the insurance?"

"I don't know. And I don't want to know. I just watch this place for five dollars a day."

"Five dollars. That guard up in the shack only gets a dollar. Why's it worth big money like five dollars a day to watch this pile of mildewed cotton?"

"I don't know, and—"

"Well, that's too bad, because it means I'll just have to feed you to the—"

"Don't blame me! I told you all I can. What do you want, a pack of lies?"

"No, Ed, I don't. I think you've been real cooperative. In fact, if you don't say anything, I won't say anything. You can go right on keeping your job, and earning your five dollars a day."

VI

"Did you hear some shooting over there?" the Angel asked when Jarrett came back to the boat.

"I heard it, and felt it. There's a fellow in there with a buckshot pistol guarding some sea-rot cotton. Does that seem peculiar to you?"

The Angel was an intelligent man, and he waited for Jarrett to finish what he had to say, but it was plain from his expression that he had a bit of information to fit in.

"Also," said Jarrett, "I learn that the *Spindrift* sailed with a cargo of it. Re-baled, I'd imagine. It looks like Zach and Harvey have a little insurance business going."

"Did you ever hear of Bronson Monk, the chief engineer? A big squatty fellow. The one they arrested in Charleston? Well, he's in Galveston, hiding. Somebody tried to kill him."

"That sounds interesting. As if they tried to shut him up."

"Yes."

"Why, then, we've got to save that poor fellow's life. Do you know where to find him?"

"No, but there's one person in Galveston who can find anybody—for a price."

"It sounds like you're talking about Aunt Pity!"

Aunt Pity was Galveston's most notorious saloon owner. Her place, located on what was generally called the Spanish Docks, was a long, low building, or accumulation of buildings, housing quite a variety of enterprises. By daylight a person would almost overlook Aunt Pity's, for there was little to distinguish its gray dilapidation among the clutter of storage houses, ship's carpenters' shops, boarding houses, saloons, and hovels that formed the waterfront there. In bright day it had an abandoned look, its small windows almost opaque from tobacco smoke and salt wind, even its door inconspicuous, set in a slot so the entrance was like the mouth of a funnel.

This feature caused some jokers to refer to it as "The Fly Trap." Their joke was not without its point, because Aunt Pity had the worst reputation in town for what the newspapers referred to as "recruitment," and involuntary recruitment was gaining Galveston a bad name as a shanghai port.

But Aunt Pity continued to operate like a queen in her domain. She was a gigantic woman, strong as a man, and on many occasions she served as her own bouncer. Actually a bouncer was little needed in Aunt Pity's for it was her boast that she ran the only place on the waterfront where everything went. "If the boys can't kick up their heels in old Auntie's, where can they?" she would ask.

It was long past midnight when Prince George swung his carriage around among the casks, cordage, and boss-man's shacks to that part of the old docks that accommodated Aunt Pity's. There was little light, but a glow came from a doorway, and the din of voices and a fiddle. The Angel went in first, and Jarrett stood just inside the door, as befitted a gentleman. It was so smoky one could scarcely see the far end of the room. At least twenty lamps burned, but the depths could not be seen, and there were a number of pillars and archways. In the lurid glow, with all the dissonance of sound and movement, one expected the room to be hot. You associated it with the entrance to a furnace, or to hell, yet inside it was surprisingly cool. There were no windows—they had all been patched with tin or boarded over, but a draft passed beneath, between the floor and the water, and found its way upward through cracks and knotholes.

A tall, graying colored man was playing a fiddle, sawing it in a violent, endless screech with his eyes closed, and men at the bar carried on a loud argument. Girls of a pretty low order were hustling. At a table in the back several men were shooting craps.

Aunt Pity saw the Angel and laid down the cigar she had been smoking. She was very fat, but obviously powerful, although her best years were past. She was big-jawed and wattled, and her arms were so slab-fatted that she could lift her elbows to the bar without moving the underflesh which hung against her sides. Her fingers were loaded with rings. Her hair was dyed the color of molten copper. She was grotesquely ugly.

The Angel engaged her in conversation, and they could be seen to argue for a while; some gold changed hands. She then turned and walked away, disappearing into another room.

"Come along," said the Angel. "We're in luck."

"You mean she has him?"

"Yes."

"You seem to know your way around here."

"I've known Pity for a long time. I knew her when she was in Natchez—she had a joint there. You wouldn't believe it, but she was pretty good-looking once."

"No, I wouldn't. She looks like Harvey Burden decked out in a dress. Her snout is like a pig's. But I suppose she's got a heart of gold."

"She'd cut you up and sell your body for bait if there was ten dollars in it. She sells sailors to the ships. A good sailor is worth fifty dollars. Of course, how often does she find a good sailor? Ordinary deck swabs are worth ten dollars."

"What does she do, drop 'em through a trapdoor?"

"That, and the kabacha powder. One pinch puts them to sleep for eight hours. Two pinches kills 'em. Depends on your size. She's good at it—she can look at a man and see just how much he can take."

They had entered the other room. "How about a drink, boys?" said Aunt Pity, who stood beside a small bar. This was obviously a special place for special customers.

"No, thank you," said Jarrett.

"Who are you, stranger? Are you that new gambling-ship fellow?"

"Yes."

"You poor son of a bitch. I feel sorry for you. Well, come around when it's all over and you can graze off my free lunch."

"When I take this town over, I'll put joints like this out of business."

He said it as a joke, but Aunt Pity was not laughing. "When you take this town over, I'll be queen of the Mardi Gras."

The Angel has gone to a stairway. "Up here?" he asked.

"Up, and all the way back, past the flops. Here's a key."

The stairway was only a narrow slot, and the roof above scraped Jarret's hat. "I don't like her," he said softly.

156

"Neither do I, but she serves a function."

"Shanghaing sailors."

"Nobody lasts long in this world unless they serve a purpose."

They were in a hall that was smelly from a smoking oil lamp. The lamp was in a bracket and the ceiling above its chimney was charred and cracked from years of heat. On one side were some cubicles with doors not quite reaching the floor. Lights were on in some of them, and the ones in use had the guests' shoes placed in sight. A colored boy in a white coat was serving drinks in one of them, and they had to stand flat against the wall so he could pass. They could hear a man telling a story, and a girl kept laughing in a high-pitched giggle, as if he were tickling her.

"Straight on," said the Angel. "Next is kind of flop house. She's got Monk hid in the loft next door."

They passed through a rancid-smelling room, with three-tiered bunks and sleeping men; then down four steps, around a turning, and up four steps, and came to a locked door. The key fitted; the door squeaked open. Jarrett did not like standing in silhouette, and he tried to make himself small against the wall. The Angel was in front of him, for which he was thankful. The Angel had a big, thick body, the kind that could stop a lot of bullets.

A man was watching them. Jarrett could feel his gaze in the dark. He could smell camphor.

"Monk!" said the Angel. "That you, Monk?"

"Who in hell are you?"

"Aunt Pity sent me."

"Who are you?" the man said again. "And who's with you?"

"I'm the Angel."

"You're the Billy Goat. Who's he?"

"Jarrett. We're here to help you."

"I may believe that, and I may not. Get the lamp and bring it in. And keep your hands clear. Don't try anything."

Jarrett got the lamp and carried it in, revealing a roof slanting down at two sides, and a gable and ventilator overhead. Bats watched with bead eyes through the louvres of the ventilator.

Monk was lying on a pallet with a pistol in his hand.

"Why'd Pity send you? Why didn't she come with you?"

"Because she figured you'd rather talk to us alone."

Jarrett said, "She trusts us. Isn't it important that good old Aunt Pity has faith in us?"

"All right—how much do you want?"

157

"For what?"

"To get me out of here. That's why you came, wasn't it? Everybody in this world is interested in just one thing—working a man for all they can get. How much?"

"You're bitter, Monk," Jarrett said. "That's not how it is with everybody. There's some folks in this world moved by the spirit of human brotherhood."

"I'm glad to hear it. But don't try anything, because this pistol has got a hair trigger."

"How bad are you hurt?"

"I took a little something. I—"

"Let me look. Have you had a doctor? I learned some doctoring up in Colorado—"

"Yes, I had a good enough doctor. The blackfellow was here. He can't speak a word, only Cajun or something, but he gave me herbs to draw the pus. I'd rather have a black any day. Except maybe a Chink. But never mind—you tell what you want."

"Who shot you? Burden? Or was it Zach?"

"Say, where do you get—"

"It must have been Burden," Jarrett said to the Angel, "because Zach wouldn't miss. Zach would have had him right between the eyes."

He put the lamp down on a box, and the light struck Monk so he could see him plainly. He had a week's beard. His face had been battered and bruised, but the swelling had gone down, leaving it scabbed purple. One of his eyes was the color of a ripe prune.

"Why'd he do it, Monk? Did you come back to Galveston looking for more money? Sure, that was it, you lost all he paid you and came back for more. And this is what you got instead."

"If you know everything, what the hell you asking for?"

"Like I said, we're on your side. Everything that's bad for Burden and Zach is good for us. They shipped mildew cotton and insured it as fair middlin'. Right? And you blew up the boilers. They paid you—let me guess—five hundred dollars."

"I collected eight hundred. I was supposed to collect fourteen, but that bastard Hiskey cheated me. I didn't want to cause trouble. But I always been a man of my word, and I expect 'em to keep their word to me. That's why I came here, not to blackmail or anything, just to get my due."

"And who tried to kill you?"

"I called at the bank. I called there as peaceful as you please, sneaking in at night and everything. I told him I

158

didn't want to make trouble, only get what was owing, plus a little for carfare, and all of a sudden he kicked my chair from under me. He kicked me in the face and picked me up and slammed me into his fist. That's how he did it—he held his fist still and slammed my face into it. Then I could see he was going to kill me—I could tell it. And I got away and ran, but that guard with the mustache followed and shot me. He came within an inch of getting me in the kidney. I know something about innards, and I was saved by a Lord's miracle, that's what I was."

"Well, wondrous are the ways of Providence!"

"So I came down here. I walked all the way, with a thumb plugging up the blood hole. I told Aunt Pity I had some money cached—more'n a thousand. I knew she'd hide me if she thought there was money in it, but it had to be a lot. People ain't going up against Burden for any fifty or a hundred dollars."

"We got to get you out of here, Monk. All you got to do is sign a statement I write out."

"I'll sign nothing. You'd get me hung off a yardarm."

"They don't do that to merchant seamen—they'd hang you in the courthouse yard. But you'll be safe. You'll be turning state's evidence. I'll hire you the best lawyers."

"They'd get to me—Zach and Burden. They'd tear the jail down stone by stone to get me."

"Yes, except for one thing. That thing being, I'm going to take over this town. I'm going to write now, and you rest for a while so you can do a real plain job on your signature. And afterward I'll get you out and across the bay where nobody will find you."

"You ain't dumping me in any bay—" Monk said, rising.

"Indeed we're not. We're taking you to the best home an orphan ever had."

VII

Harvey Burden had suffered the peculiar feeling, commencing late at night and continuing on into the day, that his chest was under the pressure of a heavy weight, encased in lead, perhaps, and that the pressure was increasing bit by bit until it threatened to stifle his breathing. And sometimes when he breathed the air had no life in it.

"Jarrett, you son of a bitch!" he whispered. It wasn't enough that he had Zach Thomas after him; now he had to have Jarrett. All the Western Steam Transportation Co. papers were out and spread across his desk. The company had gone bankrupt years ago in New Orleans, a bank there taking over as trustee for the creditors. The New Orleans claim was not legal in Texas, but it clouded things.

Was Jarrett bluffing? He didn't need to be. With only a few hundred dollars he might get some sort of an instrument from the receivers. Then, because the company had been in the ocean trade, he might start an action in Federal Court. If so, it would upset everything. Those bastards in Federal Court didn't care where the border of Texas ran—they were out to destroy the states and take over everything for Washington. That son of a bitch, Ulysses S. Grant! They'd get their gut full of him up north before his term was through.

Then there was the *Spindrift* to worry about. Fortunately he'd been able to put Monk out of the way. Catling had killed him. But Hiskey or one of the others could turn up. Why had Hiskey allowed so many survivors? Why could he never get anything done efficiently? Why did he have to do everything with his own two hands?

"Mr. Burden," said Dwight Franklyn at the door.

"Yes, yes, damn it! What do you want, Dwight?"

"That man is here."

"What man?" he shouted.

"Jarrett."

He was almost relieved. It was best to meet the problem head on. Jarrett had no principles beyond the dollar sign. Not like Zach—Zach had a code, and he aspired to be a gentleman.

"All right, what are you waiting for? Send him in." And he called out cordially: "Joseph! I'm damned sorry about my lack of hospitality the other day, but you caught me at a bad moment. This heat—this pressuring heat!"

"And the roses. I hate the smell of 'em."

"Do you, also? I'm glad someone agrees with me. But the stink we get now are autumn-blooming coreanthus."

"I tell you something I dislike worse than coreanthus. It's the smell of mildew cotton, especially if it's got a little bit of rancid seed jacket left in it."

Burden looked shot in his tracks. Jarrett went on, "The smell of it is awful around the dock, and I especially dislike

160

it on account of my boat, the *Maison Rouge,* which is having its opening tomorrow night."

"These things come and go. When the wind changes—"

"I'm afraid I'm going to have to open that warehouse."

"You will not touch that warehouse!"

"Why, Harvey, what's the matter? You act as if I'd burned you with a hot iron."

"You, sir, will not step foot in that warehouse."

"I've been told Zach has some cotton stored there. If so, I better see him moving the more obnoxious portion, because—"

"Sir, will you stop toying with me? You have come into the possession of some information, haven't you? I suspected as much the other day. Now, out with it. Pay me the courtesy of frankness."

"All right. Why would Zach have mildew cotton stored in his warehouse? Why would he *ship* it? You asked me to be honest. All right, I know he didn't ship it. I know *you* shipped it, sold it to Zach with false papers, insured it, and sunk it so he wouldn't know. Why you gave it to Zach instead of collecting yourself is still something I'm not sure of, but I can guess."

"I wanted to do him a favor if he did me a favor. The favor he did me was to take some future commitments off my hands. As for the mildew bales, as you call them, I have every intention of replacing them with sound upland fair fiber as soon as the crop is in and a present financial difficulty passes."

Burden was more in control now, and a smile settled into the great folds of his face. "Jarrett—Joseph—listen to me. Why must we struggle and strive against one another? Believe me, we will all lose. Let us understand one another. Live and let live. That is Christian, Joseph. Surely a man named *Joseph* should be inspired by such an appeal. Let live, Joe."

"That's what Monk said."

Burden slowly opened a drawer of his desk. But he closed it again and walked to look from a window.

"Ah, yes. Monk. So he managed to live. You have him, and he will testify, I suppose. You will find the others. You will prosecute. I will beat the charge, of course, but it will destroy my reputation utterly. You have me, as the saying goes, by the short hair. So what will you have of me?"

"Sell me the dock and warehouse."

"What legality—"

161

"Who in hell cares what legality? Sell me your notes on the warehouse. That, at least, you have the full power to do, adverse claims or not, and options or not."

"Yes, of course. It has to be a realistic figure, however. Ten thousand dollars."

"That's *too* realistic. I'll pay exactly twenty-five hundred. Take it, or good-bye."

Mopping sweat, Burden said, "I'm helpless to do otherwise."

Part Five

I

It was very quiet. Jarrett had never known a night to be so quiet. A breeze had blown steadily from the Gulf, commencing at sundown, and by the first light it was cool—almost cold. You could have used a wool jacket. There was a belief in the port that such breezes came directly from the Andes, with their cappings of snow.

"Nigh onto the big day, Major," a watchman whom the Angel had hired said toward morning.

"Yes, twenty-four hours from now and we'll know the tale."

"It'll be a grand opening. It'll be an opening such as Galveston and the coast has never known."

Zach had made no trouble, but that did not comfort him. You fastened a long fuse on the powder, and you waited and waited—it didn't mean the blast wouldn't come.

The sun rose, a red flare through the mists, and the mists were driven from the water. It was morning of his great day. What did the next twenty-four hours hold in store for him?

His constable came around, a square-set man named Leary. He cost $250 per day, but he was the only man willing to take a job that brought him in opposition to Zach Thomas. Quite a number of guards had been gathered by Prince George, but he wanted a man who could deputize them in case of necessity. And a constable, he'd learned from reading the old laws, was vested with that emergency power.

George's men, thirty-one strong, and running heavily to West Indians, formed in a ragged line at ten o'clock to collect their $15 for the day's work.

"No guns," said Jarrett. "I don't object to saps, and a club or two, but no guns. And no knives. I want no bullets of ours whistling through the *Maison*, endangering the customers. I don't know yet, but it looks as if I might have the Governor and his lady. I know the Lieutenant Governor will come."

"About bullets," said Prince George, "—Mr. Zach may not be so particular."

"Then on his head be it."

"Don't tell me, Major, that you're shedding your pistol?"

"I would, only with me it's not a weapon so much as an article of attire. All kinds of gentlemen are going to be here with their guns on. It would be considered amiss in me to shed mine. But my dealers aren't going to pack guns."

"Is there really a chance the Governor will come?" asked the Angel.

"He was invited. It's pretty hard to turn down an invitation printed on white satin in letters of 24-karat gold. Everybody that is anybody is coming—it's a social event. I *know* the chief judge of the Supreme Court is coming. We're going to have all the blue chips, human and collateral."

"That's wonderful news. I only wish dear old Richter could be here to see it."

"I wish he could be, too. But his daughter will look after things."

"What do you think Zach will do?"

"He'll try tearing up the dock, that's my prediction."

"And probably just when guests arrive. Or just before."

"There's where you're wrong. He wouldn't *dare* start anything with the élite and the chief justice coming! No, sir, our hours of trial run from now to sundown. If we make it till six o'clock, we've beaten Zach Thomas' hand!"

II

There was still a great deal to do. Materials littered the boat, and the red carpet, 158 feet long, had to be laid down the landing stage and across the dock to protect the gowns of the ladies. Fortunately, the town now had an abundant supply of ice, so the oysters, fruits, and all the other viands, and the Yucatan flame orchids could be kept with no chance of spoiling. There were a dozen things that had been forgotten: small things such as a string for the draw blind on the women's salon, and large ones such as getting the ivory-finish square piano aboard that had been brought over from New Orleans. And the piano had to be tuned. In the headlong rush of all this, Jarrett actually forgot about Zach Thomas. Then, suddenly, it was twilight, and only a couple of hours from the opening.

He made his last trip from town, which seemed unusually busy. An excitement like the magnetism of storm, could be felt in the air. The Congress Hotel was lighted and busy in a way that indicated an unusual influx of important guests. Carriages waited their turn in the drive. It was the first great social event of the season, given a special blessing from the fact that Jarrett had had the idea of calling it a benefit, all profits to go to the Lanternlight Orphanage.

Miss Ermaline had arrived somewhat earlier and had already taken charge of the main bank. Jarrett stopped to compliment her, and then went in to shave and dress, emerging elegant in tails, white shirt, and new, deep red carnelian studs as big as keno balls. Maxine joined him, and she was stunning. Prince George, magnificent in a scarlet uniform with silver braid, was out front to announce the guests, and to make certain nobody entered, at least in the early part of the evening, unless he was the bearer of a gold-on-satin invitation.

Jarrett gave a signal, and the orchestra commenced to play. After a long period of waiting, with no arrivals, he commenced to worry that Zach had perpetrated some devilish trick, and that nobody would come after all; but later he learned that all the hacks in the city were in use, driving back and forth and around, as nobody wished to be first to appear.

Finally a group of about thirty congregated and came all in a body, and they had to wait turns being introduced, the first ones, of course, to only the dealers, waiters, and musicians. Their first stop was at the buffet with its chilled oysters, assorted cakes, and the Widow's extra dry. Inside they were greeted with a scene of stunning magnificence, the old grand promenade and passengers' salon having been combined into a many-pillared hall from which a double, curving staircase mounted toward what was obviously the starry sky —a sky bluer than the sky of the Mediterranean, with stars as large as dollars, an effect obtained by stretching blue crêpe with silvered apertures backed by camphene lamps. Out of sight, Negro boys waited with buckets of water to extinguish the possible conflagration.

"Colonel and Mrs. Dewitt Bateman!" Prince George announced in large mellow tones at the door.

"Mr. and Mrs. Gregory T. Greene!" "The Honorable Clifton R. Venable, and his niece, Miss Caroline Marsh."

The curiosity was then extreme, for "Miss Caroline Marsh" was known to be a member of the demimonde Venable had been seeing in Sabine.

"The nerve of him!" said one gentleman. "Boys, you got to admire him."

"We're a success," said Jarrett when he could get over to Maxine. "We already have a scandal going."

"Mr. and Mrs. Harvey Burden!"

Burden in his tails and vast white vest was an awesome sight. One looked at him as at a mountain rising from the Colorado plains. He was grotesque, but you couldn't laugh at a human force of such dimensions. His wife proved to be fifteen years younger, and was garbed in what was obviously the most expensive gown in the room.

"Overdressed," said Maxine.

"I wonder if she's a Sabine gal also?"

"Oh, there you are, Joseph," Burden said, breathing hard as he came up. He had a handkerchief tucked discreetly under his starched collar to keep it from turning completely limp before the night was done. "Joseph, my boy! And Miss Maxine—or should I say Mrs. Messimo? Where is my wife? Ah, she seems to have secured some chips. All for the sake of charity. An excellent idea, having Miss Ermaline in charge of the bank. Who would wish to win from an orphanage? We came to contribute, my boy."

"You came here to win, because those games are backed by my own sweet cash."

Actually Jarrett was a little short of cash, but he would back any large payoff, if it became necessary, with checks on the Merchants and Planters, and Burden was in no position to refuse payment. He expected no dangerous play early in the evening. The big money would come later in the private rooms where the red-meat faro was set up, and big-time gamblers like Moncure, the ship owner, and Big Ed Phipps, the cattle and hide baron, would commence coppering the jack, as the saying went, and plunging on the case cards.

"May I see you a minute, my boy?" Burden said.

"You're seeing me."

"Not to upset the young proprietress"—he bowed to Maxine—"but have you heard anything of Zach?"

"No, and I sent him an invitation. It's more'n I can understand, unless he feels this would be too high-toned a gathering for him. I did expect he'd be here with the lady barber. On the other hand, her being a lady barber, he might think she'd not fit in with the Governor's lady."

"Are the Governor and his lady here?"

"No, they haven't come yet either. But I've got a couple of future governors in the crowd."

Burden looked around. "Yes, indeed," he said. "It will be terrible if anything happens."

"Why, what could happen?"

"Well, I don't want to alarm you. But Zach is not beaten —no. He is not going to sit passively and let this continue. He is not a man who will be relegated to second place. I might as well tell you that he has a large gang of toughs, hooligans of the very worst order, armed with clubs and sulphur stinks, out along the docks at this moment."

"That's nothing new. He's always got them at his beck. Blow a whistle and they'll come pouring out of his joints and brothels like rats smoked out of a Paris sewer. But I've got a few men myself. And they'll meet Zach at some considerable and discreet distance off *my* dock. So if the orchestra strikes up real loud and joy reigns unconfined, these people will never know the difference."

"I hope you're right. I do hope you are. But, frankly, I'm afraid you have underestimated the enemy. That was the fatal weakness of us in the South, sir, the fatal weakness. I told them when the first Yankee gunboat appeared off South Pass and the Chandeleurs that we would have to act, but they would not listen to me. General Lovell, Beauregard, none of them. Don't underestimate the enemy—"

"Well, I've got quite a bit of military and naval skill right here in this room. They're pretty full of good bourbon and high spirits, and they might take it hard if a gang of plug-uglies commenced smashing the buffet and tossing stink bombs under the skirts of their womenfolk. In fact, if Zach is as good a general as you seem to think, he'd pull up before coming to grips with this kind of talent. But thanks, Harvey. Nobody can say you didn't warn me."

"I have much to lose. Much! You forced me to choose, and I have chosen your side. I fall or rise with you, Jarrett!"

"Have a brandy. We've not only got five star—we've got seven star. I ordered *nine* star, but they don't make it. Not even for Emperor Napoleon the Third, they don't."

Jarrett sent him off with a slap on the shoulder. He smiled and spoke to late arrivals. He walked among the guests.

"Announcing" said Prince George—it drew Jarrett's attention because it was the first time he had said, "announcing" —"announcing Mr. Zachariah Thomas! And the Countess, Madame Elya Carlson!"

And there he was, Zach Thomas, lean, smiling his half-contemptuous smile, and dressed to the nines. And Elya! Good God, what a woman!

"Welcome," cried Jarrett, quickly recovering. "Welcome to the soirée for sweet, sweet charity."

"You son of a bitch," said Thomas from one side of his mouth while managing to look polite from the other, "you got your hand in that till, too?"

"Believe me, every cent goes to the orphanage."

"If that's so, I won't break the bank."

"Use no mercy, Zachariah! I will pay all losses from my own financial reserves. These at present include not only this boat, but the dock against which it rests, and the warehouses beyond."

"I assume there's a limit?" said Zach.

"For you, the blue sky."

"I'll buy ten thousand as a starter."

Jarrett managed to keep his composure. "As you say, Zach. Blue chips for Zachariah Thomas," he cried, escorting him to Miss Ermaline.

She cut out the stacks of blues without a change in her charming smile.

Zach strolled about. He tried a chip here and a chip there, winning and losing and moving on until he stopped at the chuck-a-luck. The man tipping the cage was a gambler from Houston. Jarrett had been careful to go out of the city for all his dealers, fearing Zach's spies, but now he had a sudden hunch. Everything here was *too* casual.

"Two thousand on the four-to-one," said Zach.

"Give me the honor," said Jarrett, taking over the cage.

"No, I wouldn't have you bother. I'll take the regular dealer like everyone else."

"But it's no bother at all," Jarrett said.

He tilted the cage, and Zach lost, but he had already picked up his chips.

"I don't like your dealing, Mr. Jarrett!" Zach said.

"I don't like your dealer."

"What do you mean by that?"

"You bet two thousand dollars and lost. I'll have that bet, Mr. Thomas."

"You will have the bet when I get a turn-of-cage from the regular dealer. Judgment, gentlemen!" he said, turning to the others. "I'll go by your judgment. Regular dealer? My winnings this turn will go to charity! Regular dealer?"

"Touché!" said Jarrett.

"What?"

"Touché, that's a French term, meaning you got me, and it hurts."

The dealer came back and turned the cage, and Zach lost again.

"Ah, well. Charity was bound to get it one way or the other. Now let's gamble you against me, Jarrett." He stacked out more chips. "Let's double up. This is my suicide system. Four thousand dollars. Next time it'll be six. Next time, eight. You always win if you have money enough."

The dealer turned the cage, and this time the dice fell for Zach.

"Why, look at those wonderful six-sided cubes!" he said. "They've gone and won me eight thousand dollars. Why, this is a red-blooded game you run here, Mr. Jarrett. Just how red-blooded are *you?* How would you like, say, this eight thousand on the ten-to-one? That would just about make a hundred thousand, all total. Give or take a few thousand. A hundred thousand! Where have I heard such a figure before? You wouldn't know, would you, Mr. Jarrett?"

Play had stopped at the other tables. A lancers schottische was being danced, but couples were leaving the floor to see what the excitement was. Jarrett was more certain than ever that the dealer had been planted, and he didn't intend to lose everything that easily. On the other hand, he wasn't going to back down.

"On the ten-to-one," said Zach, stacking the chips in blue pillars. "Now, it's my understanding I end up with your ship and not an orphan asylum. The little lady at the cashier's wicket is just getting your profits, none of your losses?"

"Right."

"Oh, you've got sporting blood, Mr. Jarrett! How about it, folks, don't you agree that Jarrett, here, has sporting blood in his veins?"

The crowd was tense and quiet. The orchestra was still playing, but not a couple remained on the dance floor.

"What's keepin' you, Jarrett? Are you calling this bet? Oh, come, now! I'll tell you what—if you want to turn the cage, go ahead."

The dealer, at a signal from Zach, stepped away from the cage. Zach motioned for Jarrett to take over, and he smoked his cigar. Beneath drooping eyelids his eyes were as intent as a stalking cat's. His teeth showed a very little in his smile.

"You turn it, Jarrett. Yours the cage, and yours the hand. What more could a gambler ask for?"

How had he done it? Jarrett didn't know, only that he *had* done it. The game was fixed, and just as certainly as he turned the cage it would come up Zach's number. He killed time by taking a cigar of his own and lighting it. His fingers were very steady. He hoped everyone noticed how steady they were. What'll I do, he thought. Oh God, what will I do?

A bell seemed to be ringing. In his extreme preoccupation, he thought it was ringing in his brain. He shook himself to drive the sound away. Then he noticed that the spectators were turning to listen. In the distance he heard shouting. A man was at the door saying something to Prince George, who hurried away with him. The bell was coming closer and closer. Clang! clang! clang! It was a fire bell. It was the steam pumping engine.

"There it is!" a man shouted. "The whole warehouse is going!"

At the door there was a press of people trying to get outside. All he could feel was relief. He proceeded to close down the game. He walked around the table, and Zach was standing there all by himself.

"Turn it once," said Zach, "just for fun, and see if the number comes up."

"Zach, I wouldn't do it. Because it'd work out one way or the other so one of us could never get a whole night's sleep again in this wicked world!"

III

The darkness in front of the warehouse was thickened by a layer of smoke. You couldn't see the smoke at first, but it choked you. Behind, a ruddy glow silhouetted the roofs. Smoke billowed upward on a strong current of heat, but no flame could be seen. On the dock the suck of the draft could be felt around your legs. There was nothing in the world that burned as fast as an old dock-set warehouse, because the draft came up from beneath and through the floor like the draft in a stove with an open grate.

Jarrett saw the Angel and tried to reach him. He wanted to find out how the fire started. Down the dock a small riot was in progress, blocking the fire engine that clanged and steamed, and waited. Zach was making sure, he thought. He wanted it all to go, everything. It was his cotton, his insurance. And by a wonderful accident it was the destruction of Jarrett's opening, maybe of the ship, everything.

Nearly everyone had come off the boat by now. There were signs of excitement when the dock exits proved to be blocked. He could not see the Angel now, for he was in the midst of the fight with Zach's bully boys. But he saw Prince George.

"Get these people back on and we'll have a tug push us out in the bay. We better do it in a hurry. It's getting pretty hot, and all hell will be loose when those roofs start to cave."

"It's low tide," George said. "We're in the mud."

Of course it was low tide. He could tell by the slant of the landing stage as he came ashore.

Zach was shouting, "Chad!" He had a voice like a trumpet when he cared to use it, and when he cupped his hands. "Chad! God damn you, break it up!"

"I'm trying to break it up."

"Stop the fight and get the engine through."

"That's what I'm trying to do! But these men of Jarrett's are stopping me."

Zach saw Jarrett coming toward him, and he turned to meet him. "Get your men away! What the—"

"Why, you God-damned—"

"Later, Jarrett. I'll fight with you later. Right now—"

"You had it planned to the minute—to the second. You got everyone around that chuck-a-luck table—"

"What are you talking about?"

"I'm talking about snakes. The kind that scuttle steamboats to collect insurance on mildew cotton. The kind that, when he couldn't ship all of it for scuttling, left it in a warehouse to burn. And at *just the right time!*"

"I didn't set that fire, and I didn't scuttle any boat."

"Zach, I might as well tell you that you're a two-bit Yankee liar."

Zach made a move, and Jarrett smashed him to the dock. He was down on hands and knees trying to retreat crabwise and get some room, room to stand, to go for his gun, but Jarrett followed him closely.

Zach finally got up. His lip was bleeding. A knee was torn out of his dress pants. His coat hung open, as did Jarrett's. They would go for their guns apparently even—but only apparently. The advantage was all with Jarrett, who had his balance, who was on the prowl, who was ready. But, unaccountably, Jarrett didn't want to do it—he didn't want to kill Zach Thomas. He wanted to beat hell out of him.

171

Zach, still retreating, and playing for time to recover, bumped a pile of cordage. He half sat, catching his fall on his back-thrust hand. Then people were all around them, excited and pushing, and the two men were caught in it. Zach was rammed over the cordage again, and Jarrett was reeling, fending people away.

An elderly man, in a biting anger, was pulling Jarrett's arm. "What's the matter with you, suh? Answer me! What manner of proprietor are you, fightin' here while leavin' yo' guests to perish?"

"You're right. You're right, Colonel Bateman," Jarrett said.

"Well, act, suh, *act!*"

People were trying to get back on the boat, and he saw the first signs of terror. He called out:

"Folks! Take your time. We'll pull out into the bay and watch from there."

It was as useless as shouting at the fire. A woman fell midway on the landing stage, and people began to trample over her. From above, Prince George grabbed her and lifted her free.

Finally all the people were aboard, except for Bateman, Jarrett, and Zach—and the Angel, who was at last getting the fire engine through. The flames were high through the roofs now, and embers were flying. The silk crêpe sky above the stairs was aflame, and the bucket brigade, after failing in trying to douse it, tore it down and threw it overboard.

"Get this hulk out of here," said Zach. "Do you have any steam?"

"Steam! For God's sake, don't be a fool! In *those* boilers—"

"What'd you spend my hundred thousand dollars on?"

"Get the hawsers out. Do it from on board. We'll have to pole it away."

Poles, boat hooks, even pieces of timber ripped from the lower deck were put into use, nearly every man aboard lending a hand, but the boat only dipped and rubbed its side against the dock fenders.

"Heave-ho! heave-ho!" They got to shouting and ramming in unison, but still to no effect. The prow swung a few feet away, but the stern only drove itself more firmly into the dock, chewing the pilings.

"It's stuck in the God-damned son-of-a-bitching mud," said a man with his coat off and his shirt loose. "That's Galveston for you! Every tide comes in thicker'n Creole gravy with *mud*."

Embers fell and burned on the decks, and the boys, dipping water by means of buckets on ropes, ran and dashed them out, but more and more landed. The heat had become blistering. Overhead, above the stacks, the flags were aflame.

Jarrett ran below to see about getting the hand pumps working. The hold was blue from smoke. He found the hoses, but they were stiff, and broke when he tried to unfold them. The smoke tore at his lungs, and he had to get back topside. They hadn't closed the doors and windows, and the draft would quickly carry the fire into the main salon.

Their only chance was to get a boat up to the far side, and take the people off there. He heard the fireboat coming, blowing its whistle in repeated short blasts.

"Toss us a line!" Zach was calling.

"No time for that!" the fireboat skipper called back through his megaphone. "We'll come alongside and take you off."

People gathered along the rail. It caused a shift in weight, and the big boat was moving. At first there was a foot or two of water between it and the dock, and this grew wider. A cheer went up. There was a gurgle of tide against the side of the dock. The fireboat towed them into the bay, and then steamed back to the dock and commenced playing futile, long-range streams at the slumping warehouses.

The fire shrank rapidly after reaching its crest, and great clouds of steam rose when the burning timbers began to sink into the water. By that time the men, with new spirit born of their common experience, had gone back to the buffet for champagne, and to the tables for profit, and the dancing resumed. A tug nudged them up to the new W. & H. Co. wharf. More and more champagne was carried up in ice tubs, and the Angel had to get Sterling, of Sterling & Vass, to open his wholesale liquor house to replenish the supply.

The stakes rose at the faro games. The orchestra played. Jarrett circulated among the women and charmed them with his courtly manners and his witty remarks. At last, when it was almost dawn, he was able to have a quiet cigar.

"Thought you'd have enough of smoke by this time, Major," said Prince George.

"It calms the nerves. Where's Zach?"

"What you going to do, Mr. Major? Kill him?"

"Yes, but I'm undecided whether to do it all at once, or by inches."

"He worked awfully hard to save this boat. For anybody out to destroy it, he worked awful hard."

Jarrett tossed his cigar over the side. "I wouldn't want you to be wrong about that, Prince."

"I wouldn't want to be, either. But I spent all night at this landing stage. I saw everybody that went ashore and came on. And you know the only man not interested enough to stay when you were having your duel of the chuck-a-luck with Mr. Zach Thomas?"

He thought back. He had taken time to look at the crowd when Zach had challenged him with the big bet, and it had seemed that everyone was there, or coming up. But one person he could not remember seeing—the man who should be easiest to remember. Harvey Burden. He hadn't been there!

"Yes," he said. "Yes, I should have known."

"Mr. Harvey Burden, that big banker, he walked right down that plank, Major. He walked right straight down it and didn't stay for the gambling at all. And you know what he did? He stood on the dock with his handkerchief and waved it around."

"He always has his handkerchief."

"That may be so, but not signaling with it."

"You're sure?"

"I'm sure."

"Thanks, Prince. I don't know what forty kinds of damn fool I'd be without you."

IV

Jarrett got off the boat, leaving the people there who were still having a good time, and he started walking. The dock and warehouses had become blackened heaps that were seas of smoke. Fire still burst out occasionally, and the pumping engines spurted water. A wet, tarry smell filled the air. The dredge end of the warehouse remained intact, and the fireboat was there, its engines beating, and the hoses pulsating with it.

A man had been killed—his back was broken. Somebody said his name was Smith. That was the guard Jarrett had exchanged shots with. His death shouldn't have angered him so much, but it did. The poor devil probably had a wife and family. He needed the five dollars a day, so he had taken the job. That son of a bitch, Burden! Burden had hired him, and Burden had killed him, to keep him quiet. Dead men tell no tales. They never testify.

He kept on walking. He walked through the night-quiet business district, shutters drawn over the fronts of the cafés, and ended up in a dark alley behind the bank.

He had not realized he was going there, but it had been in his mind, the unthinking part of his mind. The bank had a barred and lighted front, but there was a small verandah in the back, upstairs. Burden's office opened onto it. A tree grew near, and there was a pillar to brace one's foot against. He climbed until he could grab the wooden drain gutter, pull himself to the railing, and with a final effort, up and over.

It was a good place to get shot, if there was a guard, but there was no guard. All was quiet. A small metal table and a couple of metal chairs stood beneath an umbrella. The French windows were locked. Inside, by moonlight from another side, he could see the shapes of a desk, chairs, a brass spittoon, a couch, a water cooler.

He had no knife, nothing to pry with. Laying his hat brim over one of the panes, he broke it, and reached inside to the latch. He found it, opened the windows, and went in. He closed them again and felt for a match. He started to close the draperies, thinking someone might see the light, but on the other hand closed draperies might seem more suspicious. Often the best way was the bold and open way. He let down the lamp on a counterbalance mechanism, and lit it. You could light it without touching the chimneys. It had four wicks, and a battery of silvered reflectors adjusted to cast light on the desk, some filing cabinets, and an area of the carpet, leaving Burden's big chair in shadow.

It had seemed important to search Burden's office, but now that he was inside, what did he expect to find? He didn't know. He had an idea Burden might choose to hide evidence here—documents, anything very strictly private— rather than in the vault where some snooping employee would find it. He looked in all the desk drawers except one, which did not open. That was the important one, he felt sure, and he tried to pry it, using the point of a large dagger letter-opener.

The letter-opener was poor steel and bent over like a piece of tin. He needed a jimmy, some sort of bar. He looked around the room, and inside the filing cabinets and in the closet. Then he heard a door open, and the heavy tread of a man's feet on the stairs.

It must be Burden. Nobody else could shake the floor as he did. Burden, alone—almost certainly alone. Jarrett let down the lamp and blew it out. It had swung back up on its counterbalance when a key rattled and the door opened.

Jarrett could get down behind the couch, or he could hide in the closet, but the idea of hiding repelled him. Like being caught in a bedroom and hiding under the bed—degrading. No, he was not going to hide from Burden. He sat down in the chair at the desk. Burden came in breathing hard, wheezing, muttering. He struck a match, and let the lamp down and lit it. Then he saw Jarrett facing him across the desk.

He jumped and took two steps backward, both hands up, evidently expecting the crash and powder flame of a pistol. He commenced to shake violently, until he seemed almost ready to fall. Actually, he was not shaking from fear, but from the sudden release of his taut nerves.

"Hello, Harvey," Jarrett said quietly.

"What the devil? How did you— Oh, my God! Don't ever do that again. Never, never!"

He sagged and sat down and mopped his face. He stayed with his head down and his eyes closed. At last he took a deep breath and spoke.

"What do you want?"

"I was looking for evidence, Harvey. Something to show a court."

"Evidence! Ha-ha!"

"You've got no secrets from me, Harvey. I know where you went tonight. You left when the crowd was all in there around the chuck-a-luck table. That was a mistake. Your boys could have burned it. You didn't have to go make sure."

"Go make sure of what? I may have had something to do with that unfortunate *Spindrift,* but why would I burn up my own warehouses? So Zach could collect more insurance for cotton? Do you think I have nothing to do but make money for Zach? I've done Zach enough favors already. I'm going to do you some favors for a change. I thought we had an understanding—partners, sort of."

"I'd as soon be partners with a boa constrictor. My goodness, how you were going to toss the coils around Zach! First the *Spindrift* goes down under suspicious circumstances, and then the warehouse burns, ditto. Both fully insured under policies certified to Zach Thomas. Arson! A penitentiary crime. And scuttling—worse. Oh, I know you admitted a little something to me, but who would believe my testimony—me, a gambler? You'd deny all, and toss Zach in the pen. It was wonderful scheming, Harvey. It was genius. I'll admit I might be tempted to go along with you, because I despise Zach so much. And I would, only you were so underhanded dirty."

"That is ridiculous. Positively far-fetched and ridiculous. All that was based on only one fragment of truth—the unfortunate *Spindrift* incident. What was your real purpose in coming here? Was it blackmail? Did you think that by coming here with that outrageous defamatory tale you could blackmail me into refinancing your floating casino?"

"Explain to me about Claude Saigon. I've heard rumors. How come all his cotton disappeared? It just vanished—and no records."

"He never kept records. I am trying, sir, to save something for his poor widow from the debacle—"

"I'll bet you killed Saigon right in this office."

"Get out! Get out, or I will call the police. There happens to be a burglary gong in this bank, and at this very second my foot—"

"The mistake you made was in trying to kill your man Smith."

Burden stared at him, aghast.

"That's right, Harvey, you didn't quite do it. He dropped pretty limp when you gave him that old-time wrestler's bar, but this time you didn't quite do it. He's alive, Harvey. Smith is alive, and he identified you."

"No! He couldn't identify me!" he shouted. "He was beyond identifying anybody."

The desk was between them, and Jarrett relied too much on it as a barrier. He saw Burden start for him and took a backward step, avoiding the chair, his hand coming up with the pistol. But Burden did not try to get over the desk, or come around it. He simply used the desk as a weapon, lifting it, thrusting it, almost hurling it. Jarrett was carried backward, and was nearly pinned against the wall. He managed to get away, but he rammed the water cooler, which fell with a crash.

He had his gun drawn, and he tried to turn and use it. Water spoiled his footing, and he went down with one leg out and the other folded beneath him. He had to avoid the large pieces of broken glass—one of them could cut a tendon or an artery. He got up, and turned and fired, and realized that at five or six feet he had managed to miss. The biggest target in the city, and he had missed!

He did not get a second chance. Burden hit him a sweeping blow, lifting him off his feet and driving him to the wall. He lost the gun, and as he turned for it Burden reached out to seize him.

He got away, but it had been a close call. His only chance was somehow to hold this man off, this gorilla of strength —this power and weight that was inhuman. He had to avoid grappling with him until he could recover the gun. Once in the power of those hands and arms, all was finished.

He retreated, and Burden followed him. He kept him off with a long left, but he came on, and Jarrett set his heels and smashed him in the face. He continued to retreat around the room, swinging right and left and right, Burden's face a target he could not miss, and Burden simply absorbed the blows. His face became a bloody mess, his nose was smashed, and his teeth were hammered through his lips, but he came on. Blood ran down his chin and neck, mixing with sweat, blood-streaking his shirt front. But he kept coming on.

Jarrett could see the gun. It was between the wall and the overturned base of the water cooler. He made the mistake of trying to reach for it, and Burden kicked him against the wall. He attempted to roll with the blow and dodge beneath Burden's hands, but the big man was too quick, and he was in Burden's grasp.

Jarrett drove a knee upward to the groin. He attempted to rip with a thumb at Burden's eyeballs. He resorted to every savage trick of the barroom brawler, but the man's mass of flesh was his protection. It absorbed all the force of Jarrett, and engulfed him. He was being borne down and broken. He had the sensation of being crushed and smothered.

He attempted to get between the man's legs, and Burden had him in a scissors, a massive hug. Burden had opened his shirt, and now he forced Jarrett's face into his great, soft belly. He could not breathe, and a wild terror seized him. He found himself flailing without purpose.

A last instinct for survival made him stop. He gathered his strength, managed to make a bridge of his legs and roll over. He came free for a half-breath, and glimpsed some jagged pieces of glass from the cooler. He seized one and brought it up and around in a short, carving arc, with Burden's own strength against it pushing it into his belly.

With a scream, Burden released him. He retreated, looking down at his abdomen. Starting at his right hipbone and slanting upward to his ribs, the glass had cut him like a whale under the flensing knife. In the seconds before the blood came, Jarrett could see the deep fat, the opened muscle wall, and his guts like a nest of pale snakes.

Jarrett crawled and got the gun. He could not stand. He braced himself with shoulders against the wall and feet out.

He cocked the gun. Then he got his breath, and as he breathed, waves of darkness passed over him.

He must have passed out for a few seconds, because when he opened his eyes Burden was not in view. He got to his feet ready to shoot him, but he was not in the room. He went to the door, and saw Burden standing in the corridor trying to hold his fat together. With both hands bloody, he was trying to close the gaping hemispheres of his huge middle and keep his intestines in. He stared at Jarrett and did not recognize him. His brain was preoccupied with the horror of his plight.

"Oh God!" he whispered. "Oh God, oh God, oh God!"

He ran heavily down the stairs. He had no hand to use on the door, so he merely collided with it, his weight ripping the latch off. Jarrett followed him. Burden went reeling down the sidewalk at a lunging half-run, a blind, gargantuan gallop. He struck out slantwise across the cobbled street, and commenced hammering at a door. It was the door to a doctor's office. At last a man looked from an upstairs window and called down that the doctor was not there.

"It's the middle of the night!" the man added, but Burden did not hear him. He ran on.

A carriage carrying men and women from the boat stopped as if to look at him, but he ran past unheeding. He ran until he had to lean against a wall from exhaustion, and then ran on again. He climbed the outside stairs to a second doctor's office and, holding his wound with one hand, beat on the door, but there was no answer.

When he came down the steps he collided with Jarrett, and pushed him away. Other people were there—a couple of sailors, an old woman with a bucket of slops, and a bleary-eyed streetwalker.

"Harvey! Listen to me!" Jarrett said.

"I need a doctor," Burden said. He looked around dully.

"Harvey, sit down! You're cut bad, but it won't kill you if you sit still. I'll get a doctor."

"I have to find a doctor. I don't want to die. I tell you, I don't want to die in this awful town. I don't want to be buried here in this heat. Oh, God, the heat, and the stink of the flowers! The funeral flowers. I don't want to rot here in this moldy, dirty ground forever."

"I was saying, Harvey, I'll get you a doctor. Sit tight and I'll get one."

He ran and caught up with a carriage. The passengers got out so that he could use it to bring Dr. Vansin, who was still up, having been at the *Maison Rouge*.

179

"You say Burden? Harvey Burden? Did he keel over, or something?"

"No, he's been in a fight. He's slashed across the belly."

"What a target! You look as if you'd been in a fight, too."

"Come on and see Harvey."

The doctor got some things from his office and they rode back, but Burden was not there. The old woman with the slops motioned up the street. They found him lying flat on his face across the cobblestones. He was unable to speak, but he moved when they insisted, and got in the carriage, and rode sitting with his head wobbling. He passed out in the doctor's office.

"I'll tend to you next," said Dr. Vansin.

The glass had dug into the heel of Jarrett's right hand, and there was blood all up his arm, hardening in his sleeve. His knuckles had oozed blood. His face was swollen, and he had to turn his head to see things, because only one eye seemed to be working.

"All I need is a drink," he said.

"I'll give you a drink. Sit down there."

He obeyed and let the doctor take stitches. After that he put his coat on and was driven back to the boat.

Half a dozen big-time gamblers were bucking a faro game, and a check showed the house well ahead.

"What happened to you, Joseph?" cried Miss Ermaline. "Oh, dear God, Reverend Lantern always said you'd come to a violent end."

"My end is not yet. Do I look that bad?"

He went to the bar.

"Champagne, sir?" asked the mulatto bartender, carefully ignoring his bruised appearance.

"No. I need a *drink*. Give me a great big bourbon."

"With seltzer, sir? With—"

"With bourbon. Give me bourbon, with a bourbon chaser."

He had it, and stood looking at the bartender.

"Why in hell would a man want to own a gambling ship when he could be a nice, cool, comfortable bartender?" he said.

"I wouldn't know, sir. It does look, beggin' yo' pardon, like as if you been through it, Mist' Jarrett. I expect you have it very rough—in the fire and all."

"That 'and all' was the rough part."

"Oh, my darling!" said Maxine.

"Don't start that—I couldn't stand that. I love you, but stay clear, woman. I expect to father your children, but stay away from me *now*."

All he wanted was to stand by himself and let the whisky take effect. Just stand there by his very lone self, with nobody to talk to him.

Things seemed very quiet. There were voices, but as long as they were not directed at him, he seemed to be existing in his own island of quiet. Finally he felt his strength returning, and it was then Zach Thomas came into the room.

"Have a drink, Zach," he said.

When Zach did not answer, he turned to ask what was the trouble—and the next memory he had was from the floor.

"Why, he hit you!" a voice, his own, seemed to say. He looked up and saw Zach standing over him. "Jarrett," the voice seemed to say, "without any cause he hit you."

"Get up and fight!" said Zach.

"I've had enough fightin' for tonight. Come around tomorrow."

"Get up!"

"I'll get up, Zach, but I don't want to fight with you."

"Why not? Are you yellow?"

"No, I'm just tired. I'm drawn out and tired. I don't want any more fighting. I just fought with a fellow that would make you look like—" He couldn't think what Burden would make Zach look like. "Anyhow, I fought with him. I don't want ever to fight again. Anyhow, not till tomorrow."

"I think you really mean that."

"I *do* mean it, Zach. I just want to stand up and have a nice, peaceful drink with you."

"Well, I'll be damned!"

Jarrett got to his feet. Zach could hit him if he wanted to. He didn't want to be on guard. He didn't want to do anything.

Zach didn't hit him. He just stood looking at him, letting him get to his feet and back to the bar, where he braced one foot on the rail and his elbow over the molding.

"By the gods, I'm tired!"

"You must be."

"I've been fighting with Harvey Burden. He burned the warehouse. He scuttled the ship, too. He robbed Saigon's widow. I can prove it—proof irrefutable. I got witnesses. We can hang him—if he lives."

"Did you actually think I set that fire?"

"Yes, I thought you did. I thought you were a dirtier scoundrel than you really are."

Zach just stood there looking at him.

"I really went out and saved your hide again, Zach. Harvey would have had you—like they say, right by the short hair. He'd have had you for arson. Good old big fat Harvey! He was going to send you to jail for fraud and arson and scuttling, and probably break me in the bargain. He figured the warehouse would go, and my ship along with it. But he tried to make double sure. That's always a mistake, Zach."

They drank in silence.

After a while Zach said, "You going to repair this ship?"

"I'm broke."

"I got money."

"That's what I was afraid of."

"I got insurance money. It doesn't say I can't collect the insurance if somebody else sets a criminal fire. It doesn't so state in the policy."

"Right!"

"I got a few other dollars floating around. And I hear the cotton market is due to go up."

"You mean you'll *lend* me the money?"

"Better'n that, I'll give it to you. For a share."

"How big?"

"Half."

"Half what you got, or half what I got?"

"We'll work that out."

"Let's work it out now."

"You can't expect—"

"I can! I got floating here the biggest money-maker ever in the history of Texas! Of the whole Caribbean!"

"Half of what you got and I got." Maxine and Elya were watching, and Zach added, "Including women. But I get first choice."

"That I don't grant."

"Who would I choose but Elya?"

"Why, then we have no differences," said Joe Jarrett.

"No differences whatsoever," said Zach Thomas.

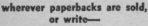

Exciting Books—Interesting Movies

Another list of books which are so important, they have been or will be made into movies in the near future.

☐ **F2211** **MARIANNE, Frederic Mullally**
(50¢) She was death and desire, sheer delight and utter depravity. A woman possessed by good and evil.

☐ **F2205** **PIONEER, GO HOME!, Richard Powell**
(50¢) The funniest novel you'll read this year and soon to be a hilarious movie.

☐ **N2178** **HAWAII, James Michener**
(95¢) This is Hawaii in all its beauty, splendor and exotic mystery. These are the men and women who loved it, from the first Polynesians to the Japanese who fought in the Nisei battalions in World War II.

☐ **A2164** **THE DARK AT THE TOP OF THE STAIRS, William Inge**
(35¢) The powerful drama about a woman who was afraid of her love and desire for her own husband. This great movie stars Robert Preston and Dorothy McGuire.

☐ **H2152** **THE FINAL DIAGNOSIS, Arthur Hailey**
(60¢) The whole fascinating story of a great hospital, where life begins and life ends. This novel reveals the dramatic techniques of modern medicine.

☐ **S2130** **THE WAR LOVER, John Hersey**
(75¢) Through the taut drama of one aircraft, one crew, one woman, John Hersey shows us the whole enormous spiritual wreckage of war.

☐ **F2126** **MURDER, INC., Burton B. Turkus & Sid Feder**
(50¢) The whole terrifying true story of the national crime syndicate. This startling and revealing movie stars Stuart Whitman and May Britt.

☐ **A2112** **LET'S MAKE LOVE, Matthew Andrews**
(35¢) A hilarious yarn about the world's prettiest girl, the world's richest young man and an utterly whacky duel between the sexes. The movie stars Marilyn Monroe.

☐ **A2110** **THE ENTERTAINER, John Osborne**
(35¢) The story of Archie Rice, wise cracking, self-loving and foul mouthed, with his irrepressible stream of dirty words, now a motion picture starring Laurence Olivier.

☐ **A2105** **PORTRAIT IN BLACK, Richard Vincent**
(35¢) A tale of mystery that will leave you breathless in your seats. This motion picture stars Lana Turner, Anthony Quinn and many other stars.

☐ **H2104** **BUTTERFIELD 8, John O'Hara**
(60¢) O'Hara's famous portrait of a beautiful, defiant girl and the fabulous speakeasy era. This smash movie stars Elizabeth Taylor, Laurence Harvey and Eddie Fisher.

☐ **A2103** **PLATINUM HIGH SCHOOL, Irving Shulman**
(35¢) Divorced, degenerate or just plain neglected, wealthy parents sent their boys to Platinum High as a last, desperate measure.

☐ A2102　INHERIT THE WIND, Jerome Lawrence & Robert E. Lee
(35¢)　The tense drama of a great trial, the clash of two giants of the courtroom—a brilliant movie starring Spencer Tracy and Fredric March.

☐ A2085　SERGEANT RUTLEDGE, James Warner Bellah
(35¢)　Under charges of rape and murder, Sergeant Rutledge was still top-soldier of the Ninth Cavalry. This exciting movie stars Jeffrey Hunter and Constance Towers.

☐ F2077　WAKE ME WHEN IT'S OVER, Howard Singer
(50¢)　From a tiny Pacific island to the Pentagon, here's the wild, wonderful, uproarious circus of laughs about the Air Force. This hilarious movie stars Ernie Kovacs, Dick Shawn and Margo Moore. This is one you shouldn't miss.

☐ A2055　THE PRIVATE LIVES OF ADAM AND EVE,
(35¢)　　　　　　　　　　　　Albert Zugsmith & Robert Hill
This is the story of modern Adam and Eve, with the same old Devil and the same old temptation. This great movie stars Mickey Rooney, Mamie Van Doren, Tuesday Weld and many others.

☐ N2026　FROM THE TERRACE, John O'Hara
(95¢)　Alfred Eaton got everything he wanted, but somewhere along the way he left something very important out—the one thing that gave his life meaning. This hit movie stars Paul Newman and Joanne Woodward.

☐ A2018　OUR MAN IN HAVANA, Graham Greene
(35¢)　"Our man in Havana" had a uniquely adventurous imagination, a cooperative assistant and the unshakable conviction that a few lies never really hurt anyone.

☐ F2014　THE LAW, Roger Vailland
(50¢)　This great book is now a movie, "Where the Hot Wind Blows" starring Gina Lollobrigida and Yves Montand.

☐ H1985　SPARTACUS, Howard Fast
(60¢)　Magnificent novel, the Gladiators' revolt against Imperial Rome. This great movie stars Kirk Douglas, Laurence Olivier, Jean Simmons, Tony Curtis and a host of other great stars.

☐ F1754　CIMARRON, Edna Ferber
(50¢)　The world famous novel about Oklahoma and the men and women who tamed the wild frontier. Now a great movie starring Glenn Ford, Maria Schell and Anne Baxter.

BANTAM BOOKS ARE AVAILABLE AT NEWSSTANDS EVERYWHERE

BANTAM BOOKS, INC., Dept. M-60, 657 W. Chicago Ave., Chicago 10, Illinois

Please send check or money order. NO CURRENCY PLEASE. Allow 10¢ per book to cover the cost of postage on orders of less than 5 books.

NAME ....

ADDRESS ....

CITY ..........................ZONE......STATE..........

M60—3-61